MY DAUGHTER'S SILENCE

CAROLINE FINNERTY

B

Boldwood

First published in Great Britain in 2025 by Boldwood Books Ltd.

Cover Design by Head Design Ltd.

Cover Images: iStock

A CIP catalogue record for this book is available from the British Library.

Paperback ISBN 978-1-80549-768-4

Large Print ISBN 978-1-80549-770-7

Hardback ISBN 978-1-80549-766-0

Ebook ISBN 978-1-80549-769-1

Kindle ISBN 978-1-80549-767-7

Audio CD ISBN 978-1-80549-762-2

MP3 CD ISBN 978-1-80549-763-9

Digital audio download ISBN 978-1-80549-771-4

This book is printed on certified sustainable paper. Boldwood Books is dedicated to putting sustainability at the heart of our business. For more information please visit https://www. boldwoodbooks.com/about-us/sustainability/

Boldwood Books Ltd, 23 Bowerdean Street, London, SW6 3TN

www.boldwoodbooks.com

For my baby, Charlie

1

Ali Daly looked at the queue of people standing in the restaurant foyer as they waited to be seated with a sinking feeling. She could tell from the way they shifted from foot to foot, their eyes burrowing into her, that they were growing impatient. As the restaurant manager, it was her job to keep the tables turning but the guests from the earlier sitting were languishing in their seats and she really didn't want to have to ask them to vacate their tables. She knew from experience that this never went down well with their guests and one of the reasons Riordan's Grill was one of Dublin's longest established eateries was because they prided themselves on making their guests feel welcome.

Today was Father's Day, which was always one of
their busiest days of the year as people celebrated
with their dads and grandads. Ali thought about her
own dad in Achill with a pang. She had called him
earlier to wish him a happy Father's Day, but he wasn't
great on his mobile phone. He had been out working
on the farm walking into the wild Atlantic wind and it
had been hard to hear him. Ali watched on as cards
were handed over and metallic-foiled gift bags were
exchanged. These tables had been booked three
months in advance and Ali wanted their guests to
enjoy their dining experience. Riordan's had a reputation as a family-friendly restaurant where they always
served good, wholesome food. It was where people
went to celebrate special occasions, birthdays, gradua-
tions, christenings and communions. The restaurant
was family run and owned by Lisa and Patrick Riordan. They also owned a wine importation business
which Patrick ran while Lisa looked after the day-to-
day running of the restaurant. Although Lisa didn't
appear much during service, she was usually found
upstairs in the office going through paperwork and for
the most part, she left the running of the place to Ali.

Ali had put her hand up to work a double shift
today. Some of the other waitresses wanted to treat
their fathers and husbands and Ali had volunteered to

do two shifts so they could have the day off. She had no plans anyway and Charlotte would be holed up in her bedroom studying. Her sixteen-year-old daughter had the last of her Junior Certificate exams taking place this week. Charlotte hadn't volunteered much information as to how the rest of the exams had gone but Ali knew she would do well. She worked hard in school and always achieved top marks. Friends of Ali's would moan about how difficult it was to get their children to knuckle-down and study; they would complain about the endless battles they faced to get them to open a book, but Ali had none of those problems. Charlotte had always been diligent about her studies. Nearly *too much*, at times, Ali thought. Sometimes, Ali worried about how much time she spent studying instead of doing normal teenage things like meeting friends or playing sport or going shopping, but books consumed Charlotte's life. While Ali knew it was important that Charlotte get a good education, she would have preferred if her daughter had some more balance in her life. She couldn't help but worry that Charlotte was so focused on getting good results that she was missing out on the fun parts of being a teenager. She never seemed to meet friends or want to go anywhere. Everything revolved around her studies. Sometimes on a Friday evening, if Ali had the night off work, she would call Charlotte downstairs, she'd make a big bowl of popcorn and buy a bag of Maltesers and sugary jellies and call Charlotte to watch a movie, but lately, Charlotte had started saying, 'I can't, Mum sorry, I've so much to do', leaving Ali to watch the movie alone. She would end up eating all the junk food by herself, questioning if she was getting this parenting thing completely wrong.

'You were bookish too,' her mother often reminded her. 'Aren't you lucky she's studious and not out drinking and smoking and giving you sleepless nights? That girl has never given you a day's worry; you should be counting your blessings.' And while it was true, Ali had done well in school, she had definitely not spent any longer than was necessary holed up in her room studying. She had had friends, she had gone to discos, she had played camogie, but with Charlotte, it all seemed a bit more... *intense*. When she had been Charlotte's age, she couldn't wait to get home from school every day. She would do her homework, eat her dinner as quickly as she could before heading out the door again to meet her friends. It was the best part of her day. In the summer months, they would take advantage of the longer evenings and head down to the beach, they would mess around on the rocks, sometimes, they would drag piles of driftwood across the sand to make a bonfire and play dares. Someone had once dared her to take off all her clothes and run into the sea and she had done it. She tried to imagine Charlotte doing the same and found she couldn't. She couldn't picture her daughter doing anything as silly or carefree. Even laughing. It hurt her to think that she couldn't even remember the last time she had heard the sweet sound of Charlotte's laughter. She kept waiting for the phase to pass. For things to get better. For Charlotte to make friends, to become more involved in things but if anything as time wore on, she was just retreating more and more into herself.

Ali knew Charlotte was a very bright child and she had always encouraged her to do well in school, she knew how important getting a good education was, but maybe she had pushed her too hard?

Just then, a woman seated at a nearby table flagged her down as she passed, dragging her from her thoughts. 'Would you mind taking a photo of us?' she asked, holding out her phone. Plates of juicy steaks with chunky chips, side orders of tender-stem broccoli and pan-fried asparagus sat before them.

'Sure,' Ali said as she placed the stack of menus that she was carrying down on the table. She took the woman's phone and held it up so that the family appeared on the screen before her, all smiling widely.

'We've four generations here,' the woman added proudly after Ali had finished snapping. 'We have my dad, my granddad and my daughter.' She nodded to the toddler who was bouncing on an older lady's knee.

As Ali looked at the smiling family before her, she thought about her daughter Charlotte, who had grown up without a father. Ali had raised Charlotte alone since day one; he had never been in their lives. Ali wondered if days like this bothered Charlotte; did she ever think about her dad and question where he was? If she did, she didn't ask.

When Charlotte had been small, she had come home from playschool and asked Ali if she had a daddy. Ali could still remember her hazel eyes staring up at her, her innocence as sweet as a fragrant summer rose. Ali's breath had hitched in her chest, her heart hammering as she deliberated about the best way to answer her question. Eventually, she had simply said, 'No, you've no daddy, but you have a mummy who loves you as much as two people.' Charlotte had giggled at her reply and seemed satisfied with this response. Ali could still remember how she had then pulled her into a hug and tickled her, breathing in her intoxicating scent. Charlotte had never mentioned him again. But Ali knew now that at sixteen years of age, Charlotte must have questions. Teenagers were at the age when they tried to forge their own identity, one that was separate to their parents; for the first time in their lives, they began questioning the beliefs and values that they had grown up with and examining it all under a new lens. They began soul searching and exploring new things as they figured both themselves and their place in the world out, and Ali expected there would soon be a time when Charlotte would start asking questions. Ali had been dreading the day when she would have to tell her daughter about her father; she had always said she would be honest with her – or as honest as she *could* be – and yet Charlotte didn't ask. Ali wondered if Charlotte felt unsure about how best to approach it with her or perhaps she felt the topic was off limits. Or there was also a possibility, which Ali always felt guilty about because it made her weak with relief, that perhaps her daughter just didn't care? Could it be that Charlotte simply didn't miss what she had never had?

Ali handed back the phone to the woman. 'Thank you so much.' She beamed, scrolling through them. 'These look great.'

Ali smiled. 'No worries, it's important to have photos to remember the happy occasions.'

Ali saw some of the guests at a nearby table standing up to leave so she hurried over and thanked them for coming. After she had seen them off, she began cleaning down their table and signalling to a waitress that she could start showing the next group over. Just as Ali had finished sanitising the table and setting it with fresh cutlery and glassware, Lisa came up alongside her.

'How are we getting on?' she asked, hands on hips as she surveyed the restaurant.

Ali nodded towards the queue which had finally died down as tables had eventually been vacated. 'Once these guys are seated, it'll all be under control again.'

'You run this place like clockwork.' Lisa smiled and squeezed her arm tenderly. 'I don't know what we'd do without you.'

Ali blushed, unsure how to take the compliment.

'Oh, by the way, did you hear anything back from St Thomas's?' Lisa asked eagerly.

Lisa was referring to the scholarship application that Ali had sent to the private school on behalf of her daughter almost a month ago now. St Thomas's was the most prestigious school in the country and both of

Lisa's children, Megan and Ollie were students there. Every year, the school governors awarded a scholarship to an incoming fifth-year student, which allowed the recipient to attend with free fees for fifth and sixth year. They received hundreds of applications annually and it was very much sought after. It was Lisa who had told Ali about the scholarship in the first place and suggested that she should apply for Charlotte. Ali had been unsure initially, Charlotte seemed happy in her current school, but Lisa had told her about the opportunities St Thomas's could open up to a child with Charlotte's academic abilities; she had extolled the values of the smaller class sizes, the broad range of extra-curricular activities, not to mention the social network. St Thomas's boasted turning out high achievers and it was proud to have the best third-level progression rates in the country. If Charlotte went there, it would open so many doors for her. She would be on a level playing field with the children of Ireland's most powerful people. The fees were eye-wateringly high and Ali knew that only very wealthy people could afford to send their children there. Ali did wonder if Charlotte was accepted, would she fit into a school like that, but she knew her daughter was so focused on her studies that she probably wouldn't even notice her wealthier classmates. In fact, Charlotte seemed to be blissfully unaware of the latest trends or brands that she knew other teenagers craved.

Ali shook her head. 'Not yet. I'm sure they've had lots of applications.'

Lisa leant in conspiratorially. 'I've put in a word for you with the principal.'

'You did?' Ali was stunned.

'I just mentioned how I knew you and Charlotte and that she was an extremely bright and determined young lady and how I believe she'd be an asset to our school.' Lisa winked.

'Thanks, Lisa,' Ali said gratefully.

'I know I can't sway their decision-making, but I like to think I've *some* influence there as I sit on the Board of Management so hopefully, it might help them take notice of her.'

'Well, fingers crossed.' Ali felt a hopeful seed start to flicker inside her. She hadn't dared allow herself to hope that Charlotte's application might be successful but maybe with Lisa's connections, they might just be in luck.

2

It was almost midnight by the time Ali left the restaurant that evening. She climbed into her little Renault Clio and drove the short distance towards the ex-corporation estate where she rented a two-bedroomed terraced house with her daughter. Wheely bins littered the road and Ali groaned as she remembered that it was bin day in the morning and she would need to put theirs out before she could go inside. As she pulled into the driveway, she saw Charlotte's bedroom light was on upstairs which meant she was still studying. Her heart sank like a stone. Charlotte had her French exam in the morning and she'd be exhausted if she didn't get some sleep soon.

After she had managed to drag the weighty bin

out onto the road, she went back towards the house and put her key in the lock. She went inside and climbed the stairs, like she did every evening when she came home from work. She knocked gently on her daughter's bedroom door, before pushing it open. She felt her heart beat a little faster as it always did whenever she entered her daughter's bedroom. Would that fear ever leave her? she wondered.

She saw Charlotte sitting at her desk, her head buried in a textbook.

'Hey there,' she greeted. 'Still at it, huh?'

'Hi, Mum,' Charlotte said, without lifting her head from the book.

'How's it all going?'

'I just want to go over the tenses one last time before the exam in the morning.'

'I don't want you overdoing it,' Ali chided. She thought back to that awful period they went through last year. She hoped Charlotte wasn't slipping back into her old ways. 'You need to get some sleep or you won't be able to keep your eyes open tomorrow.'

'Just five more minutes, Mum.' She turned around and flashed a smile at her. A smile that was so rare these days that whenever Ali did manage to get a glimpse of one, her heart pulsed and twitched and sang for hours afterwards.

'Okay, five more minutes, love and then I want you to go to bed. Promise?'

'I promise.'

She turned to leave the room before pausing. 'I'm proud of you, Charlotte. You're working so hard; you're going to go places.'

'Thanks, Mum,' she said again, without looking up.

She went back downstairs and headed into the kitchen. It was her ritual to have a cup of peppermint tea to unwind after a hectic shift. She boiled the kettle and flopped into a chair while it grumbled to life. Her feet ached from all the steps she had walked to and from tables over the course of the evening. She circled her neck and shoulders, trying to unravel the knots that seemed to be as hard as marbles sitting in between her muscles these days. When the kettle had finished boiling, she plopped a teabag in the mug and poured water over it. Then she sat back down and clasped the mug between her palms. She heard footsteps on the stairs and then Charlotte appeared in the kitchen.

'Finished?' she asked.

'I think so.'

'You've done enough now, love. Time for you to go to bed.'

Charlotte placed a gift-wrapped box down on the table in front of her.

Ali cocked her head to the side in surprise. 'Oh, what's this?'

'I wanted to give you something, Mum,' Charlotte explained shyly.

Ali took the box up in her hands and it examined it. 'What for?' Ali asked, confused by the unexpected gift.

'Open it,' Charlotte urged.

Ali tugged her finger beneath the Sellotape and tore open the paper to reveal a jewellery box. She pulled back the lid and saw a friendship bracelet, with the letters M U M as charms.

'Oh, Charlotte, it's beautiful.' She looked up at her daughter, who was studying her for her reaction. 'But I don't understand?'

'It's Father's Day today.'

'Okay...' Ali said uncertain where Charlotte was going with this.

'Well, since you do both jobs, you're my mum *and* my dad, I thought it would be nice to get you something.'

'Oh, sweetheart.' Tears pressed forward in her eyes. It was so thoughtful of her to do this, to appreciate the job Ali had done raising her alone for all these years but a part of her heart broke for her daughter, for not having her dad around and for Ali's role in all of that. She wanted the best for her daughter; she had wanted a traditional two-parent upbringing for Charlotte, just like she had had growing up but unfortunately, life hadn't panned out that way for either of them. When she saw other families like those in the restaurant today, sometimes, her heart twisted. Her daughter deserved that too; she deserved the love of two parents.

'It's okay, Mum,' Charlotte rushed over. 'I don't want you to cry. Don't you like it? I just wanted to make you happy.'

'Of course I'm happy. I'm just a little emotional, give your silly mum a hug.'

Ali squeezed her daughter, pulled her close to her chest like she was three years old again and breathed her in. 'How did I get so lucky?'

These types of cuddles were scarce nowadays which made her want to savour it all the more. Despite all the times where she doubted herself and questioned the life she was able to give her daughter as a single mum, she knew she must be doing something right. Charlotte was a remarkable young woman and Ali was so proud of her.

3

Ali pulled up at the set down area at Riverdale Community School. She leaned across the gearstick and placed a kiss on her daughter's hair. Charlotte wore it in the same style every day, tied back in a low ponytail secured by an elastic at the nape of her neck.

'Best of luck in the exam, I know you'll be your usual brilliant self.' She smiled.

'Thanks, Mum,' Charlotte mumbled, pulling open the door handle on the car.

'Have a great day, sweetheart. I'll collect you later.'

Then her daughter climbed out, slung her school bag over her shoulder and pushed the door closed behind her.

Ali didn't pull off immediately like she did most

mornings. Instead, she waited there for a while watching the other girls entering the drab, 1970s, flat-roofed building. It was a diverse school with almost 50 per cent of the children having parents who emigrated to Ireland, hailing mainly from Eastern Europe, during the Celtic Tiger years. The school had reached capacity and had been expanded with prefabs in recent years to accommodate the growing number of children in the catchment area. Some of the girls were bathed in fake tan; they wore heavy make-up with false eyelashes. They had chunky, gold hoops hanging from their ears and their hair was either carefully styled into a sleek ponytail or else perfectly straightened and left loose around their shoulders. Ali guessed from the effort they made, that they must get up very early to look so well turned-out before school. They all seemed so confident and self-assured. They walked in groups of twos and threes, chatting and laughing as they showed one another things on their phone screen. Charlotte looked so at odds beside them; she walked alone, keeping her head down to avoid eye contact and her shoulders were hunched over as if she was trying to make herself invisible. Ali couldn't help but think how childlike her daughter looked beside them. She was painfully thin, her build so slight that she appeared several years younger than the other girls her age. Charlotte had no interest in applying fake tan or putting make-up on her pale skin. She didn't try out different ways to style her lank, black hair; instead, she slung it back in her usual ponytail. She wore thick-framed glasses; even though Ali had bought her contact lenses to try, she never bothered with them. The other students took liberties and wore trainers with their uniform and left shirts untucked, some of the girls even rolled up their skirts but Charlotte wore her uniform correctly, even choosing to wear the neat brown loafers that were stipulated in the school's uniform policy but which nobody actually wore. Charlotte had almost finished third year and she had still never invited anyone home. Ali used to think it was because teenagers didn't do that any more but when she chatted to other mums, they told her that their daughters were forever hanging out in their friends' houses or hosting girls for sleepovers. Charlotte had always been quiet; in primary school, she had had one friend and they had stuck to one another like glue but the other girl had gone to a different post-primary school and Charlotte hadn't made any new friends in Riverdale.

Eventually, when all the students had disappeared

inside the school building, she signalled, pulled out into the traffic and headed for home. She was looking forward to having the day off after a hectic weekend in work. She worked nearly every Saturday and Sunday so while most people hated Mondays, it was always her favourite day of the week, as it was the start of her time to relax.

She arrived home and dragged the bin back in from the road and into the front garden. Then she put her key in the door and went inside. She saw from the letters lying scattered before her on the doormat that the postman had been. She lifted them, scanning through the envelopes. She knew from the standard-issue envelopes with cellophane panes that they were mostly bills. She dreaded getting the ESB bill with the way utility prices had sky-rocketed lately. Alongside the bills, she spotted a plush, cream envelope with her name neatly printed on the outside. Intrigued, she ran her finger beneath the gummed seal and pulled out the letter that was inside. She unfolded it and immediately saw the logo of St Thomas's school at the top of the page. Her heart rate quickened as her eyes scanned the text. The words seemed to bounce around before her so she read it again, slowly this time:

Dear Ms Daly,

We wish to thank you for your recent application to our scholarship programme for 2023. As you may be aware, we receive hundreds of applications each year and have a very extensive and exhaustive list of selection criteria. Scholarship students are not only selected on their academic record but also on what value we feel they can bring to St Thomas's. I must commend you and your daughter on your submission which was very impressive and as a result, on behalf of the governors for the school, I wish to award the 2023 St Thomas's scholarship to your daughter, Charlotte Daly. The school will be in touch with further details and to arrange an appointment to meet with Charlotte in anticipation of her starting in our school. We wish to congratulate you both and we look forward to welcoming Charlotte into the St Thomas's school community.

Best Wishes,

Mr John Franklin

Headmaster

'Oh my God!' Ali squealed aloud, even though she was at home alone. She couldn't believe it. She had done it! Charlotte had been awarded the scholarship. Ali had only applied on a whim because Lisa had suggested it but she never actually believed that she would get it. She hadn't even mentioned it to Charlotte because she didn't want to get the child's hopes up. In fact, she had filled out the whole painstaking application form by herself, even the bit where the student was supposed to write to the governors and state in their own words how they felt they could benefit from the scholarship and also what they would bring to the school. She had felt underhand doing it at the time but she had never expected Charlotte to actually be awarded it. St Thomas's was one of the top schools in the country. Only the wealthiest people in Ireland could afford to send their children there. It had educated Taoisigh and many of the CEOs of Fortune500 companies had been schooled there. This would open up so many doors and give Charlotte opportunities that Ali could have only dreamed about. Never in a million years could Ali have afforded to send her child to such a prestigious school but the governors of St Thomas's had recognised her brilliant, clever daughter's abilities and thought she was deserving of the chance. It made all those years struggling on her own seem worthwhile. Charlotte was so talented and now thanks to her hard work, she was going to have a chance to get a leg up in life. Tears of pride pushed into her eyes as she read and re-read the letter. She couldn't wait until Charlotte got home from school later to tell her.

4

Ali collected Charlotte at the school later that day. On the days that Ali was working, Charlotte usually cycled so she liked to drop and collect her on her days off. For the rest of the day, as she had pottered around at home doing laundry and catching up on housework, she had been buzzing. She felt like she was going to explode if she didn't tell her daughter soon. She had counted down the hours until it was time to collect Charlotte from the school, dying to share the exciting news.

'How was your French exam?' she asked as soon as her daughter sat into the car.

'Not great.'

'I doubt that somehow,' Ali replied dismissively.

She was used to Charlotte downplaying her achievements.

'No, Mum,' Charlotte said shaking her head anxiously. 'It was really bad.'

'Hey, come on,' Ali soothed. 'You've never done a bad exam in your life. You always get the top marks.'

'Well, not this time.'

'You're too hard on yourself.' She was used to this roleplay. Charlotte coming out of an exam, focusing on the negatives and telling Ali how badly it had gone only for her to get an A when the results came out. It was a familiar routine for both of them.

Charlotte fell silent and looked out the window for the rest of the journey home. Ali decided that now probably wasn't the best time to tell her daughter about the scholarship. She was too wound up after the exam. Ali would wait until they got home and had something to eat and hopefully, Charlotte might have relaxed a little by then.

When they got home, they went inside the house and Ali took the container of curry that she had brought home from work the night before out of the fridge. She emptied it into a saucepan and began to heat it on the hob. She looked around the small kitchen at the dated cabinets that she and Charlotte had received permission from their landlord last summer to repaint a light grey, in a bid to brighten up the room. There was only space for a small, circular table that would sit four at a push but was fine for when it was just the two of them.

'Is that Keith's curry?' Charlotte asked.

'Uh-huh. I got him to make it in work especially for you yesterday.' Keith's curry was Charlotte's favourite dish in Riordan's and whenever it was on the menu, Ali always took some home for Charlotte too. She filled a saucepan with water to boil the rice.

'Thanks, Mum,' Charlotte said, slinging her arms around her mother's neck. 'I'm sorry for being grumpy earlier.'

'Don't worry about it,' she said.

When the food was cooked, Ali heaped it onto two plates and they both sat down at the table.

'Mmmh,' Charlotte said appreciatively as she tucked into the food.

'I have some good news for you,' Ali began.

'What is it?' Charlotte asked through a mouthful.

'Well,' she began excitedly, 'Guess who won a scholarship to St Thomas's?'

'What's St Thomas's?' Her glasses were slipping down the bridge of her nose but she didn't seem to notice.

'You know, the school in town,' Ali prompted.

'Oh,' Charlotte replied disinterestedly, as she shrugged her shoulders. 'I don't know.'

'Only my blindingly clever daughter of course!' Ali gushed.

'Me?' Charlotte was looking at her blankly. 'But how?'

'Well, I sent in an application for you a few months back. I didn't want to say anything to you at the time in case you got your hopes raised but I can't believe you actually won the bloody thing!'

'But I'd have to change schools,' Charlotte said in confusion.

'Well, yeah,' Ali laughed. 'That's generally how scholarships work.'

'So you want me to leave Riverdale Community School?'

'Well, yes... This is a once-in-a-lifetime opportunity, Charlotte. They only give out two scholarships every year, one for Junior Cycle students and one for Senior Cycle. I hope you realise how lucky you are to have been awarded it.' She needed to impress upon her daughter just how amazing this was.

'But it's in the city centre. How would I get there?'

'Well, we can figure that out in time but you'd probably have to take the bus.'

'But I like Riverdale; why do I need to change?'

Ali couldn't help feeling irked by her daughter's muted reaction. She had expected a better response to the news – excitement at least. 'Because St Thomas's is a very sought-after school. They have the best teachers and smaller class sizes, not to mention the sports facilities – they even have their own pool!'

'But I don't play sports.'

'I'm just saying Charlotte, it's a very prestigious school,' Ali said tersely. 'People pay tens of thousands for their children to go to school there and you're getting it for free!'

Charlotte remained quiet and Ali could see she still didn't understand the significance of the opportunity that had landed at her feet. She almost seemed ungrateful.

'Imagine having it on your CV when you're older?' Ali went on. 'People will hear you went there and sit up and take notice. It will open doors for you, trust me.' She was trying hard to suppress her frustration. 'I thought you'd be excited,' she added, trying but failing to keep the churlish tone from her voice.

'I am, Mum. It's just it's a really big thing... I need to think about it.'

'Charlotte, love, when you get an opportunity like this, you don't "think about it"!' She raised her index fingers to make air quotes. 'You need to grab onto it with both hands. There are hundreds of kids who would kill to be in the position you're in right now.'

'Okay, Mum, I get it,' Charlotte retorted, clearly irritated. 'So that's it, you're making the decision to send me there whether I like it or not?'

'Charlotte, I'm doing this for you. You need to step out of your comfort zone; there's a whole world out there far bigger than Riverdale.'

'I've been in Riverdale for three years; it's a good school!' she retorted.

'I know it is but I want more for you. You are so smart and talented. I want you to have all the opportunities that I never got. I don't want your life turning out like mine where every day is a struggle. I want your life to be easy.' Charlotte knew that as a single mother, Ali had had to make sacrifices over the years, as she struggled to make ends meet.

'Cheers, Mum,' she snapped. 'Sorry if I ruined your life!' She stood up from the table, pushed her chair back across the tiles with a screech and stormed out.

Ali's earlier excitement rapidly evaporated; this was not how she had envisaged this conversation going.

'Charlotte!' Ali called after her daughter. 'That's not what I meant; please come back.'

5

After she had done the washing up and cleaned up after dinner, Ali sat down and called her mother. She needed to hear Maura's soothing voice down the phone after the argument she had had with Charlotte. This is what she found hardest about being a single parent: there was no sounding board to talk things out with. There was no one to share the mental load with. No one to ask whether you were doing the right thing or to offer another perspective. It all fell on her shoulders and at times like this, she began doubting herself. Was attending St Thomas's the right decision for her daughter? But then another voice, louder and more insistent, would quash those worries and tell her that this opportunity was too good to pass up and even if

Charlotte didn't realise it right now, she would thank her in time.

'Mam, it's me,' Ali said when her mother answered.

'How's all up in Dublin?' Her mother always asked her this question, as if Dublin was the far side of the world instead of being on the east coast of Ireland.

'It's good, Mam.' She paused. 'You'll never guess what?'

'Go on?' her mother replied cautiously.

'Your very clever granddaughter has been awarded a scholarship to St Thomas's,' she announced proudly in a sing-song voice. She was conscious that she was trying to frame this positively for her mother, but Ali knew that if her mother voiced the doubts that Ali herself was feeling, her resolve would fall apart.

'What's that, Ali?' Maura asked, sounding confused.

'It's a school – a private school – you know, the one where all the government ministers send their kids.'

'Oh, I think I've heard of it...' she replied vaguely. 'Was she not happy in the school she's in now?'

'She was – she *is* but this will open so many doors for her. The fees are over twenty grand a year but she's getting it all for free!'

'Oh, that's great news, lovey. She was first in the

queue when our Lord was giving out brains, that's for sure. She takes after her mother.'

Ali felt herself blushing on the other end of the phone. 'She's way smarter than me, Mam. She has brains to burn.' Although Ali had done well in school, it was because she worked hard; she didn't have the same natural ability that Charlotte had. The lightning-quick speed that Charlotte's mind worked at never ceased to amaze her. Charlotte could think several steps ahead, when Ali was just figuring out the first step.

'She must be thrilled,' Maura continued.

'Well, yeah... it was a bit of a shock to her, actually.' Ali could never lie to her mother.

'Doesn't she want to go?' Maura asked, picking up on the note of hesitation in her daughter's voice and picking at it, like a hangnail that you know you should leave alone but can't.

'She does – well, she *will* – it's just she doesn't do well with change.'

'Well sure she doesn't have to move, does she, Alice? Would you not be worried that she might not fit in in a place like that?'

Ali felt herself bristle. She knew her mother didn't mean any harm but she still held old-fashioned beliefs about class and social standing. 'Why wouldn't she fit in?' Ali challenged.

'Oh, you know yourself, love, mixing in those circles, she might feel...' She paused to choose the right word, '...a pressure on her to keep up...'

'Times have changed, Mam; money doesn't define you any more. My daughter is as good as anyone else. It doesn't matter if she doesn't come from money; she got that scholarship because she deserved it!'

'I know, love, sorry, sure don't I know she is. It's just you need to be careful after everything that happened last year...'

'That's all behind her now, Mam.' She knew Maura meant well but Ali hated being brought back to that awful time in their lives. 'She's doing so much better.'

'I know, love. All I'm saying is if she's happy where she is, then why would you uproot her? A happy child is one of life's blessings. Aren't you making life more difficult for yourself?'

'But, Mam, an opportunity like this doesn't come around every day. They had thousands of applicants and they chose her. She can't let it pass her by.'

'Well sure you know her best. She'll do great wherever she goes. You're blessed, Alice. That girl never gives you an ounce of trouble.'

'I know, Mam. Look, I'd better go here but I just wanted to let you know the good news.'

'Thanks, love, goodnight. Tell Charlotte I said well done.'

After Ali had hung up from her mother, she climbed the stairs to Charlotte's bedroom. She stood outside her door and knocked gently, holding her breath.

'Charlotte, sweetheart, can I come in?' she called out.

'Go away!' came the muffled response from behind the door.

She steeled herself, then pushed the handle to enter the bedroom.

Her daughter was lying facing away from her, curled up like a prawn on her single bed. The room was painted a sunny yellow colour. Charlotte had chosen it herself three years ago. It was crazy to think how much her daughter's personality had changed in that time. Gone was the sweet, young girl who would snuggle up beside her on the sofa and ask how her day was and instead, her daughter seemed to have withdrawn into herself. It was like an invisible barricade had been built between them. Ali wasn't sure when the wall had been erected but lately, she felt a distance between them that had never been there before. She could see her daughter, she could touch her but she couldn't *reach* her. She missed the way they would bellyache with laughter as they watched reruns of *Friends* or how Charlotte would creep into her bed in the early hours of the morning and lie beside her without saying a word. People had warned her that the teenage years were tricky, that Charlotte would pull away from her and Ali would have to let her go. Ali understood that but she had never imagined they'd be this hard. Charlotte seemed to have the weight of the world on her young shoulders. Ali felt as though she couldn't say or do anything right these days. When she looked at other teenagers, although they might withdraw from their parents and be moody, they usually turned towards their friends but Charlotte had nobody.

'She just needs to find her tribe,' Lisa regularly assured her. 'It took my Megan until fifth year before she found her group of friends and she's been like a different child since. It'll happen for Charlotte too, trust me.' Maybe a change of school was exactly what she needed.

She looked around the orderly room. Schoolbooks were stacked in a neat pile on her desk, a container with pens and highlighters all with their lids on was beside them and ring binders stood vertically with their edges all in line. There were no clothes thrown around the floor or mugs and plates left on every available surface like she had done as a teenager. She heard other parents complaining that their teenager's bedroom was like an environmental health hazard but everything in Charlotte's room was tidy and in its place. She used to be proud of how clean her daughter was but now she was starting to wonder if it was normal. At the back of her mind, a voice questioned whether she should be worried that her daughter wasn't doing regular teenage things yet.

Ali sat down onto the edge of the bed and immediately, Charlotte shunted away from her. She placed a hand on her daughter's skinny shoulder; even through the black hoody she was wearing, Ali could feel the cut of her bones.

'I'm sorry, love. I don't like it when we fight. I swear you are the best thing to ever happen to me bar nothing. I love you more than you'll ever know. Don't you ever doubt that. You are my reason for everything. I'm sorry if it came across like I was complaining or saying that you were a mistake because that's simply not true. It's me and you against the world.'

She felt her daughter's body soften beneath her palm and she exhaled heavily as she continued. 'You know I only want the very best for you. I'm doing this out of love. I would give you the whole world if I could, but this seems like too good an opportunity to pass up. I just want you to be happy, love.'

Charlotte turned around to face her and Ali saw tears brimming in her eyes and her heart plummeted. She hated when her daughter was upset; it was like a part of herself was wounded too. She had been that way since Charlotte was young; she always wanted to fix the problem. In those days, it had been easy, a kiss or a hug, maybe a Band-Aid or a sneaky packet of Haribo, but nowadays, her problems felt so much more difficult to fix.

'Come here.' She pulled her into a hug and felt tears come hot and fast.

'I'm sorry too, Mum. I know you only want the best for me.'

She wiped her dripping nose with the back of her hand. 'If you don't want to take the scholarship, then I'll understand. You are the most special person I know and I just want you to have the best. I want you to have whatever you want in life.'

'I'll accept the scholarship,' Charlotte said in a small voice.

Ali pulled away from her daughter and sat upright. 'Are you sure? It's a big decision; you should take some time to think about it.'

Charlotte shook her head. 'I know it's for the best.'

Ali nodded, feeling relief flood through her. 'Oh thank God,' she exhaled. 'This is the opportunity of a lifetime; the fees are almost my annual salary. I know you're nervous about leaving Riverdale but I really think you're making the right decision.'

Charlotte pulled her lips back into a smile but it didn't quite reach her eyes.

'I promise you, Charlotte, trust me, this is going to open so many doors for you. You won't regret it. Just you wait and see.'

6

10 JUNE 2023

Charlotte's Journal

Today was a bit of a weird one. Mum was so excited telling me that I had won the scholarship to St Thomas's. I don't think I've ever seen her so thrilled about anything. I was so shocked that she went and filled in the application form without even telling me and then to hear I'd won it was an even a bigger surprise. We were sitting at the kitchen table having dinner when she told me. I could see she was annoyed because I wasn't jumping up and down about it, but it was the first time I had heard about it. The thing is though that I like Riverdale but Mum reckons St Thomas's is a much better school and she keeps saying it will 'open doors' for me, whatever that means. I know it bothers Mum that I don't really have friends and do the stuff that other teenagers do like hanging out or going to parties. Mum worries about me and I hate myself for not being the type of teenager that she wants me to be but I'm okay on my own. I keep telling her that I'm fine. I just don't like big groups.

Because it's only just me and Mum, we're very close. I know she is proud of my good grades and always praises me but then I get scared that if I flunked a test, I'd be letting her down. 'You're going to go to college,' Mum always says. 'You're going to get a degree and get a really good job and your life won't be anything like mine.'

Or, 'You're not going to be doing this,' Mum will say whenever the heating oil has run out and we can't afford a refill and we have to drag the electric radiator from room to room. Or whenever her car won't start in the morning, she'll say, 'You're going to have a great career and be able to afford to drive a brand spanking, new car. You won't ever have to worry about your car not starting.' I know she doesn't do it on purpose but I feel all this pressure on me to keep it up. She wants the best for me but it makes me feel claustrophobic. Sometimes, I want to scream at her to stop but I never would because I know she's doing it out of love for me.

She's raised me all by herself for my whole life and I know she's made a lot of sacrifices over the years. She works hard managing the restaurant for the Riordans and although she gets okay money, I know she struggles every month so I get why this is such a big deal to her. I'll go to St Thomas's if it means that much to her. I just want to make her proud of me.

7

The summer went by in a blur and soon, the cooler evenings of August started to push in as a back-to-school chill spread through the air. Today was Charlotte's first day in her new school and Ali was equal parts excited for her daughter's new adventure and also anxious about the changes it would bring. She steered the car through the imposing gates of St Thomas's, feeling her heartbeat start to ratchet up. Majestic oak trees lined the avenue where beyond, Ali could see acres of rolling green fields where she guessed the playing pitches were.

'You've to meet Mr Franklin, the principal at nine,' she chattered, trying to keep the nerves at bay as she drove uphill along a winding avenue. They had been invited to meet him once before, after Charlotte had been awarded the scholarship and Ali recalled how he had explained that St Thomas's wasn't just a school; that they prided themselves on being a community and that long after their students had left, they still looked out for one another in life. 'It's the St Thomas's way,' he had said proudly. Ali had been impressed. This was what she wanted for Charlotte: this ease of networking and connections in all the right places. Doors automatically opening for her without needing to be pushed.

Charlotte's face was screwed up anxiously. 'They don't call him a principal, Mum; he's the headmaster.'

'Sorry, yes, got it... I keep forgetting that. Everything is so formal.' She flashed a smile at her daughter, dressed in her woollen blazer with the St Thomas's crest embroidered on the pocket and navy plaid skirt. When Ali had received the school's mandatory uniform list, she had nearly died when she discovered the prices for each piece. It wasn't just a standard uniform like the students at Riverdale wore; St Thomas's had a crested jumper, another uniform for P.E., a smock for art – the list had been endless. Lisa had come to her rescue with some of Megan's old uniform pieces that she had outgrown and Ali was very grateful for the hand-me-downs. 'It's going to take me a while to wrap my head around it all.'

They came to a stop outside an intimidating, ivy-clad, Georgian building. Range Rovers and Porsches were parked in the spaces alongside her. There were several AstroTurf pitches as well as a tennis court to her right and she saw a signpost that read *Swimming Pool*. This place looked like a five-star country manor hotel compared to Riverdale Community School with its rundown building and leaky prefabs.

They saw the other pupils walking in small groups together, chatting and laughing and generally being at ease with each other and Ali felt her heart twist. That's what she wanted for Charlotte. She wanted her to have friendships; although learning was important to her, she also wished sometimes her daughter could lighten up a little and see the fun side of life. She really hoped she would get to experience that in her new school.

'Oh, look, there's Ollie,' Ali said excitedly as she spotted Lisa's son walking by the car, surrounded by a gang of his friends. They were tossing a rugby ball to one another as they walked. Charlotte and Ollie didn't know one another well; they had only met a few times over the years in the restaurant and at Lisa's fiftieth birthday party. Ali winced as she saw the brand name on the coat that Ollie and his friends seemed to be wearing like a uniform. She had seen them on sale in Brown Thomas for almost a thousand euro. Although she wouldn't usually have the money to shop in the exclusive department store, Lisa had given her a gift voucher for it last Christmas.

'Why don't you go and say hi to him?' Ali suggested.

Charlotte turned to her as if she was crazy. 'No way, Mum!'

'But Lisa said that she's asked him to introduce you to his friends,' Ali protested. 'I can go over with you if you want?'

'Please, Mum, just leave it,' she begged.

'Okay, that's fine if you don't feel comfortable.' Ali fell quiet, chastened. She looked out the window and saw some of the girls using designer handbags as school bags. She felt like she had stepped into a different world, a world where people didn't lose sleep over paying the rent or hoping that their card wouldn't be declined when they popped into the shop for milk. Ali could never in her wildest dreams have afforded a handbag like that, let alone buy one for her daughter to use for school.

'I don't know if I belong here,' Charlotte said

doubtfully, clearly having the same thoughts as her mother.

'Of course you do. St Thomas's is lucky to have you.'

Charlotte's hand lingered on the door handle but she still didn't open it.

'You'd better go; you don't want to be late on your first day,' Ali encouraged.

Charlotte finally pulled the handle and stepped out onto the gravel. She slung her Tesco-bought school bag over her shoulder and began walking towards the red-bricked building.

Ali didn't pull off immediately; instead, she watched her daughter as she walked. Charlotte kept her gaze lowered, avoiding eye contact with the other teenagers. Ali gulped as she observed her. It felt like she had taken out her heart and handed it over to her daughter; why was she so anxious, she wondered? She just hoped she'd be happy and find friends; all she wanted was for her daughter to be happy. *Please, like it,* she prayed internally.

* * *

At 4 p.m. that same day, Ali sat waiting in the car park of St Thomas's watching as Charlotte approached the car. Her head was down, her shoulders sunken. She could tell before her daughter had even got close to her that the day hadn't gone well and she felt the familiar creep of disappointment pulling her down.

'Well, how did it go?' Ali asked eagerly as Charlotte opened the car door. She desperately hoped that if she sounded positive, her daughter might follow suit. 'Were the other students nice?'

Charlotte tossed her school bag into the footwell before climbing into the passenger seat. 'I don't belong there, Mum.'

Ali looked across at her diminutive daughter sitting adjacent to her. Her features screwed up anxiously. 'Of course you do,' Ali reassured.

'Nobody wants me there.'

Ali started the engine, checked her mirrors before pulling out of the car park. 'Look, I get that it's a big adjustment. It's hard being the new girl but just give it a little time and you'll find your tribe, I promise. Why don't you join one of the sports teams or maybe one of the after-school clubs?' Ali had been impressed as Mr Franklin had listed off the extra-curricular activities that were on offer to the students: there was hockey, rugby, basketball, soccer, tennis, swimming and badminton amongst others and for children who weren't interested in playing sport, there were drama, debating and chess clubs too – 'Something for every-one.' He had chuckled.

'You might meet some new friends that way?' Ali suggested hopefully.

'No way. I don't want to spend any longer than I have to in that place.'

The fine hairs on Ali's neck stood to attention. This reaction seemed extreme, even for Charlotte. 'Did something happen today?' Ali probed.

'No, I just don't like it.'

'Charlotte, come on, it's too early to judge it. It's only your first day. Give it a chance.'

'I was happy in Riverdale, Mum.'

Ali felt the knots in her shoulders wind ever tighter and she clenched her fingers around the steering wheel. Although she knew she needed to be patient, she couldn't help feeling frustrated by her daughter's unwillingness to engage or help herself. She wished Charlotte would get out of her own way sometimes and just allow herself to be happy.

'You have to try, Charlotte. In life, you get what you put in, so you can take this opportunity that you've been given – think of it like a stepping stone to a better life – or you can sabotage it for yourself; it's your choice.' Ali hated speaking so bluntly but she needed Charlotte to realise just how lucky she was.

Maybe she was too young to see it yet but this was a route out of poverty, a way out of the hardship that Ali endured on a daily basis. This scholarship represented so much; she just wished her daughter could recognise that.

8

Two weeks later, Ali was making her way across the car park in Riordan's when she heard her name being called.

She turned around to see Lisa waving at her. She pressed a button on her keys to lock her jeep before coming over in her direction.

'Hi there,' Ali said, as Lisa reached her.

'How was your day off?'

'Well, it was very exciting. I cleaned out my fridge, then I hoovered the house.'

'Productive.' Lisa laughed. 'How's Charlotte doing?'

'She's okay. It's a big adjustment moving schools.' For some reason, she found herself not being com-

pletely honest with Lisa. She didn't want to seem ungrateful for the opportunity that had been afforded to
them by telling Lisa just how much she was struggling
to settle in at St Thomas's.

When Charlotte had started primary school, it
had taken her months to settle. She cried without fail
every day when Ali had dropped her off in the
mornings.

'Don't worry,' her teacher had assured her. 'Some
kids just take a little longer to adjust. She'll be running in the door by Halloween, just wait and see.'
But Halloween came and went and then Christmas
too, with Charlotte still screaming every morning in
the car park. Even the teacher had grown frustrated
when Charlotte was still crying after the Easter holidays. Ali had never been able to drop and go at
birthday parties like the other parents could and
Charlotte refused to go on playdates unless Ali went
along too. The handful of times when she had been
invited to another child's house, Ali would hang
around making small talk with the other mum,
drinking a cup of coffee that neither of them particularly wanted, feeling like she was intruding on her
home and time. Eventually, the other parents
stopped inviting Charlotte around. Well-meaning
people used to give her advice and tell her she

should just drop her off and leave, let Charlotte cry it out. They told her that Charlotte was too clingy and that she needed to be able to deal with new people and situations, but this seemed too harsh to Ali. She had never been able to walk away when her daughter was upset. Even back then, Ali knew that Charlotte was different to other children her age. Charlotte was quite sensitive, her needs greater. It always took her a little longer to adjust to change. She had only been in St Thomas's for two weeks; Ali knew she needed to be patient and give her more time.

'Well, it's only been a couple of weeks. It's still early days, isn't it?' Lisa said kindly. 'It's not easy starting a new school at sixteen.'

'I really hope she finds her tribe, Lisa. She's a good kid, she's so quiet, she doesn't give me a moment's trouble so I don't know why I worry about her so much... I guess I just want her to be happy.'

'Oh, Ali, she will be. Just give her some time.' Lisa linked her arm and they began walking towards the building. 'The joys of being a mum: we worry about everything, even when we've nothing to worry about. If she was staying out late partying, you'd worry or if she's at home studying, you worry that she's pushing too hard.'

They reached the door and Ali held it open for her boss to enter, before following after her.

'That sounds about right.' Ali groaned. 'I guess I had hoped she'd love it from day one. I just pray that I made the right decision in moving her.'

They headed to the kitchen and Lisa went over to the coffee machine and began making coffees for both of them. The machine hissed and whirred as it came to life.

'Of course you did: just think of the opportunity that this is. As parents, we know what is best for our kids even when they don't realise it themselves. Charlotte is out of her comfort zone but unfortunately, that's life and we can't fix everything for our kids even if we wanted to. Charlotte needs this push, Ali.'

'You're right. Thanks, Lisa. For everything.' If it wasn't for Lisa, Ali would never have even been aware that the St Thomas's scholarship programme existed, let alone applied for it. She felt better having spoken to her boss about it. Lisa had put it all into perspective. She was doing the right thing, she just had to trust herself and although it might take Charlotte a little longer to realise that, she was confident that she would see it in time.

'How about I have a word with Ollie? I can ask

him to keep an eye on her. Make sure she is included in things and not left on her own.'

'Oh, could you?' Ali asked gratefully. 'That would be amazing.'

'No problem. Oh, by the way, Ali, are you going to the St Thomas's coffee morning next week?'

Ali had received an invitation for a coffee morning charity fundraiser that was being hosted in the school. 'I, eh, I wasn't going to...' Ali admitted. She didn't know any of the other parents except for Lisa and she assumed Lisa would be too busy with work so she hadn't planned on bothering. The thought of going into a packed hall where everyone knew one another made her skin crawl. Ali wasn't usually good in situations where she didn't know people. She wished she was one of those women that oozed natural confidence and could go up and talk to anyone but it just wasn't her. Maybe she was more like her daughter than she realised.

'You should come, Ali. They host it every September in aid of a different charity and it's always a good catch up with the other mums after the summer holidays. I'll be there and it would be a great way for you to meet the other parents.'

It sounded like the conversation she had recently had with Charlotte about making an effort. Hadn't she said the same words to her about pushing herself out of her comfort zone and being open to new things? She knew if she was doling out similar advice to her daughter, surely she should be making an effort as well. Perhaps if she got to know some of the other parents, then it would help to integrate Charlotte.

'Okay then...' she agreed reluctantly. 'I suppose it would be good to meet some of the other parents.'

'Brilliant! I can introduce you to everyone. They're all lovely, I promise you.'

9

When Ali's car had miraculously started first time that morning, she wished it hadn't. She was hoping for an excuse – anything that could get her out of going along to the St Thomas's coffee morning. She was dreading it and had nearly talked herself out of going twice already. Only that she'd promised Lisa that she would meet her there, she knew she couldn't back out.

She drove through the city and eventually entered the impressive grounds of St Thomas's. She met Lisa in the car park as arranged and followed her up the steps and into the building. Lisa led her down a corridor towards a large assembly hall. Her heart began racing as they entered the vast space with parquet flooring. The walls were covered in antique panelling punctuated with photos of famous past pupils. There was a table inside the door with a bucket that had a sticker for the Irish Cancer Society displayed on its front. She winced as Lisa opened her handbag, removed her purse and shoved a wad of fifty-euro notes down through the hole. Ali had only brought a ten-euro note with her; it was all she could afford until she got paid on Friday. She quickly pushed her money down into the slot, hoping no one could see the rusty hue of the note.

'Lisa!' someone squealed as she followed her over to a group of women standing in a circle. 'It's so good to see you!'

Ali stood hovering beside her while Lisa hugged and embraced the women.

'How was your holiday?' Lisa gushed.

'It was amazing. Have you been to Mauritius?'

'We were there a few years back; it's a fabulous spot.'

'How about you? Did you get away?'

'We were at our house in Portugal for a month,' Lisa replied.

'It feels like an eternity since I've talked to you.'

'The school holidays can feel like that all right.' Lisa laughed. Lisa stood back then, as if only remembering her, and brought her into the group. 'I want you all to meet a friend of mine,' Lisa said, gesturing to where Ali was standing beside her. 'This is Ali. Her daughter, Charlotte, has just moved to St Thomas's for fifth form.'

'Hi, Ali,' they chorused and a line of manicured hands went out to meet hers. She tried not to look intimidated as she watched the Chanel and Louis Vuitton handbags dangling from every arm. They were all towering over her in heels and smart tailoring and Ali wished she hadn't chosen to wear jeans and trainers. As she had been getting ready that morning, she hadn't wanted to look over-dressed but now she realised she would never have that problem when standing beside these women. She felt dumpy and unfashionable in her floral blouse and bootcut jeans.

'So how do you two know each other?' A tall woman with voluminous hair extensions asked.

'Ali works in the restaurant – she's our manager.' Lisa leaned in conspiratorially, enjoying being the centre of attention. 'Don't tell our chefs but she's the real reason we're still in business after all these years. Now, if I could bring her home and get her to manage my life, I'd be sorted.'

Everyone rewarded her with a laugh.

'Sounds like we could all use an Ali in our lives.' A woman held out a slender, manicured hand to shake

Ali's. 'Hi, I'm Kyra. You look really familiar; do I know you from somewhere?'

'I don't think so,' Ali said politely. She didn't think she had ever before seen this woman.

'Hmm, that's going to annoy me now for the whole day. I never forget a face.' Kyra smiled showing dazzling, white teeth.

'So, what school did your daughter move from, Ali?' Another woman with a blunt, black bob asked.

'Riverdale,' Ali replied.

She saw all the heads swivel in her direction. She watched the woman's brow furrow as she tried to work it out. She had clearly been expecting Ali to say she had transferred from another private school. 'The community school?' she asked.

'Yes, that's right.'

The woman quickly rearranged her features into a smile. 'So how is she getting on? I bet she loves our school.'

'It's a big change,' Ali said. She didn't want to tell these women how much Charlotte disliked it.

'Is she into swimming?' One of the mums asked. 'The new pool is amazing. It's good to see something useful coming from all our money.' She winked and everyone laughed.

'I guess...' Ali laughed along too even though she felt like a fraud.

She was relieved when the coffee morning was finally over and she could go home.

'See?' Lisa said as they walked across the car park towards their cars together afterwards. 'Didn't I tell you they were all lovely?'

'You were right. They were all very welcoming.' Ali smiled because she didn't want her boss picking up on her insecurities. She knew that Lisa with her natural confidence and ease with people, not to mention stacks of cash, would never understand. Although everyone had been nice to her, it still didn't explain why she felt she didn't belong there. Was it because her daughter was on a scholarship? she wondered. Was the reason she had felt like an outsider standing amongst those women earlier because she wasn't paying fees like they were? Suddenly, she could see things from her daughter's perspective and how it might feel to have to face this every single day. She was reminded of the words she was forever telling Charlotte: 'You belong there as much as anyone.' But she still felt like an imposter.

10

Charlotte's Journal

I hate my new school. I hate going in every day not knowing what they'll do now. Today, when I went into the classroom, they were all standing around the doorway. They keep doing it; every class I walk into, they're already there waiting for me to arrive. My lungs felt so tight, like my ribs had seized and were pressing down so hard on my chest that I couldn't breathe properly. I tried to act brave. Don't let them see you're scared, I told myself. I pushed my glasses up and kept my head down as I tried to go past them to get to my seat. Suddenly, I felt someone reaching out and pulling back my school bag. I froze. That was the first time they had physically touched me; up until then, they'd just called me names. I twisted my shoulder away from her and managed to wriggle free from her grip but someone else stuck out their foot then and I stumbled forward over it, causing them all to laugh.

One of the girls called Sofia wrinkled her nose then. 'Can you guys smell something?'

'Oh yeah, it stinks in here,' another girl said, sniffing the air.

'It's coming from the scholarship kid. Poor thing probably doesn't even have hot water to take a shower in the mornings.'

They all laughed and I felt water sting my eyes. Don't cry, I told myself. Don't let them see that they're getting to you.

'Ew, she probably has nits too,' Sofia said. 'They shouldn't be allowed in here. Every year, it's the same: they bring their disgusting diseases into our school.'

The girl beside her – Penny or Polly, I think her name is – clamped a hand over her mouth. 'Oh my God!' she squealed, pointing towards my feet, 'Look, her runners are Nike dupes.'

'Let's see!' they all chorused. They rushed over and circled me, staring at my P.E. trainers.

I looked down at the shoes which Mum had

picked up for me somewhere. They had probably been on sale or maybe she got them in the supermarket. I don't know what brand they are but that's because I'm not into brands.

'We don't want you here,' Sofia said then, coming right up into my face. 'Why don't you go back to your poor friends at your poor little school.'

The rest of the group sniggered.

Don't react, I told myself. I know I should just ignore them but I was shaking so badly and trying my best not to cry.

They are getting braver. What will they do next time? I've been in this school for almost a month now and Mum keeps saying, 'Just give it time,' but it's only getting worse. I wish I could go back to my old school. They don't want me in St Thomas's and I don't want to be here. Although I didn't really have any friends in Riverdale, at least people there left me alone. Nobody bothered with me once I didn't bother with them. Nobody cared that I never spoke in class or that I preferred to read in the library at lunchtime but in St Thomas's, I feel like a novelty – a fun, new toy for them all to poke, prod and play with.

I was in the middle of doing my maths homework just there when my phone vibrated with a message. I opened it and saw an image of a shanty town and someone had edited the picture with an arrow pointing towards a tin shack with a sign that said, Charlotte's house. Ever since Ollie Riordan added me to the fifth year Snapchat group, they keep spamming me with pictures. I thought he was being nice by trying to include me but now I think he's getting a kick out of it too. I keep leaving the group but they keep adding me back in.

I know Mum really wants me to make some friends; every day after school, she asks me about my day and who I sat with for lunch. She looks so hopeful, so desperate for me to say I've found some friends, that I just lie and make up some names because I know it makes her happy. She was really hoping I'd 'find my tribe' as she calls it in St Thomas's and I feel bad now because I'm letting her down again. I can't tell her about any of this because she is so thrilled that I'm at the school and has everything pinned on my life being a success.

11

Ali watched her daughter cross at the pedestrian lights as she made her way to the bus stop the next morning. It was a damp, drizzly, grey morning and Charlotte was standing there looking miserable. Office workers dressed in smart tailoring hid beneath umbrellas, standing back from the road in case they got splashed by the puddles from the passing traffic. Charlotte had a longer commute now as she travelled into Dublin city centre and couldn't cycle to school like she used to when she had been in Riverdale Community School.

The conversation she had had last night with Charlotte had been playing on her mind all night. She still couldn't work out whether Charlotte was exaggerating or not.

'How was school today, love?' Ali had asked as she heaped a ladleful of beef tagine over a plate of rice for her dinner.

'Not good.' Charlotte had responded glumly, playing with a forkful of rice.

'Why? What happened?'

'They all know I'm the scholarship kid.'

Ali had been stunned. 'B-but that's impossible!'

'I swear, Mum, they do,' Charlotte retorted.

'But Mr Franklin told me that it's entirely confidential. Even the teachers aren't told who is awarded the scholarships; they want everyone treated equally.'

When Charlotte had first received the award, Ali had called Mr Franklin to discuss how it all worked. One of Ali's biggest concerns was that Charlotte would be singled out as the token scholarship kid, which she really didn't want to happen, but Mr Franklin had been at pains to assure her that the awarding of the scholarships was entirely secret and that not even the teachers were made aware of which children were scholarship recipients. They didn't do a public announcement or an award ceremony; the whole thing was kept under wraps. He had explained it was because they wanted every child on an equal footing and Ali had been impressed.

'Well, that's a nice idea and all, but it doesn't work that way in reality.' Charlotte's tone was heavy with sarcasm and Ali was taken aback; it wasn't like her daughter to speak like this.

'What's that supposed to mean?' Ali asked in bewilderment.

Charlotte shrugged. 'I think it's just obvious.'

'How do you mean?'

'I don't dress like them or wear the same designer coat or shoes.'

'So you're telling me that they know you have the scholarship because of what you *wear*?' Ali was incredulous.

Charlotte nodded.

'Oh, come on, love, are you sure you're not imagining it?' Ali retorted. It sounded like Charlotte was being a little over-sensitive. How could anyone guess she was the scholarship recipient based on her clothes alone? Surely not every single kid in St Thomas's was clad head to toe in designer gear. Were they?

'I swear, Mum, they know it's me.'

'Well, that's their loss if they're going to be so shallow and judge someone they don't know simply by what they're wearing. The world would be a boring place if we all dressed the same.' She knew she was being dismissive but if Charlotte was being a little dramatic, the last thing Ali wanted to do was add more fuel to the fire and make a big deal of it.

'They really seem to hate me, Mum,' Charlotte went on. 'They hate that I'm *there*.'

'Charlotte, love, I doubt that. I know it's hard being the new girl but are you sure you're not exaggerating?'

'It's true. I stand out a mile. I don't like it.'

'Look, love, you won that scholarship fair and square; you belong there more than anyone. That school is lucky to have you. It's the best place for you, it will just take some time to settle in but once they get to know how beautiful and smart you are,' she reached across the table and tickled her daughter beneath her chin, 'they'll fall in love with you too.'

'Can't I go back to Riverdale?' she begged. 'I was happy there.'

'Don't you know how lucky you are to be at St Thomas's, honey? It's the best place for you. Do you know how many kids would kill to be in your shoes – to get a scholarship for the most prestigious school in the country?' Ali had tried to keep the annoyance out of her voice but Charlotte just didn't appreciate the opportunity that had landed on her plate. 'Keep your head down and forget about them. It's the best place for you. You'll show them when you get stellar results in your exams.'

Now, Ali looked at her daughter standing there getting soaked by the soft mizzle that seemed to be coming from every direction, the kind of rain that looked innocuous enough but would have you soaked through in minutes. Earlier that morning, Charlotte had emerged from the house without her coat and when Ali had told her to go back in and get it, she had refused, which wasn't like her. Ali wondered was this something to do with what she had told her about the other students identifying her as the scholarship recipient based on the clothes she wore? She was starting to second-guess herself; had she done the right thing in persuading her to change schools? Ali wondered. She just wanted the best for Charlotte; she wanted her daughter to seize the opportunities presented to her. Surely that didn't make her a bad mother. *Did it?*

12

Two weeks later, Ali stood in the restaurant kitchen getting ready for lunchtime service when she felt her phone vibrate in her pocket. She placed down the pile of dirty plates she had in her hands, wiped them quickly on her apron before fishing it out.

'Hello?' she answered.

'Hello, is that Mrs Daly?'

'Ms Daly,' Ali corrected.

'Apologies, *Ms Daly*. This is Mr Franklin from St Thomas's. I wanted to have a quick word with you about something and was wondering if this was a good time or perhaps you might want to call me back at a time that suits you better?'

'No, no, now is fine,' Ali replied quickly. She

hoped everything was okay with Charlotte. 'Just give me a sec, I want to step outside.'

She left the bustle of the kitchen and hurried towards the back door of the restaurant. She stepped out into the bin yard where the restaurant waste was collected. Recycling bins overflowed with empty wine and beer bottles. The balmy October air warmed her face. They had been experiencing something of an Indian summer over the last few days. She sat down onto a white plastic patio chair that was used by the staff when they went out to smoke or catch some fresh air on their break.

'How can I help you, Mr Franklin?'

'There was an incident in school involving your daughter Charlotte yesterday. A teacher overheard a couple of girls giving her a hard time.' He paused for a moment before continuing. 'It was in relation to the fact that she is a scholarship recipient.'

'I see...' Ali said, processing what he was telling her. A flash of guilt seared her for not taking Charlotte seriously when she had told her about it initially. 'But how would they know? I thought you said that nobody was told who the scholarship students are?'

'It absolutely is treated with the strictest of confidence, but I guess... sometimes... well, sometimes, students work these things out for themselves... I'm sorry, it isn't a nice thing to have to tell you.'

'I see...' Ali said, feeling her heart sink. She thought back to the conversation that they had had two weeks ago and felt a wash of guilt. Charlotte had told her this but she hadn't believed her. It seemed outrageous that even though her fellow students hadn't been told expressly that Charlotte had received the scholarship, they had been able to identify her simply based on the clothes she wore. The thought of her daughter being teased because she didn't have as much money as the rest of them stung. Why hadn't Charlotte told her about what had happened yesterday? she wondered. Had she not been paying enough attention to her? Or worse, had Charlotte felt unable to approach her mother because she hadn't believed her last time? If that was the case, Ali would never forgive herself. Ali tried to remember how Charlotte had seemed the night before, whether she had been acting any differently or been upset, but she hadn't noticed anything out of the ordinary with her. If she thought about it, Charlotte had been quieter than usual over the last few weeks but she hadn't complained again about St Thomas's. Ali had thought she was beginning to settle in her new school and deliberately hadn't mentioned anything else about their conversation, hoping that Charlotte had moved on. Now she knew that that wasn't true.

'She never mentioned anything about it to me yesterday when I came home from work,' Ali said.

'We want to assure you that the matter is being dealt with and we take incidents like these very seriously. I have personally spoken to the children involved and with their parents too. The students will all be detained after school on Friday. Their behaviour is unacceptable and is not a good reflection on the students or the wider community of St Thomas's.'

'Well, thank you, Mr Franklin for bringing the matter to my attention. I'll talk to her tonight and try to get to the bottom of it.'

'While I'm speaking with you, I wanted to check in on how you feel your daughter is settling in at St Thomas's?'

'Good,' she lied. The truth was that Charlotte had been in the school for over a month but save for the conversation they had had where Charlotte told her that she believed everyone knew she was the scholarship recipient, she didn't say much. Whenever Ali asked her a question about how her day had gone or if she had got much homework, she would generally respond with a one-word answer like, 'Fine' or, 'Okay.'

'That's good, I'm glad to hear that. Her teachers are all very happy with her and her work; the only thing they said is that they wished she'd participate more in class but I'm sure that will come in time.'

'Of course, thank you Mr Franklin. I appreciate you keeping me in the loop.'

Ali hung up the phone feeling heaviness fill her body. She went back inside and looked around at the restaurant which was starting to fill up with lunch-time diners.

'Everything okay, Ali?' It was Lisa.

Ali rearranged her features into a smile for her boss's sake. 'I think so...' she said anxiously pursing her lips together. 'That was Mr Franklin from St Thomas's.'

'Oh yeah, how is Charlotte getting on? I bet she adores it. My pair love it there. They'd board, only we live ten minutes away.' She laughed.

'Well, you know Charlotte, she doesn't say much... Mr Franklin said there was an incident in school yesterday but Charlotte never mentioned anything to me about it.'

'Oh yeah?'

Ali sighed. 'Apparently, some girls were giving her a hard time about being a scholarship student.'

'I'm sorry,' Lisa said. 'That's horrible. How did they

know, though? Aren't these things normally kept confidential?'

'Yes, Mr Franklin assured me that nobody is told who gets the scholarships so that's why I'm baffled by the whole thing. Charlotte seems to think it's down to her lack of designer clothing but I hardly think they could identify her from that alone.' A thought occurred to Ali then; it seemed so unlikely to her that they had identified Charlotte as the scholarship recipient based on her lack of designer apparel. Could Lisa have told some of her friends who had children in the school? Or maybe Lisa had let it slip to Ollie that Charlotte had been awarded the scholarship and it was possible that he had spilled the beans to his friends. Ali studied her boss's reaction looking for any tell-tale signs that she had told someone. But all she saw was sympathy in her eyes. She chastised herself for doubting Lisa; she was her friend, she was on her side. God, she hated this situation; it was ruining her trust in everyone.

'Well, you shouldn't worry,' Lisa assured her. 'Now that Mr Franklin is aware of it, he will be keeping an eye on things. That's the difference between St Thomas's and other schools; they're on top of everything, even before us parents hear. They really care about the students' wellbeing.'

Ali nodded, taking on board what Lisa was telling her. 'I hope so. He did seem very proactive in how he was dealing with it, in fairness.'

'Us parents need something to show for those extortionate fees.' She laughed easily.

Ali blushed and Lisa realised her faux pas. 'Oh, I'm sorry, Ali, I didn't mean it like that... What I was trying to say... but doing a very bad job of it... is that the fees are so expensive and the school governors are aware they have to keep parents happy. There is a certain standard to be upheld and anything sub-par won't be tolerated...' The explanations spilled out of her mouth. 'I didn't mean to make you feel excluded.'

'Don't worry, Lisa, I didn't take offence. I knew what you meant.'

Lisa smiled gratefully and shook her head. 'I'm always digging a hole for myself.'

Ali felt reassured. Lisa was right, St Thomas's wealthy parents were paying for the privilege of attentive teachers and a zero-tolerance approach to bullying and although Ali wasn't actually paying fees herself, as a scholarship recipient, Charlotte would be treated as though she was. 'I'll have a chat with Charlotte when I get home tonight.'

'I wouldn't worry, Ali,' Lisa said, placing a reassuring hand on her arm. 'I promise you, Mr Franklin will keep a close eye on her.' Then she headed back upstairs to her office and Ali went back to making sure the restaurant was running smoothly, that the kitchen were pulling together, guests were attended to promptly and tables turned over efficiently.

* * *

When Ali got home that evening, Charlotte was upstairs in her room studying as usual. She saw her hunched over her desk, dressed in her favourite black, baggy hoody with the hood pulled up around her head, her glasses slipping down her face.

She stuck her head around the door frame. 'Hey, love, how was your day?'

'Okay,' her daughter replied without looking up from her textbook. She would need to have a word with Charlotte about pushing too hard with her studies. She didn't want to end up in the same situation as they had been in before. She had only just started fifth year; if she was putting this much pressure on herself now, what would she be like by the time her Leaving Cert exams came around next year? She decided to let it go for tonight but she knew she'd need to keep a close eye on her.

'Did you get the dinner I left in the fridge for you?'

'I wasn't hungry—'

'Well, would you like me to heat it up for you now?' Ali offered.

Charlotte shook her head. 'I'm okay, Mum.'

Ali entered the room and made her way over to the desk. She stood beside her daughter, peering down at the page in the math's textbook that she was studying. It all looked like double-Dutch to her; there were equations there that made her shudder. Ali had always marvelled at her daughter's aptitude for maths; she did not get it from her.

'Mr Franklin called me today,' Ali began tentatively.

At this, Charlotte swung around to face her. 'What did he want?' she asked quickly. Too quickly. Ali knew immediately that there was something she wasn't saying.

She came up alongside her. 'He mentioned there was an incident in school yesterday. Were some of the girls giving you a hard time?'

'Just leave it, Mum. It's okay.'

'Well, I don't think he'd go to the trouble of phoning me if it was nothing, Charlotte. He mentioned that some kids have been giving you a rough time about being a scholarship student. I'm sorry for not believing you when you told me a couple of weeks back.'

'It's okay, Mum.'

'I'm so sorry, honey but when people are mean to someone, it's only because they're insecure about something in themselves,' Ali went on. 'You need to know that.'

Charlotte looked at her sceptically.

'I mean it,' Ali continued. 'People are only ever mean to others when they're jealous of somebody.'

'Why would they be jealous of me, Mum?' she asked.

'Because you're so smart.'

Charlotte rolled her eyes and looked back down at her textbook.

'I wish you'd told me,' she continued.

'Look, Mum, can we just not talk about it?'

'Right, well, if it happens again, please tell me. You know you can come to me about anything.'

Charlotte stayed silent, pretending to be engrossed in her book.

'All right, then,' Ali said eventually, knowing her daughter didn't want her there. 'I'll leave you alone.' She crept out of the room, pulled the door closed after her and left her daughter to study in peace.

13

A few days later, Ali was sitting with Lisa in her small office up above the restaurant. They usually sat down together once a week to go through the previous week's takings, stock ordering, the staff roster and any other issues that might have cropped up.

'How's Charlotte doing?' Lisa asked, closing her diary when they had finished. Her reading glasses were perched on top of her head. 'Did you get a chance to talk to her?'

Ali nodded. 'I did, but she clammed up and more or less said I was overreacting.'

'At least she's okay about it all.' Lisa shook her head. 'I'm telling you, teenagers are a nightmare. I don't know how my pair haven't put me in an early grave. The latest in our house is that Ollie has us hounded to have a party for his birthday. He'll be sixteen on Friday and he wants to have it at ours. He has already invited everyone!'

'How many are going?'

'Practically the whole year. Boys and girls. I miss the simple days of letting them run riot in a soft play centre for a couple of hours, handing out a few slices of pizza and party bags and then everyone went home happy. It's a whole other level nowadays.' She groaned.

'Good luck with that!' Ali laughed.

'Actually, Charlotte should come along too,' Lisa suggested.

Ali gave a dismissive wave of her hand. 'Oh, I don't think it would be her scene...'

'Come on, Ali,' Lisa cajoled. 'It would be a great way for her to meet people. I promise, I'll make sure everyone makes her feel welcome and included.'

Ali thought about it. Lisa was probably right. If Charlotte went to the party, she might meet some new friends, which would help her settle into the school or at the very least, she would feel included for the first time.

'Well, I'll ask her,' Ali said to appease her. 'Thanks, Lisa.'

'She just needs a little push out of her comfort zone. I'm telling you, Ali, once she gets to know them and they get to know her, I'm sure they'll all get along great together.'

'I hope so, Lisa... It's just, well... Charlotte... she's a little bit different to other teenagers; she isn't very social.'

'Well then you need to insist she goes. You're not doing her any favours allowing her to remain holed up in her room studying, you know. It's like a baby bird when they're ready to fly the nest and the mother has to give them a push; you need to do the same for Charlotte. A kid like that needs a little nudge in the right direction.'

A flood of guilt washed over her; was this her fault? Because Ali's family were in Mayo and she only had a very small circle of friends in Dublin, it had always just been her and Charlotte. That was enough for Ali, and they were happy in their unit, but had she harmed her daughter without realising it by making her world too small? Did Charlotte lack social skills because Ali had never shown her how? She realised that she wasn't helping her daughter by allowing her to remain introverted. Maybe Lisa was right; Charlotte needed a little help to launch and it was up to Ali to guide her. That was part of a mother's job.

'You're right,' Ali agreed.

'When she was sick as a baby and you gave her medicine, did she cry and spit it back out?'

'Well, yeah...' Ali replied, uncertain where Lisa was going with the question.

'And did you stop giving it to her because she didn't like the taste?'

'No, of course not. I knew she needed it to help make her better.'

'Exactly. As parents, we know what is best for our children and we sometimes have to make them do things that they don't want to do because we know it is in their best interest.'

'I've never thought of it like that before. You're right, of course. Thank you for the invitation. I'll make sure she'll be there.'

'Great.' Lisa beamed. 'And I'll make sure Ollie introduces her to all his friends and that they look after her.'

* * *

Ali went home that evening and as she lay in bed, thought about how she was going to convince Charlotte that she should go to the party. She knew it was a big ask. Charlotte never went anywhere, let alone to a party for a boy she only knew through her mother. They weren't even in any classes together and Ali didn't think they had ever properly spoken to one another. She would need to approach it carefully, catch her daughter when she was in a good mood, which seemed rare these days.

'How was school?' she asked over dinner the following evening.

Charlotte shrugged.

'Did you get the results of your math's test yet?'

'I got 97 per cent.'

'Well done, that's amazing. I'm so proud of you and how hard you're working.' She paused. 'Did you know that Ollie is having a party for his birthday? Lisa was telling me all about it today; sounds like the whole year are going to it. What about you? Are you thinking of heading along?' She held her breath for her daughter's response.

'Me?' Charlotte thumbed her chest.

'Yes, you,' Ali said.

'Why would I be going to his party?' Her brows were hiked in disbelief.

'Because you're in his year and from what Lisa tells me, practically everyone is going. Boys and girls.'

'Except me.'

'But you're invited.'

'By who?'

'Well, Lisa...'

'I am not going to the party.'

'You have to.'

'No I don't. I don't want some pity invitation, Mum; I know there is no way he would want me there anyway.'

'Charlotte,' Ali began sternly. 'Lisa was very kind to invite you; I can't very well be rude and turn her down.'

'So lie and tell her that I've got something on.'

'She's my boss, for God's sake! If she finds out that I lied then it will make things really awkward in work. Please don't put me in that position; I'm the world's worst liar and she'll see right through me.'

'And I'm your daughter! How would she find out anyway?'

'Oh I don't know,' Ali sighed in exasperation, 'but it would be Murphy's Law that she would.'

'I don't want to go.'

'It will be a good way for you to meet some new people and besides, you never know, you might hit it off with some of the girls there.'

'Hardly.'

'I'm begging you, Charlotte; just go along for a couple of hours and I'll pick you up early.'

She felt bad but then she remembered what Lisa had said about pushing her daughter out of her comfort zone and although Charlotte would not realise it yet, maybe she was actually doing her a favour in the long run by insisting that she go along. As the saying went, *you have to be cruel to be kind.*

14

On Friday night, Ali waited as the electric gates parted, then she turned the car into the Riordans' driveway. She had never been to Lisa and Patrick's house before and as her car's tyres crunched over the biscuit-coloured gravel, she swallowed down a lump in her throat. Black estate fencing bordered an immaculate lawn as the driveway snaked along until an enormous, two-storey contemporary house came into view. It had a zinc roof shaped like a barn with white rendered walls and panes of glass so large that Ali imagined the views must be spectacular. This was the kind of home that wouldn't look out of place in an interiors' magazine.

Ali parked up her little Renault Clio with its faded

red paintwork and looked around at the flashy cars parked alongside her. On her right, a teenage girl stepped down from an impressive jeep while on her other side, a Maserati was parked. A group of boys were making their way up the front steps wearing t-shirts, jeans and white trainers which looked like they had just been taken out of the box. They were dressed in a way that said they wanted to appear effortless but had actually put a lot of time into styling themselves. The girls, on the other hand, had no problem letting the world know that they had put a lot of effort into dressing up and all looked like they were auditioning to be Victoria's Secret models. They wore short, tight dresses, bandaged to their toned bodies in bright colours, they all seemed tall and had tanned legs that stretched up to their shoulders. Their hair looked as though it had been styled professionally and their make-up would give any make-up artist a run for their money. There were so many young people entering the house that Ali realised Lisa hadn't been exaggerating when she had said that Ollie had invited his whole year group. She glanced across to the passenger seat at Charlotte, who looked just as nervous as she was. She was dressed in a cute top Ali had picked up for her in Penney's with her usual loose-fitting jeans. Not wearing one of her baggy hoodies was the only concession to dressing up that her daughter had made and that was only because Ali had begged her to make an effort. She wore her black hair slung back in the same low ponytail that she wore every day going to school and her blemish-free face was without a trace of make-up. Her naturally fair skin seemed almost paler now beside these girls who were bathed in fake tan. Ali knew that Charlotte was nervous coming here this evening so she hadn't wanted to push her into dressing up in clothes that she might feel uncomfortable in. She was choosing her battles carefully and it was enough for her that her daughter had actually come tonight. Ali was excited that Charlotte was finally going to a party like every other teenager. How many times had she longed for her to go out with friends and although Charlotte didn't want to go, at least she was here. *Baby steps*, she reminded herself. She spotted Lisa at the door dressed in a white, linen shift dress. Patrick, Ollie and their eldest child Megan stood on the step beside her greeting the guests. At sixteen, Ollie was already towering over both of his parents and had the well-defined shoulders of a rugby player. Ali guessed he must be at least six foot tall. All the young men here tonight had the same broad-chested build as him and she remembered Lisa telling her that when they weren't on the rugby field, they spent a lot of time in the gym and sipping protein shakes, trying to bulk up.

'It wasn't like that in our day.' Lisa had shaken her head and laughed conspiratorially to Ali as she filled her in about the weights bench Ollie had wanted last Christmas.

'Ali!' She heard Lisa call her over.

'Ready?' she whispered to her daughter, who looked like a lamb to the slaughter as she made her way towards the house surrounded by the other teenagers.

They ascended the steps and Lisa pulled her into a warm hug before turning to Charlotte. 'I'm so glad you came,' she gushed before nudging Ollie.

'Yeah, thanks for coming,' he mumbled.

'Thanks for inviting her,' Ali interjected when her daughter remained mute. Behind Lisa's head inside the house, Ali could see an architectural staircase with steel spindles and floating steps that led to a mezzanine at the first-floor level. Brightly coloured art popped off the stark white walls. It was the kind of house that Ali could only dream about living in. 'Oh, here, I nearly forgot,' Ali said, taking out the envelope with the birthday card she had written earlier and handing it to Ollie. Lisa had insisted that she wasn't to bring a present but now as she looked at the gift bags being presented to the boy by the other guests, she began to second-guess herself. She wished she had ignored Lisa and brought a gift anyway.

'Thank you, Ali,' Ollie replied.

'I'd better go check on the caterers,' Patrick said, excusing himself. 'These kids will be getting hungry soon.'

'Ollie, why don't you bring Charlotte into the house and introduce her to your friends,' Lisa suggested.

Charlotte shot a pleading look in her mother's direction, begging Ali not to do this, but Ali pretended not to notice. Her daughter needed to start mixing with kids her own age.

'Eh, do you want to come in?' Ollie offered awkwardly, as prompted by his mother.

Wordlessly, Charlotte followed after him and Lisa winked at Ali as they walked across the marble floor inside the vast entrance foyer.

'Bye, love,' Ali called after her. 'Call me when it's over and I'll come pick you up.'

'She'll be fine once she gets in there and meets everyone,' Lisa assured her.

Two women made their way up the steps and hugged Lisa. 'We brought a little something,' one of them sang in a cut-glass accent, dangling a bottle of wine in front of her. 'We thought you could use some moral support.'

'You girls are lifesavers! I think I'm going to need it.' Lisa laughed, before turning back to Ali. 'Ali have you met Joan and Shelly? Ali's daughter, Charlotte just moved to St Thomas's for fifth year,' Lisa said by way of introduction.

Ali noticed how the women's eyes ran her up and down before one of them offered out her hand. 'I don't think we've met,' the woman she had been introduced to as Shelly began. Designer sunglasses were perched on top of caramel-coloured waves. Ali shook her slender hand that was studded with diamonds. 'My son, Bryant is good friends with Ollie.'

'Nice to meet you,' Ali said.

'Nice to meet you,' Joan said next, smiling to show teeth so white that they could only be veneers. 'My daughter Lucy is in the form too. I've heard about Charlotte,' she began in a way that made Ali wonder if her child had been one of the ones who had worked out that Charlotte was the scholarship recipient.

After the pleasantries had been exchanged, Ali stood there awkwardly with the three women.

Lisa thumbed over her shoulder. 'Do you want to come in and have a glass of wine with us, Ali?'

'No.' Ali shook her head. 'I'm going to go while the going is good. Thank you for inviting her, Lisa.'

'No problem. And don't worry, I'll look after her and make sure she gets introduced to everyone. I bet you after tonight, she'll make loads of new friends, you wait and see.'

Ali went down the steps and climbed back into her car, feeling the women's eyes on her the whole way.

15

Ali returned home and found it felt strange to be in the house on her own at night-time without her daughter in it. Charlotte never normally went anywhere so Ali was used to having her around, even if she usually was studying in her bedroom. As she entered her compact kitchen, she thought about the size of Lisa's home and how Ali's entire house could easily fit into Lisa's hallway alone. She made herself a cup of tea, turned on the TV and flicked onto the *Late Late Show*. She never usually got a chance to watch it as she normally worked on Friday nights but Lisa had given her the night off so she could take Charlotte to the party and the assistant manager Lauren was holding the fort. She hoped Charlotte was getting on all right but she knew Lisa would look after her.

She must have nodded off because when she woke next, the *Late Late* was over and there was a movie on instead. She picked up her phone to check it and saw she had several missed calls from Charlotte.

'*Shit*,' she cursed out loud. She looked at the time and saw it was almost midnight. The party was probably over by now and Charlotte would want to go home. She called her daughter back straight away.

'Mum,' Charlotte sounded panicked. 'I've been trying to call you—'

'Sorry I fell asleep.'

'Mum,' she repeated. 'Can you come get me? Now.'

'Sure, I'll leave right away. How was the party? Did you have fun?'

But Charlotte had hung up.

Ali got into the car and headed towards the coast with a sinking feeling curdling in her stomach. It hadn't sounded like Charlotte had enjoyed herself as much as she had hoped.

The roads were quiet at this time of the night and it wasn't long before she was back on the Duncloyne road where the Riordans' house was located. She saw a dark figure lurking in the shadows before she got to the property and as she got closer, realised with a start that it was Charlotte. Ali would know her diminutive frame anywhere. She slowed the car, pulled up alongside her and rolled down the window.

'Hey, what are you doing out here?' Although this was one of the nicer parts of the city, it was still dangerous for her daughter to be wandering around the streets at night on her own. 'And why didn't you wait for me in Lisa's house?' Ali had hoped to thank Lisa for inviting Charlotte to the party.

Charlotte opened the car door and climbed into the passenger seat. 'I want to go home,' she said in a small voice.

'Did something happen?' Ali asked, concerned. 'Were those girls who were giving you a hard time there?'

'Please, Mum, I just want to go home.'

Ali decided to bite her tongue and swallow down the barrage of questions that were making their way up her throat. Charlotte clearly did not want to talk right now. Ali knew her daughter; she knew that she needed to give her space and she would talk when she felt ready. Although she was tempted to ask questions like, how did the party go? Did she make any new friends? Had something happened or did she just not enjoy it? Ali knew that if she bombarded Charlotte, she would clam up.

Disappointment coursed through Ali and her fingers clenched the steering wheel as she drove them home. It was only then that she realised how much she had been pinning on this night going well. Ali had had high hopes that tonight might have been a turning point for her daughter, that she would go to the party, make some new friends and start to be a bit more social but it sounded as though Charlotte hadn't enjoyed herself. They both fell quiet as Ali drove. Charlotte looked out the window where the inky sea blended with the navy-blue sky.

When they eventually returned home, Charlotte climbed the stairs for bed and Ali let her go without making a big deal of it. She knew from experience that she would talk when she was ready. Perhaps tomorrow, her daughter would be willing to open up to her.

16

13 OCTOBER 2023

Charlotte's Journal

The party was a nightmare. I didn't want to go but Mum made me feel so guilty that I had no choice. The Riordans' house is like something out of a dream. I've never been in a house like it – they even had an outdoor pool which is a bit ridiculous in Ireland because I don't know when they get to use it, but I don't think that's the point. It was so awkward when I followed Ollie outside and saw everyone there; some of them I recognised from school but there were loads I had never seen before.

'What's she doing here?' I heard somebody ask Ollie as soon as we got outside. I saw it was one of the girls from my class, the ones that surround me every day and seem to really hate me being at St Thomas's.

Ollie went red, shrugged and said, 'Blame my mum.' I knew he was embarrassed that Lisa made him invite me; he hates that he is connected to me because of our mums.

'Ollie, why don't you introduce Charlotte to your friends,' Lisa instructed. She had followed after us but had obviously missed what he had just said.

He shot her a hateful look and didn't budge.

'Come on.' She nudged him in the side. 'Don't be rude.' It was obvious that Ollie Riordan didn't want me there any more than I wanted to be there.

'Everyone, this is Charlotte,' he mumbled eventually.

Sofia laughed. 'We know who she is.'

'Let me get you a drink, Charlotte,' Lisa said. 'What would you like? I have beer or some of those awful sugary Smirnoff Ice things that you young people seem to like... or would you prefer a soft drink?'

I thought I had misheard her but when I looked around, I realised that some of the other teenagers had bottles of alcohol in their hands. 'A Diet Coke would be great thanks, Lisa.'

She went over to the bar area that they had set up

to one side of the pool and took a can of Diet Coke out of an ice bucket and added some ice cubes to a glass. 'There you are,' she said, pouring it and handing it me. 'Do you know something?' she said, smiling at me. 'You're actually so pretty when you take all those baggy clothes off.'

'Thanks,' I mumbled and pushed my glasses up onto the bridge of my nose. I know she meant it as a compliment but it didn't feel like one. Mum wouldn't let me wear a hoody like I normally wear and instead made me wear a top she had bought for me in Penney's with a pair of jeans. The top was tight-fitting with a tiny rose pattern – something I would never wear in a million years and when I told her that I didn't feel comfortable in it, she had practically begged me. 'Come on, honey. Lisa is my boss so I want you to look like you've made an effort,' she had cajoled. 'It's only for one night. Please, Charlotte. It won't kill you to leave off the baggy hoody for a few hours,' she had countered when I had protested. So reluctantly, I had worn the top.

'Why don't you go mingle with some of the girls over there?' Lisa said, pointing over to the gang from my class. They were standing around in their tiny dresses, flicking their hair constantly, trying their best to get attention from the guys who were more interested in rugby tackling and horse-playing with one another. 'Sure,' I said because I knew Mum would kill me if I wasn't polite to her boss. I moved away from her and pretended to make my way over to them but I stood to the side and wrapped my arms around myself. I didn't want to be there. I didn't fit in with them. They were all falling around the place and the sound of high-pitched, fake laughter punctured the air. It was hell. I don't know why Mum forced me to go – oh wait, I do: it's because she wanted to keep her boss happy. I saw Lisa heading back inside the house to drink wine with some of the other mums who had stayed on, so I was just left standing on my own. But that wasn't the worst part about the night, what happened later was horrible; I was too stunned to realise what he was doing until he had launched himself on me and everyone was jeering him on. His hands were everywhere and I panicked. I can't tell Mum about it though because she might not believe me. I can't tell anyone.

17

Ali rose the next morning to get ready for work. She showered and dressed in smart trousers and a blouse. She secured her curly, dark hair back off her face with a claw clip and applied a quick covering of foundation to put a bit of colour into her skin. She left her bedroom and stopped on the landing outside Charlotte's door and listened out for a sign of life but her daughter appeared to be sleeping on after her late night. Ali found she was relieved; recently, Charlotte had taken to getting up early on weekends to study and would remain at her desk all day long, only taking a break to use the toilet or get a drink or snack. Ali decided to leave her sleeping and not to wake her to say goodbye. She continued on downstairs into the kitchen. She pushed a slice of white bread down into the toaster and when it had popped, she gripped the dry toast between her teeth, grabbed her keys and handbag and made her way out the door.

She sat into her car and turned the engine over. It didn't start so she tried again. *Please not today, little car,* she begged. She knew her Clio was on its last legs but she couldn't afford to replace it. It had broken down a few months ago and it had cost her a small fortune to repair it. She had been telling Lisa her tale of woe and had been mortified when her boss had offered to loan her the money to pay for it. Lisa had insisted that she didn't need to repay the money but Ali had always paid her own way so even though it had taken her three months, she had repaid every cent. She tried starting it another time and she said a silent prayer of thanks as it grudgingly came to life.

In the restaurant, she saw Lauren was busy carrying an armful of plates over to a table as she looked after the breakfast rush. It was clear from her hurried demeanour that she was run off her feet.

'No sign of Lisa?' Ali asked, immediately jumping straight to work and helping to clear off tables. She was dying to ask Lisa about how Charlotte had been at the party. She wondered if Lisa had observed her daughter mixing with the other teenagers or had she stayed by herself for the night? She knew Lisa would give her the full story.

Lauren shook her head. 'No, not yet.'

'I guess they have a big clean-up after the party.'

'Oh, yeah, I forgot that was last night. Did Charlotte enjoy herself?' Ali had told Lauren about Charlotte being invited to Ollie's party and how she was reluctant to go. Lauren's children were younger and as Ali filled her in on Charlotte's life, she would often remark how she was glad that an addiction to *Bluey* and getting them to stay in their own beds at night were her biggest battles.

Ali shrugged. 'You know Charlotte, she doesn't say much.'

'Well, at least she went, Ali; that's a step in the right direction and hopefully, it will help her settle into the school,' Lauren said kindly.

'Here's hoping.' She noticed the eyes of customers boring into her. 'I'd better get this lot their food before the *h-anger* takes over.'

She hurried over and began taking an order.

The morning rush soon spilled into the lunchtime rush and in the lull between lunch and the dinner guests arriving, they finally had time to catch a breath. Ali went into the kitchen and sat down for five minutes. It was filled with the heavenly smell of beef roasting in rosemary for that evening's service. The radio was playing as the chefs prepped for the night ahead. She filled herself a bowl of chowder, then sat down at the small staff table and checked her phone. The hourly news came on the radio. She was half paying attention to it as she scrolled through her phone.

When she was finished eating, she stood up and put her plate in the washer as she heard the news-reader say: 'A teenager has been taken to hospital in a critical condition following an incident in the north of the city overnight. Gardaí are appealing to any witnesses who may have been in the area to come forward.'

'The poor parents getting that call,' Lauren remarked, coming up alongside her.

'I can't imagine,' Ali replied. 'It's every parent's worst nightmare.'

'Well, hopefully whoever it is will make a full recovery.'

'No sign of Lisa yet?' Keith asked them from across the kitchen. 'I wanted to add a few things to the meat order.'

Ali shook her head. 'No, I haven't heard a word from her or Patrick today.'

'Me neither,' Lauren said. 'It's not like Lisa to not

be in contact. Even when she's on holiday, she always checks in to see how things are going.'

Ali shrugged. 'I guess they probably had a late night. I'm sure she'll be in soon.' She stood up and stretched. 'We'd better get going; the dinner crowd will be here before we know it.'

* * *

Ali got home from work and from the driveway saw that the house was in total darkness. Usually, there would at least be a light on in Charlotte's bedroom, which faced onto the road. Ali had called her daughter during the day but she hadn't answered. Then she had been so busy in work that she hadn't thought any more about it. Maybe Charlotte was in the kitchen; you couldn't see the light from the front of the house.

She took in the wheely bin that had been standing outside her gate for three days now and dragged it into her garden, then she let herself into the terraced house. She flicked on the light in the hallway and looked down it to see the kitchen was in darkness too, so she climbed the stairs. She turned on the landing light and came to Charlotte's bedroom door which was closed. She opened it and peered inside. Her heart quickened as it always did when she entered her daughter's bedroom. Through the darkness, she could make out Charlotte's shape underneath the duvet. Perhaps she had gone to bed early after a day of studying, Ali reasoned. She was about to creep back out so as not to disturb her when she heard something. It sounded muffled, like a sniffle – or was it a cry?

'Charlotte?' she said softly. 'Are you awake?'

She noticed her daughter tensing beneath the duvet and she knew then that she wasn't asleep.

'Charlotte, is everything okay?' she tried again.

No reply came.

'Did you get much study done today?' she tried.

Her daughter remained stubbornly mute. Ali switched on the lamp beside her bed and saw Charlotte was entirely covered by the duvet; even her head was beneath it.

'Charlotte, love, did something happen last night?'

'Just leave me alone, Mum; I'm really tired,' came the muffled response.

'Okay, I'll give you some space but you know you can come to me any time if you want to talk.'

As she crept out of the room, pulling the door after her, an uneasy feeling washed over her. Something was up with her daughter; she was sure of it.

She could feel it in the marrow of her bones. Charlotte had been acting strangely since the party but surely Lisa would have called her if anything untoward had happened?

She went back downstairs and dialled Lisa's number. She hoped her boss wouldn't mind her calling at this time but she hadn't seen her at work today so she could call on the pretence of letting her know how the day went in the restaurant and then ask if everything had gone okay at the party. She was probably overreacting; perhaps Charlotte had just had a bad day and wasn't in the mood for talking – her daughter could be moodier than the ocean on a winter's day but all the same, she just wanted to put her mind at ease and knew she would feel better if she asked Lisa.

18

The phone seemed to ring for an age. Ali checked the clock on the microwave and when she saw that it was almost eleven o'clock, she guessed her boss was probably already in bed, especially if she was recovering from a late night the evening before. She was just about to hang up when eventually, she heard Lisa's voice pick up.

'Ali,' she said quietly.

'Lisa, hi,' she began tentatively, suddenly unsure what to say. 'Look, I'm sorry for calling you so late...' She paused. 'I hope I didn't wake you...'

'No, no, I was awake.' She sounded tired.

'I just wanted to let you know that everything went

okay in the restaurant today,' Ali continued. 'It was busy but there were no issues.'

'Thanks, Ali...' Lisa said. Ali wasn't sure if she was imagining it but she was sure she could hear a note of hesitation in her tone, as though there was something holding her back or she was distracted.

'I, eh, was wondering how the party went last night? Did Ollie enjoy himself?' Ali tried to keep her tone light so that Lisa wouldn't detect the real reason for her call.

There was silence for an age until Lisa eventually replied, 'Didn't you hear?' She sounded grave. Ali could imagine her face right now: her brow furrowed, her fingers worrying at her wedding band as she sometimes did whenever something went wrong at work.

'Hear what?' Ali asked in confusion.

'Something happened last night. At the party.'

'What was it?'

'There was an accident. A boy was pulled unconscious from the pool. Didn't Charlotte tell you?'

Ali felt her blood run cold and a crop of goosebumps broke out down along her spine. 'I... I picked her up early from the party,' Ali stammered. 'I've barely seen her since, to be honest. She was already asleep when I got home from work. What happened, Lisa?'

'We don't know the exact circumstances, only that someone spotted him floating in the pool and they dragged him out. We called the ambulance straight away and Patrick did CPR but he didn't come round.' The woman dissolved into tears as she recounted the story to Ali.

'That's terrible. Have you heard how he is doing today?'

'He's in intensive care.'

'Oh my God, Lisa, I'm so sorry to hear this. What a horrible thing to happen to that poor boy and an awful thing for you all to witness too.'

'Everyone is in shock,' Lisa went on. 'We've had the Gardaí here this evening taking statements. It has been horrendous.'

Ali gasped. 'Do they suspect foul play?'

'Of course not!' Lisa was uncharacteristically brusque in her reply. 'But obviously, they have to in-vestigate the circumstances. It's standard procedure.'

'Of course,' Ali said, abashed. 'Did anyone see it happen?'

'That's the crazy thing: there were fifty kids invited here last night and nobody saw it. I keep asking my-self how it could have happened, you know?' Lisa continued in a tone that told Ali she'd been grappling to comprehend and put logic on the turn of events all day. 'He's a big guy; he's well over six foot tall. He was found in the shallow end of the pool so he would have been able to stand... None of us can understand it...'

'That's just awful. Perhaps he slipped and injured himself during the fall.'

'That's the only thing that makes any sense,' Lisa agreed. 'I still can't believe nobody saw what happened,' she repeated in disbelief.

'I'll ask Charlotte if she saw anything but I'm sure she would have told me if she'd witnessed something like that happening.'

'Thanks, Ali.'

'If I hear anything more, I'll let you know and don't worry about the restaurant; I'll keep everything under control until you're able to come back. I'm thinking of you all.'

'Thanks, Ali, I really appreciate it. I just pray he recovers.' Her voice wavered on a knife-edge of tears once more.

'Me too. If there's anything I can do, please just ask.'

'Of course. Thanks.'

Ali hung up. She thought about the boy and his poor family getting that phone call to say he had been in an accident. Then Ali remembered the story she had heard on the radio earlier and realised it must be the same incident. She recalled how she had said to Lauren that it was every parent's worst nightmare. She wondered what had happened? Had he tripped and fallen into the pool perhaps? Or he could have slipped on wet tiles maybe. There were so many explanations. She wondered if she should wake her daughter to ask if she saw anything but Charlotte would have told her about something like that. There was no point disturbing her sleep now when it had obviously happened after she had gone home. It could wait until the morning.

19

Ali didn't sleep a wink that night. She tossed and turned as she thought about the poor family that were probably sitting anxiously at their son's bedside under the dimmed lights of intensive care, watching their son hooked up to wires and monitors, begging and praying that he would pull through. She desperately hoped he would recover; a chill spread through her every time her mind wandered to the alternative.

Eventually as dawn broke over the Dublin streets and butter-yellow morning light invaded around the sides of the roller blind, she gave up the battle with sleep and pulled back the duvet. She rubbed her eyes and planted her feet on the floor. She padded across the carpet, not wishing to wake Charlotte at this hour, and crept downstairs. She filled the kettle with water and flicked the switch for it to boil. While it grumbled to life, she put two heaped teaspoons of instant coffee granules into her favourite mug. Her heart clenched as she looked at her daughter's tiny handprints and crookedly drawn love hearts that decorated the pottery and how she had painted the word *MUM* in her six-year-old handwriting. A bittersweet pang of longing hit as she remembered how she had brought Charlotte to a pottery-decorating class to make it. She could still see her daughter with her whole face screwed up, biting down on her tongue in concentration as she had hand-painted it, before the studio had glazed it and baked it in a kiln. Back then, Charlotte had adored her; she had hated being apart from her. She would come up and wrap her chubby arms around her leg and say in her sweet, lispy voice, 'I wub you, Mammy.'

She wondered when it had all changed for them? Charlotte seldom came over and threw her arms around her out of the blue or even just said, 'I love you, Mum.' All these little detachments happened so slowly that you didn't even notice it until you woke up one day and realised there was a distance there and the daughter that had once idolised you, now pushed you away. She knew it was the natural order, that our children who arrive into the world attached to us until the cord is cut and are dependent for all their needs, gradually separate a little more each day until they are ready to forge their own path in the world. It was evolution's way of preparing our offspring for adulthood but oh how she desperately missed those days when she had been the centre of Charlotte's universe.

She looked out through the patio door at the back garden with its long grass that needed to be cut. She had been planning on tackling it with the lawnmower today because she had a day off, but she'd have to go into the restaurant instead this morning as Lisa had so much going on at home, so it would have to wait a bit longer.

She had almost finished her coffee when she heard movement from upstairs and after a few minutes, Charlotte appeared in the kitchen. Her eyes were red-rimmed and at first, Ali wasn't sure if she had been crying but she hoped it was just from tiredness.

She smiled at her daughter, who made her heart soar by just being close by. 'Hey, love, how did you sleep?'

Wordlessly, Charlotte made her way over to the table and slumped into a chair opposite her. She balled her hands into fists and rubbed her eyes.

'Looks like you slept as little as me, huh?' she continued. 'Is everything okay?'

Charlotte remained silent.

'Were you studying all day yesterday?' Ali continued. 'I'm proud of you and know how hard you're working but do you think you might be pushing yourself a little too hard? Remember what your therapist said: don't let yourself get overwhelmed by the pressure.'

Ali knew they were both thinking back to the time not so long ago when the pressure had got too much for her daughter and she had resorted to drastic measures to cope. Ali had come home from work as usual and went upstairs to check on Charlotte like she always did. She had entered the bedroom, but Charlotte hadn't heard her come in. She had seen her daughter sitting at her desk, bent over something, deep in concentration. At first, Ali had thought she was hunched over a textbook that she had resting on her legs but as she got closer, nothing in all her years of being Charlotte's mother could have prepared her for what she saw. Charlotte's school skirt had been pushed up and ruby-coloured blood glistened on her inner thigh. Some of the droplets had congealed to form a trickle that was running down her leg.

'Oh my God! Charlotte!' she had cried, rushing

over to her. 'What's happened to you?' She'd noticed the light glinting off something shiny in Charlotte's hand.

Charlotte had spun around and tossed the shiny thing onto the floor. It was only then that Ali had realised what it was. It was a blade. Her mind had been slow, like it was filled with treacle; she still couldn't make the connection between the blood and the blade. Had Charlotte had an accident, or another thought crashed into her brain, unwelcome and intrusive: had Charlotte done this to *herself*? It just hadn't made any sense.

She had rushed downstairs to the kitchen and opened the cupboard where she kept the medicines. She'd said a silent prayer of relief when she found her first aid kit. She'd opened it and seen there were some antiseptic wipes and bandages. Then she'd hurried back to her daughter and started trying to clean up the blood and assess just how deep the cut was.

'That's a nasty gash,' she had said as she'd gently dabbed at the skin around the wound which was still oozing bright-red blood. She had been thankful to see that it wasn't too deep, more surface level and probably wouldn't require stitches. Charlotte hadn't flinched as she cleaned it up; Ali knew that it must have stung but it was like it didn't register with her or she couldn't feel the pain. 'How did this happen?' she'd repeated her earlier question as she'd cleaned it up as best she could.

Charlotte had remained silent but a film of fear glazed her saucer-like eyes.

It was only then that Ali had noticed the other scars. Little slashed lines up and down Charlotte's thighs.

At that moment, it had hit Ali that this was no accident. 'Did you do this?' she had demanded.

Charlotte had nodded and Ali had clamped a hand over her mouth. 'But why? Why would you do something like that to yourself?' Her beautiful daughter, her perfect, *perfect* child. Why would she want to hurt herself?

'I don't really know, Mum.'

She had thought of all the things she had spent time worrying about when Charlotte was younger. Was she too hot in her cot? Or too cold? Were there any lumps left in her food which could cause her to choke? Should she bring her to the doctor when she had a fever that wasn't coming down with Calpol and Nurofen? Would she remember to check for traffic when she was crossing a road without Ali there beside her? She never once, in all that time, could have imagined that the danger might actually come from Charlotte herself.

'I just don't understand it,' Ali had confessed, her earlier shock and anger dissipating. She'd convulsed into tears. 'Why would you do this to yourself?'

'I'm so sorry, Mum. I really don't want to make you cry.' Charlotte had started to get upset too.

'Did something happen? Are you being bullied?' Ali had asked. She'd needed an explanation. She'd needed to understand why her daughter would inflict this damage on her own body.

Charlotte had shaken her head.

'I need a reason, Charlotte,' she went on, exasperated by her daughter's unwillingness to give her the answers she desperately needed.

'I don't know,' Charlotte had whispered. 'I guess it feels good.'

'*Good!*' Ali had cried, her voice climbing dangerously higher. The rational side of her brain had told her that she needed to remain calm but how could she when faced with this? 'Good?' she'd repeated, trying to soften her tone, knowing that she risked Charlotte closing down again. 'How can cutting yourself feel *good*?'

'I can't explain it. It just helps. It releases all of the badness inside me.'

'What badness?' Ali had shrieked. 'You haven't got a bad bone in your body! Why do you think so little of yourself?' Why was her daughter saying these awful words? How had Ali gone so wrong as a mother that her daughter's self-worth was non-existent? Ali had longed to shake her. To make her see sense. To make her see herself through her mother's eyes and see how special and wonderful she was. If Charlotte could see herself like Ali saw her, she would never do anything like this.

Charlotte had remained mute.

'Doesn't it hurt?' Ali had tried. The despair so plain in her voice.

Charlotte blinked. 'I don't feel pain when I do it, just relief.'

Ali had shaken her head. She was trying hard to understand but it just didn't make any sense to her. Charlotte had sounded like she enjoyed this.

How had Ali not seen it before? She should have noticed something was wrong. But she had realised that Charlotte had been clever; by doing it on her upper legs, a part of her body that Ali wouldn't regularly see, she was deliberately concealing it from her.

After Ali had bandaged the wound, she had helped her daughter to get into her pyjamas. She had slept in with Charlotte that night, the two of them crammed into her daughter's single bed. She was too afraid to let her sleep on her own.

'We'll go to the doctor in the morning. We'll fix this, love. Whatever it is that is causing you to do this to yourself, we'll get you the help you need,' Ali had whispered into her silky hair as they lay there, too traumatised by the events that had taken place that evening to fall asleep.

The next morning, they had gone to their GP, Dr McDonagh. Even though they didn't have an appointment, Ali had told the receptionist that it was an emergency and she had kindly offered to fit them in. As they had sat in the waiting room, Charlotte had looked glum and Ali couldn't help but think she was too tiny and fragile to be dealing with such a heavy problem. When it was their turn to see Doctor Mc-Donagh, Ali had carefully explained what had happened. He was an older doctor, one more at home prescribing antibiotics or cholesterol tablets than dealing with a teenage girl's mental health crisis. He had eventually referred them to the Child and Adolescent Mental Health Services, CAMHS, and Charlotte had seen a counsellor there every week.

During the course of her counselling sessions, Charlotte had eventually confessed that the pressure she felt to do well in school had got on top of her. Ali had blamed herself; she had always encouraged her daughter to work hard in school. She wanted her to do well but had she unwittingly been putting her daughter under pressure to live up to her high expectations? If she had, she hadn't meant to; she just wanted the best for her daughter. She wanted her to achieve everything she dreamed of.

The counsellor had recommended that Ali try to keep everything relaxed at home and that Charlotte might try writing in a journal to help her process her thoughts and to explore any worries she had. Charlotte had taken the advice and had started journalling. Ali had to admit that from time to time, especially if Charlotte seemed anxious or withdrawn, she had been tempted to snoop but she knew it was Charlotte's safe space and so she respected her privacy. Ali had kept a close eye on her to make sure she wasn't putting too much pressure on herself in school or letting herself get overwhelmed by her studies. Slowly, her daughter had begun to get better; her smile returned and that pale, haunted look that had been shadowing her, disappeared. She had eventually been signed off from CAMHS but now Ali had to question whether her daughter was relapsing back to that awful time.

Once again, Charlotte made no effort to reply.

'How about I make us some pancakes for breakfast?' she suggested in order to change the subject.

Her daughter shrugged ambivalently and Ali couldn't help but remember a time when her daughter would have jumped up and down screaming with glee if she had suggested pancakes.

She stood up from the table and moved across the kitchen. She opened one of the high cupboards, lifted out the jar of flour and an egg before going to the fridge and taking out the milk. She bent down to another cupboard to remove the glass bowl she always used for making batter.

'I was speaking with Lisa last night,' she continued over her shoulder as she measured out the ingredients. 'Did you see anything strange at the party?' she asked.

'No,' Charlotte said immediately.

She glanced over at Charlotte as she sieved flour into a bowl. 'Apparently, there was an accident. A boy was dragged unconscious from the pool. Did you hear anything about it?'

Charlotte shook her head. 'It probably happened after I went home.'

'It must have,' she agreed, tapping the sieve against the side of the bowl to break down the last stubborn clumps.

'Is he okay?' Charlotte asked with genuine concern in her eyes.

'He's in a bad way from what I've heard. He's in intensive care. What a horrible thing to happen. Lisa is distraught. Nobody ever imagines anything like this happening when you throw a party.' She shook her head.

Charlotte blanched before her eyes. She reminded Ali of a wilting flower on a hot day.

'He will be okay, won't he, Mum?'

'Let's hope so. I can't imagine what his family must be going through.' Ali put down the sieve, went over and pulled her daughter close. For once, she didn't stiffen in her arms and so, Ali allowed herself to breathe in her familiar scent. 'I don't know what I'd do if anything ever happened to you,' she choked.

Just then, they were interrupted by the doorbell. Ali straightened up. 'I wonder who that could be at this time on a Sunday morning. Bit early for door-to-door salesmen.'

She went down the hall to answer it and through the frosted glass panes saw an outline of two people standing outside. She opened the door and her heart picked up speed when she saw that two male Gardaí in uniforms were standing on her doorstep. Her first thought was that they were coming to break bad news to her. She thought about her parents in Achill. She had last spoken to them on the phone two days ago; what if something had happened to one of them?

'Is everything okay?' she asked, panicked.

'Are you Ali Daly, mother of Charlotte Daly?' the smaller of the two men asked, flashing his identification badge at her. He had ruddy cheeks and little flakes of dry skin nested in his beard.

'I am. Is everything okay, Guard?' she asked, feeling self-conscious as she stood there in her fleecy dressing gown.

'I'm Detective Inspector Kevin Ryan and this is Garda Tim Waldron,' he said. 'Is your daughter at home?'

'She is.' A rush of gratitude flooded through Ali that she knew Charlotte's whereabouts. Imagine how terrified she would have been if Charlotte had been out somewhere? No matter what reason they were here for, at least she knew her daughter was safe.

'Would you mind if we came in? There's something we'd like to speak to you about.'

All kinds of thoughts entered her head. What was going on? Why did they need to come in? 'Sure... of course...' she said, stepping aside to let them in. She brought them into the living room and began fixing cushions. She lifted the throw she hadn't bothered to fold before she went to bed the night before and folded it into a neat rectangle.

'Sit down,' she instructed. 'Can I... eh... offer you tea or coffee?' She had never had Gardaí call to her home before and she wasn't sure of the standard protocol.

'No, thank you, we just wanted to have a word. Is your daughter available to speak too?'

'Can you tell me what this is about?' She felt droplets of sweat pooling beneath her armpits and soaking through her pyjama top. She had never had any dealings with the Gardaí before; the only previous interaction she had had was when she had been pulled over for driving slightly above the speed limit but the Garda had just let her go with a caution. That was the only time in her life that she had been on the wrong side of the law.

'We'd rather talk to both of you together and we can explain everything then.'

'Okay, let me go get her.' She excused herself from the room and made her way towards the kitchen. So many thoughts were whirring through her head. What on earth could this be about? Her daughter never went anywhere, never did anything... perhaps she had got involved in something online...? But Charlotte wasn't one for social media. Although she had the apps that most teenagers used like Snapchat, she rarely used them. Suddenly, another thought crashed into her mind, spreading icy fear through her veins; was this something to do with what had happened at the party? Did they want to see if Charlotte had witnessed the boy falling into the pool? Her heart started to race and her throat felt dry and scratchy as she entered the kitchen to get her daughter.

Charlotte raised her head to look at her. 'Who is it?'

'It's the Gardaí,' she whispered so that they wouldn't hear her.

Charlotte blinked rapidly. 'What? Why, Mum? Why are they here?'

'I'm not sure. They want to talk to both of us together.'

She shook her head quickly. 'No, Mum – I can't. Tell them I'm not here...'

'Don't worry, love, I'm sure it's nothing serious. Let's go talk to them.' Whatever about her lack of dealings with the Gardaí, Charlotte had had none and she knew this must be terrifying for her.

'No, Mum!'

'Charlotte, love, you have to,' she coaxed. 'We don't really get a choice. Come on, honey, I'm sure it's all a big fuss for nothing.'

20

Ali led Charlotte into the living room where the two Gardaí were sitting on the sofa with stern faces waiting for them. Ali looked at Charlotte, who was also wearing her pyjamas, and dearly wished they were both dressed. She knew she would be more confident if she was out of her pyjamas at least.

'Charlotte.' The Garda stuck out his hand towards her daughter. 'I'm Detective Inspector Kevin Ryan.' He gestured to the man beside him. 'And this is Garda Tim Waldron.'

Charlotte returned the handshake limply.

'Sit down, love,' Ali encouraged, worried her daughter was about to pass out at any moment, judging by how pale she was.

Charlotte sat in the armchair that stood in front of the window and Ali sat on its arm beside her.

'Now we just want to start by asking you a few questions if that's okay?' he began, removing his cap.

Ali nodded, wishing they would put them out of their misery and tell them what this was all about.

'There was an incident at a party in a house on Duncloyne road on Friday night and we believe you were in attendance, Charlotte,' Garda Waldron began.

Relief spread through Ali. They must be interviewing all the children who had attended the party to see if any of them had witnessed what had happened to the boy. This was just standard procedure. 'Yes, we heard about that,' Ali interjected. 'It was a really awful thing to happen.'

The Gardaí didn't look at her and instead kept their attention focused on Charlotte. 'A boy was found unconscious in a swimming pool at the property and we were wondering if you saw what happened?'

'She was gone home by that stage,' Ali butted in again. 'I picked her up early.'

'Can you let your daughter speak please, Ms Daly,' Garda Waldron reprimanded.

'Sorry,' Ali said contritely.

'My mum is right,' Charlotte finally spoke, her

voice no more than a whisper. 'I went home early so I didn't see anything.'

'So, you didn't see what happened to the boy or how he entered the pool?' Garda Waldron went on.

She shook her head.

'Are you sure?' he pushed.

'Excuse me, Garda but she has told you what she saw; I don't think it's fair to keep asking her,' Ali interjected.

'We have witnesses that say they saw the boy being pushed into the pool.'

'What the hell!' Ali gasped. 'I thought it was an accident.' Wasn't that what Lisa had told her?

'Your daughter was last seen talking to him so naturally that makes her a person of interest in our investigation.'

Charlotte's eyes grew saucer-like with fear and her whole body began trembling.

'Are you serious?' Ali almost laughed, only their faces were so grave that she knew they weren't joking. This was Charlotte they were talking about. Her meek and timid daughter. The tiny girl who was almost a foot shorter than all the guys that Ali had seen walking into the party. 'There's no way she could have! I already told you, she left before he was found in the pool so she wasn't even there when it happened. I picked her up shortly after midnight. You can check my phone's location... I don't know... but it will prove she was gone home early.'

'Charlotte, is there anything you would like to add?' DI Ryan asked.

Charlotte shook her head. She was shaking so much that Ali put her arm around her narrow shoulders to steady her.

The two Gardaí exchanged a look with one another before standing up, then DI Ryan turned and spoke directly to Charlotte. 'We will be continuing with our enquiries. We know the owners to the property, Mr and Mrs Riordan, have a top-end security system so we're hoping they may have CCTV footage of the incident but if you think of anything in the meantime, we'd strongly encourage you to let us know.'

Then he replaced his cap on his head and they made their way back towards the front door.

Ali swallowed big, heaving gulps of air as soon as she had closed the door behind them. She was outraged. She was shocked and scared too but the overriding feeling was indignation; how dare they! How dare they come to her home and accuse her daughter of doing something like that? How dare they throw their weight around and try to intimidate Charlotte into owning up to something that she didn't do! She hadn't even been there at that time, for God's sake! Ali had been so stunned and taken off guard by their line of questioning that she hadn't been able to articulate a reply to them but now her head swam with everything she should have said. She shouldn't have been intimidated by them; she should have spoken out more forcefully and defended her daughter. She turned to Charlotte then. 'Are you okay?'

'Mum, I'm scared,' she wailed.

Ali pulled her in for a hug and could feel the vibrations of her racing heart against her own. The only time Charlotte had been to the Gardaí was to have her passport form signed; this was completely new territory for her and Ali knew she had got a fright. Hell, she had got a fright too.

'You've nothing to be frightened about,' Ali consoled her. 'I know they're Gardaí and they have a job to do but how dare they come into this house and completely terrorise a child and accuse you of doing something like that!'

'But, Mum, they're trying to blame me.' She put her fingers into her hair and began pulling it from her scalp. It scared Ali to see her so distressed. She reached out and held her by her frail wrists to make her stop.

'They don't even know for sure that there was foul play involved!' Ali retorted. 'According to Lisa, it was an accident.' She was beyond furious with the Gardaí for trying to pin this on her daughter, when nobody even knew the exact circumstances.

'But why did they come here unless they think I had something to do with it? They think I pushed him!'

'Calm down, love. They're probably interviewing all the teenagers who were at the party,' Ali reasoned.

'Do you know who the boy was, who was pushed into the pool?'

Ali shook her head. 'I haven't heard his name yet.'

'Do you think it was Josh Quinlan?' Charlotte asked, her eyes wild and panicked.

Ali hiked her brows in confusion. 'Who's he?'

'He was one of the boys at the party.'

Ali felt her breath hitch in her chest and the fine hairs on her arms stood to attention. 'Why do you think it was him?'

But Charlotte's gaze flickered to the floor.

'Charlotte, is there something you're not telling me?' Ali continued carefully. It felt as though she was picking her way across a landmine-strewn field. She placed her hand beneath her daughter's chin and tilted her face upwards, forcing her daughter to meet her eyes.

Suddenly, Charlotte stood up and began pacing around the room. Ali's mind was racing with questions. Who was this Josh Quinlan boy and why had Charlotte asked if he had been the victim? It wasn't adding up. She knew all the teenagers who had been at the party were most likely chatting online about what had happened but as far as she was aware, Charlotte didn't have any friends or wasn't part of any groups, was she?

'Mum, why are you being like this? You're acting like you don't believe me!' Charlotte turned back to her with tears brimming in her eyes.

'Charlotte, love, we've just had a visit from the Gardaí to our home. This is serious. I just want to make sure I have all the facts straight.'

'Are you saying you think I had something to do with it?' Charlotte asked incredulously as a tear rolled down her cheek.

Ali came back to her senses. This was Charlotte. Her daughter. She pulled her tightly towards her chest. 'Oh, love, of course I don't. I'm sorry, it's just those Gardaí really rattled me.' Once again, she felt anger warm her veins for their call and disturbing what should have been an ordinary Sunday morning.

21

Charlotte's Journal

Oh my God, the Gardaí have just been over to our house. Someone ended up in the Riordans' pool on the night of the party and they're in a coma in hospital. The Gardaí think somebody pushed him and it gets worse because they suspect it was me. I don't know who it is but I have a feeling it might be Josh Quinlan and if it was him, then it's all my fault, but I never meant for this to happen. I'm too scared to check my phone in case I see anything online about it or if the people who were at the party are sending me stuff on Snapchat. I don't know whether to tell Mum the truth about what I know or not; it could land both of us in huge trouble and I don't want to do that to her. She has enough on her plate. And the Riordans are her bosses. The Gardaí said that they may have CCTV footage and I'm so terrified about what will happen if they find out the truth. I wish I had never gone to that damn party. I can't tell Mum what I know. It will cause too much trouble. I can't tell anyone.

22

Ali and Charlotte spent the rest of the day on edge. Charlotte lay on the sofa with the TV on but Ali could tell that she wasn't watching it. She didn't go upstairs to study and she refused the pasta bake that Ali made for dinner. Ali wasn't faring much better. She couldn't focus on anything. She would stand up to boil the kettle, then sit down, having forgot to make the tea. Or she loaded the washing machine and then forgot to turn it on and moved onto something else. She would walk into a room and couldn't for the life of her remember what she had come in for. It reminded her of the hours before she went into labour with Charlotte, when she had been restless and couldn't sit still. She had been uneasy the whole day and couldn't figure

out what was wrong with her until her waters had
broken as she climbed into bed that night. The morning's events were sloshing around her brain like a
horror movie you couldn't clear from your mind. She
had been supposed to go into the restaurant as she
had promised Lisa but she didn't want to leave Charlotte alone in this state so she had called Lauren and
begged another favour.

'Did you hear that the boy who we heard about on
the news was actually at the party in Lisa's house?'
Lauren said down the line incredulously. 'Apparently,
he fell into the pool.'

'I did,' Ali said but offered up no more information.

'Did Charlotte see it happen?' she asked nosily.

'No, she'd already gone home, thankfully.'

'Well, it's awful. It doesn't bear thinking about.
Lisa and Patrick must be so stressed. I wonder what
happened?'

'I'm not too sure...' Ali said, wishing to divert the
subject away from the party. She didn't want to go into
sordid details about what had happened in the Riordans' house because then she'd have to tell Lauren
about their visit from the Gardaí this morning. 'Look,
I'd better go. Thanks for helping me out; I owe you
one.'

When she had hung up, she looked out at the weed-strewn grass, knowing she should probably take the lawnmower out while the day was dry but she couldn't face it. Instead, she went into the living room and flopped down beside her daughter on the sofa. 'What are you watching?' she asked.

Charlotte shrugged and passed her the remote.

'Do you know what we need? *Gilmore Girls*.' The series had been a favourite of theirs. They both liked how Lorelai and Rory's family dynamic resembled their own and they would watch re-runs whenever they could. She used the remote to navigate and turned on an episode but neither of them laughed where they usually did and after a while, Charlotte got up and wandered upstairs.

Ali remained where she was and gave Charlotte some time alone. She had hoped that perhaps she had gone to study; even though she spent so much time lamenting how hard Charlotte worked for school, now it would give her some semblance of normality to see her daughter hunched over her desk again. Eventually, she decided to follow after her. She climbed the stairs and held her breath as she crept into the room. She saw the misshapen lump of her daughter beneath the duvet.

'Are you okay?' Ali asked.

She heard a muffled sob and once again, she was outraged for what had happened earlier. It was clear that her daughter had been left traumatised. Another child might take something like this in their stride but not Charlotte. Her daughter was so timid and innocent and things like this didn't happen in her world. She was angry that just as she had been trying to get her settled into St Thomas's and she had finally gone out socialising, this had happened. Ali knew the incident this morning would set her back now. She'd lose any confidence that she had and God knew she didn't have much to begin with. It would take Ali ages to get her back on track again.

'Oh, love,' she said sitting down onto the edge of the bed. 'I know you got a fright today but you have nothing to worry about, I promise you.' She pulled back the duvet to stroke her daughter's face, which was sticky with tears. 'You've told the truth and the Gardaí will realise that once they finish their investigations.'

'How can you promise that, Mum?' her voice quivered.

Ali used her fingertips to brush her hair back off her face and smooth it down. 'Because I know this has nothing to do with you. The police have to do their job, they have to investigate the incident properly but

as Lisa said, it was a tragic accident and this is nobody's fault. They'll soon find out exactly what happened when they talk to the rest of the kids who were
at the party and everyone tells them the same thing. I
know it's hard but please just try and forget about it.
There's no point in you getting yourself all worked up
over it. It might not seem like it right now but I'm
telling you, this will all blow over before you know it.
You've got to trust me on this.'

23

After Ali had finally managed to calm Charlotte down and reassure her that everything was going to be just fine, she had stayed stroking her hair until her breathing had gradually softened, the breaths becoming slower as her body relented and she drifted off to sleep. It had been a long time since Ali had sat by her daughter's bedside but although she hated seeing her so distressed, she had enjoyed the closeness of it. It was a little window back to when Charlotte had been young and night after night, she had sat by her cot, tracing circles on her hand, willing her to go to sleep. She saw Charlotte's journal lying on her bedside table and guessed she had been writing in it earlier. Ali was tempted to open it and read what her daughter had written but no, she told herself, the journal was Charlotte's only place where she could express herself freely. Ali needed to respect that, no matter how much she longed to get inside her daughter's head.

She picked herself up off the bed, taking care not to wake her daughter, then tiptoed out of the room. She crept back downstairs and went into the kitchen. She opened the fridge and was glad when she saw there was a bottle of white wine standing on the shelf inside the door. She rarely drank at home but she needed a glass after the day she had had. She uncorked the bottle, took a sip of the chilled wine and closed her eyes. Her shoulders and neck were aching and she tried to circle them to ease the tension that had seized them. She was using her thumb and forefinger to massage a particularly tender knot when she heard the doorbell go.

She left the kitchen and went out to the hallway to answer the door. She was taken aback to see Lisa standing there, and especially because her boss looked to be a shell of her former self. Lisa was a very glamorous woman and was usually always immaculately dressed but now she was wearing a baggy sweatshirt over gym leggings. Lisa got her hair blow-dried professionally twice a week but today, it was bushy and unkempt. She didn't appear to have any make-up on either and dark shadows hung like moons beneath her eyes. Ali tried not to let her face register shock at her boss's appearance.

'Lisa, I wasn't expecting you... Come in.' She had been taken completely by surprise. Lisa had never been to her home before. In fact, Ali couldn't remember ever telling her where she lived but Ali guessed that as her boss, it wouldn't have been too hard for Lisa to find her address on the computer system. She wasn't sure what Lisa must think of her modest, terraced, ex-corporation house, where seagulls scavenged the green for rubbish and local youths were piling up pallets and anything they could find to build the annual Halloween bonfire. Compared to the palatial seafront mansion that Lisa Riordan called home, Ali's house was tiny.

She led Lisa into the living room. 'I've just opened a bottle of wine; would you like a glass?'

'I'd murder one. Only a small glass though because I'm driving.'

'Sure. Sit yourself down there and I'll go fetch you one.'

Ali returned with her own glass and a freshly poured one for Lisa. She handed it to her boss and sat down on the armchair adjacent to her. 'How've you been?' she asked sympathetically.

'Honestly? It's been a nightmare. I haven't slept since it happened.'

'You must be exhausted.'

'I am, but I can't sleep.'

'How's the boy doing? Sorry, I don't know his name.' She wanted to hear the words from Lisa's mouth; she wanted to see if the name Charlotte had mentioned was the correct name.

'It's Josh Quinlan. He's a friend of Ollie's. They play on the rugby team together.'

Josh Quinlan. Ali clenched her eyes shut and felt fear curdle in her gut. She had hoped Lisa would say another name. Any other name than Josh Quinlan because that meant that Charlotte knew more than she was telling her.

'There's been no news today I'm afraid,' Lisa went on, shaking her head in despair. 'I tried calling his parents earlier but they didn't pick up. I'm sure they're out of their minds with worry. I believe he's still unconscious.' She took a sip of her wine. 'I keep checking my phone in case there's a message with an update on his condition but there's been nothing...' She trailed off. 'Are you okay, Ali?' Lisa asked, clearly noticing her strange behaviour.

'Sorry, yes, it's just so shocking.' She told herself to calm down and stop jumping to conclusions. Wasn't it entirely plausible that Charlotte had heard his name mentioned on Snapchat or on one of the social media apps that teenagers used? Although Charlotte didn't appear to engage in social media, Ali knew she had accounts.

'At least no news is good news,' Ali continued, forcing herself to sound upbeat. She hated herself for trotting out time-worn platitudes but she didn't know what else to say. Lisa seemed distraught.

'Everyone is very upset; we're all on edge waiting for the phone to ring with news on Josh or whether the Gardaí have found anything suspicious. I haven't even had a chance to check in on the restaurant.' Lisa sighed. 'My head is a mess. I just can't think straight.'

'Don't worry, Lauren filled in for me today. She would have called me if there were any issues.'

'You weren't in work today?' Lisa was surprised.

'No... Something happened, Lisa...' She paused. 'The Gardaí – well – they called here this morning...'

'They called here?' Lisa's botoxed brows gave the smallest indication of movement.

'They wanted to question Charlotte on the circumstances of the accident. I assumed they were interviewing everyone at the party.'

Lisa paled before her eyes. 'There were almost a hundred kids there, Ali, they couldn't be interviewing them all.'

'I thought you said you had only invited fifty?'

'Some kids brought friends, you know what they're like... When I totted them all up, we had over double the number that Ollie said he had invited. What did they say to you?'

Ali couldn't believe what she was hearing; *one hundred* teenagers milling around at a party, surely Lisa knew that was too much? Things were bound to get out of hand.

'She got an awful fright seeing the police here. I have to say, they weren't very friendly considering Charlotte's a teenager. I thought they might have had more soft skills rather than going around and frightening the life out of kids. Anyway, we told them that Charlotte didn't see anything because I'd picked her up early from the party.'

'That's what I wanted to talk to you about actually...' Lisa said tentatively.

Ali cocked her head.

'Well,' Lisa began. 'Some of the kids – I don't know which ones – but they've been saying stuff...'

'What kind of stuff?' Ali prompted.

'Well, that they saw Charlotte push Josh into the pool.'

'Charlotte?' Ali repeated in disbelief.

Lisa shook her head. 'I know. I can't imagine Charlotte doing anything like that either.'

'But I thought you said it was an accident?' A chill spread down along Ali's spine. She now realised that the Gardaí had called here because they had been tipped off, not because they were automatically interviewing every child who had been at the party, like she had assumed.

'That's what I thought... but then they started saying that he was pushed and that it was Charlotte's fault.'

Ali shook her head definitively. 'There's no way Charlotte would do something like that. No way. Charlotte wouldn't hurt a fly. Literally – she won't let me use fly spray or swat them away.'

'I know, that's what I keep telling myself. But why would these kids say it unless there was something behind it? At first, I was sure they were confusing her with someone else but they're all saying the same thing, Ali. They're adamant that it was Charlotte's fault. I don't know, maybe he tripped over her or something...' Lisa held her head in her free hand and exhaled loudly. 'It's a bloody nightmare. If I had known something like this could happen, I would never have agreed to Ollie having a party.'

'I picked her up before it even happened so it couldn't have been her. Didn't you see anything, Lisa?'

Lisa shook her head. 'We think it was just after half eleven when we first heard the screaming coming from the pool area. Patrick and I were inside the house. One of the kids had had too much to drink, he had passed out on the deck and we had to carry him inside and of course then he vomited everywhere, so we were helping him and cleaning up the mess. We ran out to see what was going on and that was when we saw Josh being dragged out of the water. I'll never get that image of his limp body out of my head.' Her features creased with pain as she re-lived the trauma.

'Some of the kids were drinking?' Ali asked in disbelief. 'But it was a sixteenth birthday party; weren't they were all underage?'

'Oh, come on, Ali, you know what teenagers are like,' Lisa said dismissively. 'We let Ollie have a couple of beers now and again at home and most of his friends' parents are the same. It's no big deal. I'm telling you, they're all at it.'

'Charlotte isn't,' Ali replied.

'Well, maybe not Charlotte...' Lisa conceded. 'But

all I'm saying is that it's not unusual for them to drink at house parties.'

Ali didn't want to get into an argument with her boss but she couldn't believe what she was hearing. Lisa had been responsible for over one hundred children all under the legal drinking age and she thought it was okay to turn a blind eye to the fact that they were consuming alcohol? Maybe Ali was stricter than other parents or maybe it was because Charlotte was still so innocent in terms of doing things that other teenagers did but she couldn't help but be shocked by this revelation. 'Well, if they were all drunk, how are they so certain they saw Charlotte push Josh into the pool?' Ali challenged. 'They probably couldn't see straight and now my daughter is being dragged into this mess when it had nothing to do with her!' Ali was doing her best to keep the anger from her tone but she knew she wasn't doing a great job.

'I'm not saying that's what happened, Ali; I just wanted to give you a heads up on what's being said but it seems like the Gardaí are already a step ahead of me,' Lisa said defensively before pinching the bridge of her nose and rubbing at her red-rimmed eyes.

'What about Ollie, did he see what happened?' Ali asked.

Lisa shook her head. 'He said he wasn't sure; it all happened so fast and he didn't see it either.'

Ali sighed.

'Look, I'd better go,' Lisa said, standing up and putting her wine glass down on the coffee table. 'I told Patrick and the kids that I wouldn't be long. They're all very upset. This has been a shock for all of us.'

'Of course,' Ali said, still reeling from what Lisa had just told her. She got up and walked her out to the door. She stood on the step, folded her arms across her chest to stave off the chilly night air and watched Lisa climb up into her Range Rover and reverse out of the driveway.

After the car had disappeared down the road, Ali closed the door and went back inside. A tension headache had begun pounding beneath her skull. None of this made any sense to her. She wanted to climb the stairs and rouse Charlotte from her slumber to get her version of events. She desperately want to ask Charlotte right this minute but her daughter had been so upset by the Gardaí's visit earlier and Ali didn't want to make matters worse. She was sure this had to be a mix-up or someone had made a mistake. She decided she would let her sleep on it tonight and ask her daughter in the morning.

24

Ali's head was thumping after Lisa had gone home. She pressed her index fingers into her temples and circled them. It had felt like her boss was pressing down on her chest, sitting on her lungs and squeezing tighter and tighter until she could no longer breathe. She still couldn't reconcile the version of events that Lisa had relayed to her with her timid, petite daughter. There was no way on earth that Charlotte was physically capable of pushing a strong, six-foot tall rugby player who was almost twice her size – it just didn't add up. She didn't want to be one of those mothers who were naïve about what their children got up to but she still couldn't get her head around the fact that both the Gardaí and Lisa had suggested that

Charlotte had put this child in intensive care. This didn't sound like her daughter.

It had been a shock to discover that the other teenagers had told the Gardaí that Josh had been last seen speaking to Charlotte. Then when Lisa had told her that they had first realised something was wrong was just after half eleven, that had sent sirens blaring through her brain. She checked the call log on her phone and saw that when Ali had called Charlotte back after all the missed calls, it was 11.44 p.m. and Charlotte had asked her to come pick her up. Ali did the maths in her head; if the timeline was correct, how had her daughter not seen the events that had taken place that evening? Had she left the party just before the events kicked off or had it happened before she left and if that was the case, why did Charlotte deny witnessing it? It had been almost midnight when Ali had reached the Duncloyne Road and had found Charlotte walking down the street from the Riordans' property. She had been quite a distance from their house so Ali hadn't even noticed a commotion at the property. She had assumed at the time that by walking down the street in the direction in which she would be coming from that Charlotte was trying to make it easier for them to get home faster but now she couldn't help but question if there was another reason for her to have left the Riordans' home? The fact that she had known Josh Quinlan's name had unsettled her too.

Ali's head was swimming with so many fragments of a story, she was trying to connect them but they just weren't slotting together correctly, leaving her with large gaps where doubt could infiltrate.

There was something else bothering her too. Ever since she had collected Charlotte from the party forty-eight hours ago, her daughter hadn't been herself. Charlotte wasn't the most smiley or talkative of people at the best of times but she had practically stayed holed up in her room since the night of the party. She wasn't even studying which was so out of character for her. After the Gardaí had visited, Charlotte had spent the rest of the day curled up beneath the duvet. Ali had assumed it was because the visit had upset her so much but now she was left questioning whether there was something else bothering her? Something else on her mind? Alarms bells were piercing through her skull. Her instinct was telling her that something wasn't right here.

The next morning, she crept up the stairs and pushed the door into her daughter's bedroom. It was Monday and Charlotte had school, but one look at her daughter told her she wouldn't be going anywhere.

'Charlotte, love,' she began gently. 'What's going on?' She sat down on to the edge of the bed and placed her hand on the lumpen shape of her daughter. 'I need you to talk to me,' she continued. 'I'm really worried about you. You're not eating, you won't come downstairs, you're not studying. This isn't like you.'

A muffled sob came from beneath the duvet.

'You were right; it was Josh Quinlan that was pushed into the pool,' Ali continued, trying a different tack. She was hoping to elicit a reaction from her daughter. She needed something to go on, a clue to what was going on here.

But Charlotte remained infuriatingly mute.

'Did something happen at the party?' Ali continued to push. 'You know you can tell me anything. I promise I won't be mad; I just want to help you. A problem shared is a problem halved. If you tell me what's going on, I can help you through this.'

'You could never understand, Mum,' Charlotte's strangled reply came back.

'Try me,' Ali challenged. 'I know you might not think it but I was young once too, you know. I've seen lots of things. I swear there's nothing you can tell me that will shock me. Just open up to me, honey and we can sort out whatever is going on together. I'm begging you, trust me.' She held her breath as she asked the next question. 'Were you talking to Josh on Friday night?'

Charlotte began to sob harder and Ali felt all her senses sharpen. She knew she was on the right trail. Something had happened to her daughter at the party and judging by Charlotte's reaction, it was connected to Josh.

'Charlotte, love, you have to tell me... You have to promise me that you didn't push Josh.'

'I swear I didn't, Mum!' she sobbed. 'You have to believe me.'

'It's okay,' Ali soothed. 'I can help you, whatever it is, I promise you, I'm on your side but you have to tell me what's going on. I'm begging you, tell me what you know, Charlotte and we can take it on together. No matter what.'

Charlotte remained infuriatingly quiet, her lips clamped together. Ali was torn between using threats to force her to talk or perhaps she should tread carefully and trust that Charlotte would open up when she was ready? Her parenting style had never been authoritarian, she and Charlotte had always had an open and honest relationship, but maybe this where she had gone wrong.

'I'm going to leave you now but I'm here whenever you're ready to talk,' she said, walking desolately out of the bedroom.

Ali came back downstairs feeling despair pool into her gut. She entered the kitchen and stared out at the garden which was littered with amber-hued leaves. Suddenly, an incident from years ago jumped into her head. She thought back to that time in primary school when Charlotte's teacher had phoned her to say that there had been an accident in the yard during break time. Charlotte and another child had been playing with their dolls but had started arguing over something. The teacher on yard duty hadn't seen what happened next but the other girl had fallen backwards and smacked her head on the tarmac. Through her tears, the little girl had claimed that Charlotte had pushed her. The child had ended up with a bad wound which needed stitches. She and Charlotte had called over to the other family the next day to apologise and bring a small gift – a Sylvanian Families toy, if she recalled rightly. Charlotte had been obsessed with them back then and so when they had gone to the toy shop to choose what to buy, Charlotte had chosen one to give to the injured child. The other parents had been gracious about it at the time; they understood that young children weren't in control of their emotions. When Ali had asked Charlotte about it afterwards, she had said it was an accident but now as Ali recalled the incident, a part of her was left questioning whether something had happened back then that even despite her young age, had caused her child to snap? Was there a part of her daughter that was capable of harming someone when she lost her temper? Did she really know Charlotte as well as she thought she did?

25

16 OCTOBER 2023

Charlotte's Journal

I'm so scared. I keep thinking over everything from the night of the party, trying to remember exactly the way it happened but it was all so fast. I can tell that even Mum is doubting my story. But how can I tell her the truth about what happened that night? She'll never believe me and it would have big consequences for both of us. I didn't think it would go this far but it just keeps growing and growing and now the police are involved.

My heart feels like it's beating twice as fast since all this started. From the moment I wake up in the morning until I go to sleep, it feels as though there is a concrete block sitting on my chest. When our next-door neighbour knocked on the door earlier to drop in a package that had been accidently delivered to their house, I couldn't breathe; it was like there was no air left in the room. Every time the doorbell goes, I think that it's the Gardaí, coming back to arrest me. I've brought this to our door – I've put this stress on Mum and I hate myself for it.

I've started cutting myself again. When I feel the sting of that blade piercing through my skin and the poppy-red blood start to trickle out, the pain inside me is released and it's like all the badness inside me disappears for a little bit. I know Mum will be so disappointed in me; she thought I had put all that behind me but I can't help myself. It's like the urge overcomes me and I can't make myself stop. I know Mum doesn't understand why I do this to myself, I don't even really understand it myself, but it feels good. For a little while at least, I'm out of pain.

26

In the restaurant on Monday evening, Ali stuck her head around the open door to Lisa's office. She was surprised to see her boss in work with everything that was going on. Ali hadn't wanted to leave Charlotte at home on her own but she had already got Lauren to cover for her yesterday and she knew she couldn't pull in any more favours. Plus she needed the money. As a single mother, it all fell on her and that pressure to keep up with the rent, pay the bills and put food on the table never left her.

She tapped lightly on the door. 'Can I come in?' she asked.

'Sure.' Lisa sighed and pushed her reading glasses

up into her hair. Ali noticed she hadn't had her usual weekly bouncy blow-dry. She guessed her boss had more important things on her mind right now.

'I didn't think we'd be seeing you today,' Ali went on.

'I needed the distraction. I'm better off in here where I'm busy. I feel like I'm going doolally at home.'

'Any news on Josh?' Ali asked, taking the vacant seat opposite her boss.

Lisa shook her head, full of despondency. 'He's still in a coma, apparently. I called around to the Quinlans' house yesterday – they live in the big, glass-fronted house on your way up the Cliff Road in Bally-doyle, you know the one I'm talking about – it has amazing views over Dublin Bay. I think his father is some big tech millionaire.'

Ali knew the house Lisa was referring to. She had always admired it whenever she went past it. It was flat-roofed, art-deco style with expansive glazing over-looking the Irish sea. Sometimes, she and Charlotte would drive along that road and pick their favourite house that they would buy when they won the lottery. The memory pinched at her heart.

'Did you get to talk to them?'

'They weren't at home.' She exhaled heavily.

'We're all up the walls. Everyone is going out of their minds. Our house is crawling with Gardaí. No one knows what to do. You walk into a room and someone tells you that you can't enter. I look out the window and they've put crime-scene tape all around the pool. I feel like I'm living on a movie set except this is my home.' She held her head in her hands. 'We keep telling them that there was no foul play involved, that it was an accident. We were there all night; we would have noticed if there were tensions brewing between some of the kids or we would have heard something if there was an argument but they won't listen and said that they have to treat the house as potential crime scene.'

'That's awful.'

'Patrick is in a right state about it all.' Lisa lowered her voice. 'And now, they've requested the CCTV footage...'

Ali's face lit up. 'You have CCTV?' She felt a surge of excitement and relief unwinding the knots of tension that had knitted in her shoulder blades since the Gardaí had visited the day before.

'Yeah, it's part of the security system.'

'Well, that's a good thing, isn't it? Surely it will show exactly what happened and take the finger of blame away from everyone.' If the Gardaí looked back over the footage recorded on the night, they might finally be able to put an end to the suspicion hanging over Charlotte. Her daughter's name would be cleared and they would be able to prove that this whole drama had been nothing to do with her. 'If you show them the CCTV footage then it will prove that it was just a horrible accident.'

Lisa shifted in her seat and lowered her gaze to the floor. 'Neither of us want them seeing the CCTV footage, Ali,' she said cagily.

'Why not? Have you looked at it yet?'

Lisa nodded.

'Well, did Charlotte do what's she's being accused of?' Ali pressed.

'The cameras are so far away and the images are very grainy so it's hard to make it out but the Gardaí have more sophisticated technology; they'll be able to zoom in properly and see exactly who it was.'

'But that's a good thing!' Ali protested, growing frustrated by Lisa's reticence.

'Ali, everyone there is saying that the last person seen talking to Josh was Charlotte,' Lisa explained gravely. 'You need to understand that she could be implicated in this whether you like it or not.'

Ali fell quiet, knowing that Lisa was right.

'There's something else...' Lisa continued. Her tone was pinched, like stretched elastic, and Ali could tell she was holding something back.

'How do you mean?'

'You know the way I told you that some of the kids were drinking?'

'Uh-huh.'

'We supplied the alcohol, Ali.'

Ali blinked in disbelief. 'You gave it to them?' When Lisa had told her the teenagers had been drinking, she had assumed they had snuck their own alcohol into the party with them; she didn't think her boss would blatantly hand alcohol over to underage children. Was she looking for trouble? 'Are you serious, Lisa?' Supplying underage teenagers alcohol at a party was a recipe for disaster. Ali longed to ask her how she could have been so stupid but she was conscious that Lisa was her boss and she didn't want to cross the line and risk offending her.

Lisa nodded glumly. 'It was just a few cans of beer and some of those alcopop things – sure there's barely any alcohol in them! We were there with them the whole time. We didn't think anything like this would happen.'

'Do the other parents know that their children were drinking alcohol?'

Lisa looked at her in a pitying way as if Ali was completely out of touch with the modern world and for a moment, Ali wondered if she was the one who was wrong here. Was she being naïve? Because Charlotte wasn't like other teenagers, she didn't really know what was standard behaviour for young people these days and Lisa's response made her feel stupid. 'Ali,' she said as if she was explaining the situation to a small child, 'it's what everyone in their form does when their kids are having a party. The kids almost expect it. Teenagers are going to drink alcohol and I know I'd rather they were doing it in a safe environment where they're being supervised by parents rather than in some dark and wet field somewhere...'

'I guess...' Ali said weakly. 'So, you're worried that if the CCTV footage shows that you gave them the alcohol, it could potentially land you in trouble?' Ali surmised.

Lisa nodded. 'Because the kids were all underage, it could have very serious consequences for us. Patrick is terrified. We could lose our alcohol licence for the restaurant if this comes out. That's why we don't want them to see the footage.'

'But the CCTV footage could help to clear Charlotte's name!' Ali objected.

Lisa held her gaze. 'Or it could involve her more,

Ali. We've no way of knowing for sure; as I said, the footage is really grainy.' Her voice climbed higher. 'Are you really willing to take that risk?'

Ali fell quiet as she mulled the situation over.

'Ali,' Lisa began slowly. 'If the Gardaí ask you or Charlotte about the alcohol, I need you both to say that you don't know where it came from.'

'So, you want me to lie to them?' Ali asked in disbelief.

'Not *lie*, just...' Lisa replied impatiently, with a dismissive wave of her hand. 'I don't know... just don't mention the fact that there was alcohol at the party. Charlotte didn't even drink, so for all you know, she wasn't even aware that the others were drinking.'

Ali remained silent. She didn't feel comfortable with what her boss was asking her to do. It was bad enough asking her to lie and dodge the minefield of the Gardaí's questioning but it really wasn't fair to put that pressure on her daughter. And if the truth ever came out, they could find themselves in even bigger trouble.

'I'm telling you,' Lisa continued. 'I'm not asking you to lie, just play dumb or this could have serious repercussions for *all* of us.'

Ali nodded. 'Okay.'

Lisa smiled, showing perfectly white teeth. 'Thanks, Ali.'

Ali exhaled. 'We've just got to hope that Josh pulls through quickly.'

'The sooner this nightmare is over, the better for all of us,' Lisa agreed solemnly.

27

Charlotte had been fast asleep when Ali checked on her when she came home from work that evening. As she stroked her skin in the darkness, she found her face was sticky from all the tears she must have cried before she fell asleep. Her heart ached for her daughter who was clearly distressed by what was going on. Ali had a feeling – maybe it was a mother's instinct – that there was something that Charlotte wasn't telling her, but what was it? She needed Charlotte to open up to her; if she could only get her daughter to tell her everything – no matter what it was – Ali was sure she could help her. How could she make Charlotte realise that her silence was dragging her out further into even deeper water?

Ali had tiptoed out of the room and instead of going downstairs to have her herbal tea like she usually would, she had gone straight to bed too. Even though she was exhausted, she had spent the entire night tossing and turning in bed. She was trying to process everything her boss had said – and all the *unsaid* things – the thinly veiled hints or had they been *threats*? She was trying to read between the lines but it had felt to Ali that Lisa had been warning her that they needed to be careful with what information they gave to the police. It seemed Lisa wanted to hold back as much as possible about the events that had taken place at their house that night and she had implied that Ali should do the same, because Charlotte was implicated too. She could understand that Lisa had a lot to lose if the Gardaí discovered they had supplied the teenagers with alcohol but she had suggested that Charlotte was in jeopardy too. Ali trusted Charlotte but maybe Lisa was right; if the Gardaí did a forensic analysis of the CCTV footage, who knew what they might find?

As the dawn chorus broke beyond her window, Ali had got up to use the bathroom. Then she crept into her daughter's room and was relieved to find she was still sleeping, so she left her alone and went back to bed. She lay there praying that Josh would pull through and then at least they could all start to put this nightmare behind them but with Josh's life hanging in the balance, the repercussions for Charlotte and her involvement in this mess were serious.

Her mind wandered to Josh's parents, who were going through their own anguish and torment as they sat beside their son's hospital bed. Just what part – if any – did her daughter have to play in putting him in this situation? she wondered. At least her daughter was safe in her own room; Josh's parents didn't have any guarantees that their son would recover. Her heart broke for them. She wished there was something she could do to help.

She lay there wide awake while dawn streaked the sky in shades of fiery orange and mauve. As her brain raced in chaotic circles, she eventually decided she was better off getting up. She wrapped her dressing gown around her and headed down to the kitchen. She flicked on the lights, banishing the darkness. She began pulling out ingredients from the cupboards. Baking always helped to calm her whenever she was feeling stressed. She decided she would make something to take over to Josh's parents. Something nourishing, soothing. She knew food was probably the last thing on their minds right now but they would need sustenance to keep them going during the long hours sitting at their son's bedside. She would call over to them this morning; she knew they were probably at the hospital but she could leave the loaf on their doorstep with a note to say she was thinking of them and praying for their boy. It felt like a small gesture given everything they were going through but she wanted to show her support for them and let them know that they were in her thoughts.

It wasn't long until her small kitchen was filled with the heavenly smell of freshly baked banana bread. When she had removed it from the oven, she allowed it to cool on a wire rack before wrapping it in tin foil. She left a note for Charlotte to say where she was going, then she grabbed her keys, got into her car and headed for Ballydoyle where Lisa had mentioned Josh's family lived.

The city streets were starting to come to life with traffic and throngs of gloomy morning workers filing into offices. She stopped at a red light and through the window, she watched a flock of seagulls pierce holes in a black sack of rubbish that lay on the footpath awaiting a bin lorry to collect it. Another gull swooped down, causing the other gulls to scatter. She watched how they didn't even attempt to put up a fight to defend their patch; they knew when they were beaten and just flew away, allowing the new bird to scavenge instead. Ali knew it was nature's way – it was every creature for itself, survival of the fittest and all that – but she couldn't help thinking that nature could be cruel.

The lights turned green and she soon forgot about the seagulls as she drove through the pretty fishing village of Ballydoyle. Boats bobbed on their moorings in the harbour. In summertime, the village would be thronged with day-trippers. The pubs would be deco-rated with hanging baskets filled with fecund pansies and petunias and the queue for ice creams would trail down the street but on this drizzly day in October, it was quiet. She continued along until the road climbed higher as she ascended the headland. She looked at the houses on this road with awe. This was one of Ire-land's best addresses. The Cliff Road in Ballydoyle was millionaire's row and she couldn't even begin to imagine the wealth that the people living in these homes possessed. The road climbed higher still, as did the property prices and soon Josh's house came into view. It was an architect's dream: the flat roof, its boxy design with zinc cladding that was spread over three floors with glass feature windows on all sides to maximise the views across Dublin Bay. Up above, she saw a glass balcony, with outdoor sofas and what looked to be a bar that she guessed they used to entertain their friends. This house made Lisa's mansion look ordinary.

It was only when she reached the automated gates guarding the entrance that she realised she might not be able to get into the property. She pressed the button on the intercom and was relieved when the gate slid neatly to one side to allow her access. She entered the driveway, taking in the manicured lawns and neatly trimmed box hedges. She gulped when she saw a Lamborghini parked on the gravel. She silenced the engine and stepped out of her car carrying the tin foil wrapped loaf and a card she had handwritten earlier. She made her way over to the gigantic front door and found another intercom. She pressed it and waited. Nobody answered. She guessed they were probably at the hospital. She bent down and placed the loaf on the doorstep and propped the card up in front of it, ready to leave. She had just turned to walk back to her car when she heard the sweeping sound of the door opening behind her. She turned around and saw a man who she guessed must be Josh's father standing there in his dressing gown. He had dark hair, sprinkled with salt and pepper highlights. Ali guessed he was a little older than her, probably in his mid to late forties. His face though was the face of a much older man; his eyes were red and blotchy and exhaustion creased and shadowed the hollows.

'Can I help you?' he called after her. He noticed the card and loaf then and bent down to retrieve them.

'I wanted to drop something over to you...' Ali mumbled as she made her way back over to him, suddenly at a loss for words to explain why she was here. 'I... I heard about your son. I'm so sorry.'

The man nodded a silent thanks, the raw pain etched on his face.

'How's he doing?' she continued.

He pinched the bridge of his nose between his thumb and forefinger. 'He's still in a coma but at least he's stable.'

Ali pursed her lips together. 'I'm sure the doctors are doing all they can.'

He nodded. 'My wife is at the hospital now. I'm just home to grab a quick shower and then I'll head back there again.'

'You both must be exhausted.'

The man wrinkled his brow in confusion. 'Sorry, who did you say you were again?'

'Oh, sorry, I didn't... My name is Ali Daly; my daughter goes to St Thomas's with your son.'

She watched his eyes dart across the driveway to her Renault Clio and suspected he was doing a quick mental calculation on how she could afford the exorbitant fees if that was the car she drove.

'I'm Roger.' He offered her his hand. 'What's your daughter's name?' he asked.

'It's Charlotte. Charlotte Daly.'

'Charlotte,' he repeated, the name thick on his tongue. Ali knew instantly that the name was familiar to him. 'As in *Charlotte,* the girl who pushed my son into the pool?' he asked incredulously.

'She didn't do it...' Ali rushed in, trying to explain. 'She's a really good kid... It's not in her nature to hurt someone.'

'How dare you! How dare you come here and offer me,' he pulled the tinfoil off the loaf, 'this... this cake thing. Did you think it would smooth everything over? A homemade cake to say sorry for putting your son into the intensive care unit?' He hurled the loaf down onto the gravel beside her, narrowly missing her. She watched it disintegrate over the driveway.

'I... I swear I didn't mean to upset you; I honestly just wanted to let you know that I'm thinking and praying for your son.' She bent down to pick up the pieces of banana bread and torn shreds of tin foil.

'Because of your daughter,' he jabbed a finger accusingly at her, 'my son is lying comatose in a hospital bed fighting for his life. This is all her fault!' His whole face was screwed up with rage and tiny droplets of spittle flew from his mouth like bullets.

'I understand you're angry but I know my child and she would never do something like that.'

'How can you be so naïve? All the teenagers that were at the party have the same story. They all saw her do it!' he cried. 'No one ever wants to believe that their kids might do something like this but you keep telling yourself fairy tales if you want, Ali. The Gardaí are due to have the results of the analysis of the CCTV footage today so we'll finally get to the bottom of what happened. We're in very close contact and we have given them every resource they need for their investigation. All they are waiting for is the evidence before they can make an arrest. I think you might find yourself believing it when they arrive on your doorstep later on,' he raged. 'If I were you, I'd be scared. Go on, get out of here; you've caused enough trouble.'

As she made her way over to her car, Ali thought she was going to be sick. Roger's words had rattled her. She believed her daughter, she really did, but what if the CCTV evidence showed something she didn't want to see? She might have to accept that her daughter was capable of something that she had never believed she could do. But no, another voice said, this was *Charlotte* they were talking about. There was no way her daughter could ever do something like that to another person. She believed her daughter. A mother would know... wouldn't she?

CAROLINE TANNER

28

Ali drove back home with a sickly feeling curdling in her stomach. It had been a stupid idea calling over to the Quinlans' house. What had she been thinking? What had she expected given everything that family were going through? She checked in her rear-view mirror and saw a Garda car behind her. She slowed down to ensure she was within the speed limit and continued on. It had been a shock to listen to the vitriol in Roger Quinlan's words and how he believed that this was all her daughter's fault. It had been hard to hear how he was pinning his son's precarious state in the ICU on Charlotte.

She signalled to turn onto the road where they lived and in her mirror, she noticed that the Garda car turned after her. She continued slowly down the street through the narrow spaces left between cars parked along both sides of the road. Then she indicated and turned into her driveway. She had just silenced the engine when she heard another car park behind her along the path. She checked her mirror and noticed that the Garda car had followed her home. Her heart picked up speed as she climbed out of the car and saw the same two Gardaí from the last time getting out of their car.

'Ms Daly,' they began.

'Is everything okay?' she asked, hearing the tremor in her own voice.

'We'd like to talk to you for a few minutes. Don't worry, it shouldn't take up too much of your time.'

'Of course,' she said, tightening her grip around her keys.

They followed her up to the house and waited behind her while she found the right key. Her hands were trembling as she tried to aim it for the lock; it took her several attempts but eventually, she managed to open the door and she stepped aside to allow them into her hallway.

'You know where to go,' she said, gesturing towards the living room door. A quick glance around downstairs told her that Charlotte wasn't up yet.

She followed them in and the three of them sat in the same chairs that they had taken the last time they had visited.

'Can I get either of you a tea or coffee?' she offered, knowing that they would decline. She knew the drill at this stage.

'No, thank you,' Garda Waldron said.

'Is your daughter here?' the Detective Inspector asked.

'She's upstairs in bed; do you want me to wake her?'

'There's no point waking her up. I have a teenager at home; they love their bed.' He flashed her a grin as if they were best pals and this was just any old ordinary social visit. She wanted to reach out and slap the smile off his face. She knew what he was doing; they were going to do the whole 'good cop/bad cop' routine. Well, she wasn't falling for it.

'We can talk to you,' Garda Waldron said, taking up the lead. 'Ms Daly—'

'Call me Ali, please—' she interjected.

'Okay, Ali – so we've had a chance to analyse the CCTV footage from the night of the party in the Riordans' house.' He opened the folder that he had been carrying beneath his arm and produced some grainy black and white pictures. Her eyes quickly scanned the photographs and she knew these were images taken from Lisa's security system. She noticed time-stamps in the corner. Her heart began pounding against her ribcage so loudly that she was sure they must be able to hear it too. Blood rushed and rang in her ears. What if there was something here that implicated her daughter? Wild, panicked thoughts careered around her brain. *Deep breaths*, she told herself. *Stay calm. Focus, Ali.*

'These are some stills taken from the footage which covers the rear of the Riordans' property,' he said, handing her the pictures. She took the images from him and began to study them. She could make out an outline of what appeared to be two people: one was smaller in frame, diminutive in comparison to the much broader shape of the second person who was holding a cup. She screwed up her eyes, trying to see if she recognised them but it was impossible to identify who they might be.

'We believe this person,' Garda Waldron used a pen to point at the smaller figure in the image, 'is Charlotte and we believe this person,' he moved the pen across the sheet, 'is Josh.'

'But how can you say that? It's impossible to identify who those two people are!' She felt more confident now having seen the images, that there was no way they could identify her daughter. She placed the sheet of paper down on the coffee table before her.

'We have forensically analysed the footage and can confirm the clothing matches the descriptions of what both parties were wearing on the night.'

'But you still can't be sure it's my daughter. Those cameras are notoriously grainy.'

'We're pretty certain. Charlotte was the only teenage girl in jeans that night.'

It was true; Charlotte had been the only girl in jeans. When she had dropped her off at the party, she remembered how the other girls were wearing short dresses and her daughter had been the only one casually dressed.

'If you look at the timestamps, we can see Charlotte is talking to a boy at 11.24 p.m.,' he continued, 'then we know the ambulance was called at 11.31 p.m.' He produced another image from his folder. This time, it was an image of a lonely figure heading out through the gates of Lisa's house. 'You'll see the CCTV cameras on the entrance show Charlotte exiting the property at exactly 11.27 p.m. and from the footage, it appears she wasn't walking – she was running.'

Ali's felt her lungs tighten, like someone had filled them with glue. She searched out oxygen but couldn't find air in the room.

'I know it can be hard to remember the details but what time did you collect your daughter?' Detective Inspector Kevin Ryan took up the lead.

'I... I don't know for sure, but it was after midnight.' Ali was flustered.

'And what time did she call you to come pick her up?'

'Ehm, let me check the call log on my phone.' She fished it out of her bag with trembling hands and saw the call from Charlotte was received at 11.44 p.m. that night. 'It was 11.44 p.m.'

'So, we have CCTV footage of your daughter talking to a boy, then she leaves the party in a hurry, just minutes before a body was retrieved from the pool,' the Detective Inspector continued.

Acidic bile burned its way up her throat. 'Wh... what are you saying?' she stammered. She felt her breathing turn shallow as though there was something pressing down against her chest.

'Surely it must strike you as a little coincidental?' He flashed her a smile and Ali was disgusted by his flippant attitude to such a serious situation.

'She's not like other teenagers. Going to parties isn't in her comfort zone. I guess she felt unsafe or overwhelmed by everything going on...' Ali explained.

'Or there is another possibility. Why would your

daughter leave at the exact same time the incident occurred, unless...' he broke off.

'Unless?' Ali challenged. 'You seem very confident that Charlotte was involved but do you actually have photos showing her doing it?'

'Unfortunately, they move out of shot and the cameras don't cover that area but we're confident that this CCTV footage places your daughter at the same end of the pool where Josh was found floating. This, coupled with the fact that we have several witness statements purporting an altercation involving Charlotte in the moments before Josh's body was discovered, make her a key suspect in our investigation.'

'How do you know he was pushed if the CCTV doesn't show that area? How do you know it wasn't an accident?' she protested. She thought about the cup that the boy they believed to be Josh in the photos was holding that may or may not have contained alcohol. She needed to give them something to cast doubt over their theory that Charlotte was somehow responsible for this and it wasn't beyond the bounds of possibility that he had had too much to drink, slipped and fell in. She thought about telling them that the kids were drinking but then she remembered her promise to Lisa. Her boss had instructed her not to mention the fact that she and Patrick had provided the alcohol.

She was torn between landing her boss in trouble and desperately wanting to defend her daughter.

'We have several witness statements taken from the people in attendance that night and they all support one another.'

'Well, unless you can show me the proof then I'm telling you my daughter is innocent,' Ali said, forcing herself to sound braver than she felt.

'We will be continuing with our investigation, Ms Daly but we would like to remind you that this is a very serious incident and if you are deemed to be withholding information in order to protect a suspect, you too could find yourself in hot water.' He stood up and tipped his hat in her direction. 'We'll be on our way now, but in the meantime, if you know of anything else that would help our investigation, you know where to find us.'

29

After the Gardaí had gone home, Ali went upstairs to her daughter's bedroom to see if she had woken yet. She found Charlotte still sleeping. She watched the shallow rise and fall of her chest and she hoped that she was having good dreams far away from this awful nightmare that had engulfed them both. She was still stunned by how their lives had disintegrated beyond belief in just a few days. It was almost now 11 a.m. and as it was Tuesday, Charlotte should be in school but Ali had decided to let her skip another day. Given everything that had happened over the weekend, it was understandable that her daughter was exhausted. She left her to sleep, crept back out of the room and went downstairs.

She made herself a coffee and sat down at the table. Her eyes fell upon the artwork that Charlotte had made in primary school, which still hung on their fridge. There was a Santa Claus with cotton wool beard, finger-painted houses and stick people standing beneath a rainbow. Ali's heart tore as she remembered how Charlotte would skip down the path from school to proudly show her what she had made in class that day. Even though the colours had long-ago faded and the paper was getting tatty and curled around the edges, Ali left them there because she couldn't bear to take them down. How happy her daughter had been back then; how simple their lives were compared to the situation she was trying to navigate right now. Ali could fix everything back when Charlotte was young; her problems had been smaller, more trivial. There was nothing that couldn't be made better with a kiss and a frosted cupcake spilling over with sprinkles that they had baked together.

She held her head in her hands. Her mind had been hijacked by questions and worries all morning, firstly after Josh's father's visceral reaction to what she had intended to be a kind gesture and then by getting a second visit from the Gardaí. Why were people blaming Charlotte? The old saying 'there's no smoke without fire' jumped into her mind but, this was

Charlotte they were talking about; Charlotte wasn't capable of harming someone, was she? It was hard not to let her fears run away and take over. What would happen if the Gardaí continued along the same road with their investigations and arrested Charlotte? The thought of her small, meek daughter sitting opposite Gardaí in a dimly lit interrogation room, a naked lightbulb and a table and chairs the only furnishings, sent shivers down her body. She wondered for the hundredth time how they had ended up in this situation. Why had she pushed Charlotte into going to Ollie Riordan's party? If only she had listened to her daughter; if Charlotte hadn't gone there that night then none of this would have happened. *If only.* She and Charlotte had always been self-sufficient, happy and content in their own unit. She had never felt that Charlotte was missing out by not having a father in her life but now, for the first time, how she longed to have someone by her side through this whole ordeal. How she wished she had someone to talk to about all of this. Someone who loved her daughter as much as she did and who would be just as outraged and also scared to the pit of their stomach by the events that had unfolded since the night of the party. And as much as she was lacking emotional support, she had been thinking that she should also probably get legal advice, but how could she afford it?

Just then, her phone rang on the table beside her, causing her to jump. Relief flooded through her when she saw her father's number on the screen. He called her a couple of times a week, usually on his way home from Mass.

'Dad,' she said, feeling a longing and homesickness that she hadn't felt in over twenty years since she first moved out of home.

'I was just in Mass,' he announced without a hello. Her father's routine was as comforting as it was familiar. Her parents were creatures of habit: they went to ten o'clock mass every morning, they would get the newspaper and their daily groceries in the shop across the road from the church and then head home for the day. 'How are you, love?'

'I'm good, Dad,' she lied, doing her best to keep the emotion out of her voice as the tears threatened to spill over. She pictured the cottage in Achill where she had grown up, the waves crashing below them, its craggy coves and white, sandy beaches that would rival any Caribbean island. She thought of the sweeping, emerald headland knitted with seams of crumbling, stone walls, where cattle munched on the luscious grass. Home. Her sanctuary. How she wished she could bundle up her daughter, get into her car, drive back to the village of her birth, and stay safe and secure there in her parents' cottage forever but the last thing she wanted to do was bring this nightmare to their doorstep. They were in their seventies; she couldn't burden them with this. They had never been on the wrong side of the law in their lives; hearing something like this could give one of them a heart attack.

'Your mother was asking for you,' he continued.

'Thanks, Dad, tell her that I love her and I love you too.'

'Right so,' he said, a typical Irish dad, unable to put his affection for her into words and yet she had never doubted his love for a minute. She was so grateful to have a father like this and once again thought about her daughter being deprived of that experience. Would they be in the mess they were now if she had had a male role model in her life? she wondered. Would the situation have escalated this far if Charlotte had had a father figure to wade in and fight for his daughter and be by her side as they tried to navigate these unchartered waters?

Ali and her father chatted a bit more before saying their goodbyes and when she hung up, the tears that had been threatening for the past few days finally took over.

***

It was lunchtime when a bleary-eyed Charlotte appeared in the kitchen. Ali looked at her beautiful daughter before her and remembered her first smile and how her whole face had scrunched up as if summoning all her might. She had worked so hard to do it and Ali couldn't ever remember being as proud in her whole life. That's when Ali had realised she had fallen under the spell of motherhood, the moments of sheer joy she got from simple things; it felt inexplicable when you tried to describe it – like how you could be so tired from soothing a newborn baby all night long and then their little finger would hook yours, and you'd instantly forget about the exhaustion. She had called her parents, beaming down the phone to tell them, like Charlotte had been the first baby in the whole world to smile. She recalled how Charlotte's tiny hand had wriggled its way into hers as they had walked into the classroom on her first day of school. Ali had clasped it tightly inside her own, an unspoken communication between them that everything was going to be okay. That gesture had told Charlotte that no matter what, her mother would take care of her. But Ali couldn't do that now. Their problems were much more serious. There was so much more at stake than a little separation anxiety.

'Hi, love, how did you sleep?'

Charlotte remained silent.

'Do you want some breakfast? You must be starving.' Ali stood up and looked in the fridge to see what they had. 'Maybe an omelette?' Charlotte had barely touched food for the last few days and Ali needed her to eat something. She was already skin and bone and Ali wanted her to have sustenance to keep going.

Charlotte shook her head. 'I'm not hungry.'

'I thought you could use a day off school,' Ali continued, 'so I let you sleep on.'

'Thanks, Mum,' she mumbled.

Ali took a deep breath before her next sentence. 'Charlotte, the Gardaí were here again this morning.'

Her daughter's hazel eyes widened with fear. 'What did they want?'

'It's okay, love, I handled it but they were asking a lot of questions...' Ali paused, choosing her next words carefully. 'If there's anything – anything at all – that you want to tell me, it's okay, you won't be in trouble. I swear there's nothing you can say that will shock me. I won't get mad. It would be much easier if you told me everything that you know.'

Charlotte remained mute and Ali shut her eyes tightly together in frustration. Why couldn't she get through to her just how serious this all was? The police seemed to be following a definite line of enquiry and unless Charlotte spoke up about what had really happened that night, then she could find herself pinned with the blame. She longed to shout and scream at her, to grab her by both shoulders and shake some sense into her but she knew that approach would never work with her daughter. Charlotte was like a timid and wounded animal that you wanted to help but needed to gain its trust first.

'Please, Charlotte,' she tried again. 'Just be honest with me.' Ali looked at her beautiful daughter sitting across from her and remembered the day she had been born and how she had promised she would do everything she could to always keep her safe. She had known then as soon as the blanketed infant had been placed in her arms that no matter what, she'd always put her first and love her unconditionally; it was her and her girl against the world. But now, she was starting to doubt her; her heart and everything she had always believed to be true had been shattered and she was left asking herself if she ever really knew her at all?

Charlotte's eyes were swimming with tears and Ali's heart twisted and crumpled in on itself. She physically ached seeing her daughter in this much turmoil.

'Oh, love,' she soothed, pulling her into her arms and breathing in her scent. And Ali knew that the promise that she had made all those years ago to keep her safe, mattered now more than ever.

30

Ali got up the next morning and went to wake Charlotte for school. She was due into work today and she didn't want to leave Charlotte at home alone with her thoughts for another day. It wasn't good for her being alone and brooding over her worries. It seemed wrong going back to normal routines when their world was teetering on the precipice of being turned upside down but Charlotte had already missed two days and she didn't want her falling behind in her studies and besides, staying in bed all day and moping around the house wasn't good for either of them. They had both been upset yesterday and neither of them had spoken about the incident for the rest of the day, feeling there was nothing more to be said. Ali had

woken up with a renewed sense of resolve and forti-
tude; she refused to let these people get her down.
Emotions were running high, especially as Josh's condition remained unchanged and everyone wanted to
point the finger of blame at someone, but she would
not allow her daughter to be made a scapegoat. Ali
knew the truth; she believed Charlotte and that was
all that mattered. Although she would be lying if she
said that the Gardaí's visit the previous day hadn't terrified her, she was confident the truth would win out
in the end. It always did.

She took a deep breath and entered her daughter's
bedroom. She felt her body tense up as it always did,
her senses heightened, her reactions on alert, as she
wondered what might lie in wait for her behind the
door. She could never erase the images of what had
had happened last year; they would forever be etched
on her mind as if Charlotte had taken one of her
blades and carved them there herself. The room was
dark, the air musty. She drew back the curtains and
opened the window. Cool morning air and birdsong
flooded into the room.

'Charlotte, darling, it's time for school,' she called
out gently. Usually, she didn't have to wake Charlotte
in the mornings. She woke herself and would appear
down in the kitchen dressed in her unform.

'I'm not going, Mum,' came the muffled reply from beneath the duvet.

Ali lowered herself down onto the edge of the bed. 'I know this is hard for you but you're going to have to go back to school eventually. There's no point in prolonging it because it becomes even harder then to face it. You've done nothing wrong so why should we be the ones to suffer? The best thing we can both do is go about our business as we usually do; we don't want to let anyone think we have something to hide or else they win.'

'No, Mum, I can't. I feel sick.'

Ali placed a palm on her forehead. Charlotte didn't feel hot. 'Are you sure? You feel okay to me.'

'It's my tummy.' Her hands gripped her abdomen. 'I feel like I'm going to throw up.'

How could she tell whether it was anxiety or if she was genuinely feeling unwell? But she had to trust her daughter. 'Okay,' she said uncertainly, 'I guess you'd best stay at home if you're not feeling well... I have to go to work; will you be okay while I'm gone?'

Charlotte nodded. 'Thanks, Mum.'

'If you get any worse, promise you'll call me, okay?'

Ali dressed herself and checked on Charlotte again before she headed to the restaurant. She would call her on her break and make sure she was okay although she was pretty sure it was the stress of the situation that was manifesting itself physically and causing her daughter to feel ill.

She parked out the back of the restaurant where the staff left their cars and saw Lisa's Range Rover was there too. She was glad she would get an opportunity to speak to her boss about the developments that had taken place and she hoped she might have an update on Josh's condition too. She was conscious that despite what was going on in her world, there was a boy very ill in the ICU and she had been praying for his recovery every day.

She hung up her jacket in the staff room, then headed upstairs to the office. The door was closed so she knocked gently.

'Come in,' she heard Lisa call from behind the door.

'Hi there,' she said, entering.

The other woman was sitting behind her desk with a thick wad of invoices in front of her.

'Ali, how are you?' Lisa pushed the papers to the side and rubbed her eyes. 'I can't concentrate on these.' She paused. 'I wasn't sure if we'd see you today...'

'Of course I'd be here.'

'Well, it's just with everything you... How's Charlotte...?'

Ali felt affronted; she was sure Lisa wasn't deliberately getting a dig in but it felt as though she was laying all the blame at her door. Perhaps she was being overly sensitive but it felt as though Lisa was trying to distance herself from the events that had taken place that night, however, her boss wasn't completely blameless in this situation either. Although it seemed everyone was trying to blame Charlotte, it was Lisa who had been hosting the party, she was the one who had supplied the teenagers with alcohol and it seemed unfair to Ali that she shouldn't be getting any of the culpability.

'She's okay, Lisa; we're both very upset. She hasn't gone to school for the last couple of days and she wouldn't go for me today either; she said she was feeling sick but I think the stress of the whole thing is getting to her.'

'Poor Charlotte,' Lisa said sympathetically. 'This situation has been tough on everyone. We just have to hope Josh wakes up soon.'

'Did you hear how he's doing?'

Lisa shook her head. 'Nothing since I last saw you. I believe he's stable but if he hasn't woken up by now,' she lowered her voice conspiratorially, 'it's not looking good, is it?'

A shiver broke out across Ali's body. If Josh didn't wake up then they could be dealing with a murder case. Ali couldn't bear to let her head go there. 'Of course he will. I guarantee that the doctors are doing all they can.' She had to remain optimistic about the boy's recovery because the alternative was too terrifying.

'You're right.' Lisa sighed. 'We have to try and stay positive.'

'The Gardaí called around again yesterday with some stills taken from the CCTV footage of your garden.'

Lisa's eyes widened. 'Did they mention anything about the alcohol?' she asked urgently.

Ali once again felt herself bristle. Surely her first question should be asking about its implications for Charlotte but Lisa was only thinking about herself. It seemed that all her boss cared about was minimising the collateral damage for her family. 'No.' Ali shook her head. 'But I think we need to tell them. I don't think it's fair that they're following a line of enquiry that insinuates that Charlotte pushed Josh when he could easily have drunk too much and fallen into the pool.'

'No way,' Lisa replied resolutely. She took off her reading glasses and placed them down on the desk between them. Ali noticed her eyes looked weary and she wondered if Lisa had had trouble sleeping like she had. 'You can't tell them, Ali; this could ruin us. Our reputation would be in tatters. We supplied the alcohol from the restaurant so our business might be shut down – your job would be gone... No, Ali, you absolutely can*not* tell them.'

Was this a thinly veiled threat? Ali wondered. Was Lisa trying to blackmail her into keeping quiet? Was she trying to imply Ali might lose her job if she spoke out? The balance of power rested in Lisa's hands but Ali had to fight to clear her daughter's name.

And what about my child? Ali longed to retort but didn't have the neck to challenge her boss and then hated herself for being so weak.

31

Ali left Lisa to get on with her paperwork and went downstairs to the restaurant. Although Wednesday morning wasn't their busiest time of the week, most of the tables were occupied and they were kept nicely ticking over. She met Lauren and after she had filled her in on the events of the last few days, she asked how Charlotte was doing and how she was coping with the stress.

'I can see this is really taking its toll on both of you, Ali. You look exhausted,' Lauren said, placing a sympathetic hand on her arm.

Ali found herself getting teary eyed. She was glad to have someone who genuinely cared for them, with no ulterior motives or who wasn't serving their own interests.

'Charlotte wasn't feeling too good this morning actually so do you mind if I nip outside and give her a call to check on her?'

'Aw, the poor thing. Of course I don't, take your time; I'll handle things in here.'

Ali headed out the back fire door and stood outside. A flower pot that once had held a rose bush but which had long since withered, was littered with cigarette butts floating in rainwater. She took her phone out of her pocket and dialled her daughter's number.

'Hi love, how are you feeling?' she asked when Charlotte picked up.

'I'm okay,' she whispered. There was a crack in her voice that told Ali she had been crying.

'How's your tummy?'

'I still feel sick.'

'I can come home if you want me to?'

'I'm okay, Mum.' Her voice sounded so much younger and more vulnerable over the phone. Once again, Ali found herself getting angered that her daughter was being put through this ordeal.

'Well, I promise I won't be late home; I'll ask Lisa if I can go a little early tonight.'

'Thanks.'

Ali exhaled loudly, rubbed her hands down her face and then went back inside to the restaurant. She saw Lisa had come downstairs and was over at a table chatting with a customer. Ali got to work and took down the order for a table of elderly men meeting over breakfast, then she gathered up their menus and proceeded to the entry station.

She had just placed the menus back on the shelf when she heard a woman saying to Lisa, 'I can't believe her audacity. I don't know, Lisa... I'd feel very uncomfortable if I were you.'

Something about her tone caused Ali to stay where she was and listen to what was being said. The woman had her back to her and didn't realise she was able to overhear the conversation.

'It's tricky...' Lisa sighed. 'She swears she didn't do it.'

The woman used a slender wrist to flick her hair. 'Come on! All the kids there said it was her. Don't you have security cameras?'

Ali paused where she was and bent down beneath the desk, pretending to be adjusting something.

'They didn't cover that area of the pool very well, unfortunately,' she heard Lisa reply.

'Well, everyone knows what happened; the kids are all saying the same thing: they saw her do it,' the other woman said. 'Their stories all corroborate one another. It's only a matter of time before the Gardaí put together the evidence. Aren't you worried, Lisa?'

'Of course I'm worried; I haven't stopped thinking about poor Josh and his family all weekend.'

'I mean having the girl's mother here working in your restaurant. It could bring you the wrong kind of attention...' the woman went on.

'Ali has worked here for almost fifteen years now; she's our manager. I'd trust her with my life.'

'I'm just saying be careful. That girl should never have been allowed into our school. I was never in favour of that scholarship system; all it does is attract trouble. Why should some kid get something for free when the rest of us work so hard and they use our money to pay for it?'

'Well, Patrick and I supported it. We are always telling the kids that it's important to give back.'

'Lisa, you're too naïve.' The woman shook her head dismissively. 'It brings a different... element. She would have been happier sticking with her own kind. We don't need this kind of drama in St Thomas's. These scholarship kids mixing with wealthy people; it's only natural that they'll be jealous...' She lowered her voice and changed to a sing-song tone. 'And when people are jealous, they are capable of doing anything...'

Ali felt untamed fury rise up inside her. Her fingers clenched around the edges of the black-veined marble countertop. How dare this woman speak about her daughter in this way? What was worse was that Lisa wasn't even defending her. She knew Charlotte; she knew she was innocent.

Ali didn't want to make a scene in front of their customers and so she bit her tongue for the rest of the day and waited until Lisa was alone in her office, then she went upstairs and entered the room without knocking. She saw her boss with her reading glasses on as she studied something on her computer screen.

'Is everything okay, Ali?' Lisa looked surprised to see her there and Ali knew it was because she usually knocked before entering.

'I heard what you said earlier.' Ali had intended doing this calmly but the words spilled from her mouth in a temper.

Lisa wrinkled her face in confusion. 'What are you talking about?'

'I overheard you talking to that woman from the school.'

A flicker of recognition flashed in Lisa's eyes and guilt washed over her face. 'Oh my God, Ali, I'm sorry.

I don't know what you heard but you have to understand that because she's a customer, I just let her say
her piece. You know how it is... But that's not how I
really feel about it all. You know that. I was the one
who suggested you should apply for the scholarship
in the first place. I'm so sorry, I shouldn't have let her
talk about you like that; I should have stuck up for you
both. I feel terrible.'

Lisa was mortified and Ali didn't have the heart to
leave her stewing. 'It's okay.' She sighed. 'But that
woman said some really hurtful things.'

'I know and I'm sorry. Just to be clear, that's not
how I feel.'

Ali nodded slowly, willing to accept what her boss
was saying. 'Okay then.' She nodded. 'Let's forget
about her. We've both got bigger things to worry
about. I'd better get back to work.'

32

Ali went home that evening completely wiped and with a thumping headache boring through her skull. The conversation that she had overheard in the restaurant had played on her mind in a loop all day long. The woman had spoken about Charlotte as if she was diseased and phrases she had used like how the scholarship system attracted 'trouble' and how Charlotte would have been happier sticking with 'her own kind' had left her seething. Not only had the woman emphasised the wealth difference between them but the way she had spoken about her and her daughter made it sound as though they were an entirely different species. Ali had fought hard to restrain herself and not storm over to have it out with the woman. The restaurant was her workplace; she couldn't jeopardise her job by doing something rash like that and so she had had no choice but to continue on as normal.

As she turned the nose of the car into the driveway, she saw the house was shrouded in darkness. She turned off the engine and let herself in. She found Charlotte upstairs in bed. Judging by the dank air in the bedroom, she hadn't left her bed all day. She could see light coming from her phone screen, so she knew that her daughter was awake. Ali switched on her bedroom light and looked around for dirty plates or mugs, signs that she might at least have eaten or drunk something, but there was nothing.

'How are you feeling, love?' she asked.

Charlotte hastily stuffed her phone under her pillow. 'Tired. I've slept most of the day.'

'Did you eat anything?'

'I'm not hungry.'

'I brought home some lasagne from the restaurant for you,' she encouraged. 'Come down and have some.'

Ali was relieved when Charlotte didn't protest. Keith's lasagne was another of Charlotte's favourites. The chef made the creamiest bechamel sauce and topped the dish with a thick crust of golden cheddar which would bubble in the oven; it was their go-to comfort food.

Charlotte followed her mother downstairs and Ali put the foil tray that Keith had given her into the oven to heat up and while it cooked, she flicked the switch on the kettle and made a pot of tea for them both.

'Do you think you might manage to go to school tomorrow?' Ali tried.

Her daughter's face was so pale and purple shadows hung beneath her eyes.

'Mum, please don't make me – I don't want to see anyone. I can't face them. They're all saying I pushed him into the pool but I didn't.'

'I know you didn't. That's why we can't let them win. If you stay at home, it looks like you're guilty but by facing them, you're telling them that you've nothing to hide.'

'I know, Mum but I can't. Please don't make me go back there,' she begged.

'But you're in fifth year; you can't miss school or you'll fall behind.'

'I promise, Mum, I'll study myself; I'll cover every-thing that we'll be doing in school. Just please don't make me go back there.'

Ali was torn. Charlotte was making a good case for herself. Ali could understand how difficult it would be to go back and face all her year group who, for some reason, seemed to have it in for her. They had closed ranks and were using her as their fall guy. She guessed it was because being so shy and vulnerable made her daughter easy prey for them. These entitled rich people were acting like lions on the savannah; they had spotted the weak one in a herd, mercilessly singled her out and circled until they were ready to pounce. It was disgusting.

'All right then, but only until this blows over, then you're going to go back in there with your head held high. Deal? You have nothing to hide.'

Soon the smell of the lasagne cooking filled the room and Charlotte's tummy grumbled loudly in response. *She must be starving,* Ali thought.

Charlotte nodded. 'Have you... eh... have you heard how he is?'

Ali sighed. 'Still the same, apparently.'

'What if he doesn't wake up, Mum?' she asked in barely a whisper, biting down on her lower lip. Ali noticed it was trembling.

'Don't even think like that. Of course he will. We have to stay positive.'

They both fell quiet and Ali knitted her fingers tightly around her mug. 'Can't you remember anything from that night?' she asked after a beat. She was blue in the face asking Charlotte the same question since the night of the party but her daughter was adamant that she had not seen anything. 'Are you sure you didn't see anything before you went home? Maybe someone acting suspiciously, people arguing?' she prompted. If the CCTV timings were correct, there were just minutes between Charlotte leaving and everything else kicking off.

Charlotte shook her head in the same way she had been doing every time Ali asked her this question over the last few days.

'I believe there was alcohol served at the party. Did the other kids look drunk to you?' Ali continued, clinging to her theory that Josh had been inebriated and had fallen into the pool. It was the only life raft she had left in this storm.

'I didn't notice.'

Ali let out a groan of exasperation. 'Even if it was something small. It could really help and then we could clear your name,' she pressed.

Charlotte's eyes darted to the tiles. 'I told you I didn't see anything, Mum,' she whispered.

33

Ali went into work the next day and asked Lisa the question that she always asked as soon as she saw her.

'Any news on Josh?'

'He's still the same, apparently.'

'The family must be going out of their minds. I feel like it's all I can think about.'

Lisa shook her head despairingly. 'Me too.' She sighed. 'Every time I look at Ollie, I can't imagine being in their shoes. How's Charlotte doing?'

'She still won't talk to me. She won't go to school either. I'm really worried about her. Did Ollie really not see what happened that night?'

Lisa shook her head. 'Unfortunately not, he was over the other side of the garden when it happened.'

'I just can't believe none of them captured it on their phones; don't teenagers usually film everything nowadays?' Ali said despondently.

'I know,' Lisa agreed, shaking her head. 'I checked Ollie's – it was the first thing I did but I found nothing. Have you checked Charlotte's phone?'

'Well, no...' Ali began, suddenly feeling unsure of herself. Should she have checked it?

It suddenly occurred to her that that would be the first thing that most parents would do in this situation. 'Charlotte isn't much of a phone user,' she added. 'And besides, I believe her, Lisa. I know she didn't do anything wrong.'

Lisa nodded. 'I know, but kids these days live their whole lives on their phone. You might get a better insight into what is going on inside her head. I know when mine are off form, I'll usually find the answer in their phone.'

As Ali went about her job, her mind was elsewhere. When a customer waved her over as she was passing their table and asked if she could bring them another bottle of wine, she forgot to bring it. Then, she took an order and only realised when the people at the table called her over almost forty minutes later wondering where their food was, that she had never given it to the kitchen. She apologised profusely and asked Keith to put a rush on if he could but this wasn't like her. She hated this feeling of being incompetent. Usually, she was on top of everything; she never made mistakes.

When she went home that day, she found her daughter in bed yet again. Although Charlotte had promised to keep on top of her studies if Ali didn't force her to go to school, it looked like she hadn't opened a book, which wasn't like her. She cajoled her to get out of bed and made them both some pasta for dinner. The situation with Josh in hospital was taking its toll on the two of them. The more days continued to drag past with him showing no sign of waking, the more emotions were heightened. People wanted someone to blame and unfortunately, that person seemed to be her daughter.

Charlotte's thin frame looked even tinier now as the stress of the last few days seemed to have eroded her already miniscule appetite. Just yesterday, they had been in the kitchen when Charlotte had got up to get a glass of water and as she had reached up to an overhead cupboard to take down a glass, her t-shirt had risen up and Ali had been shocked by how much her hip bones had jutted out on either side of the concave hollow of her stomach. She wasn't going to school and she wasn't studying either. She hadn't left the house since the night of the party and Ali was at her wits' end. Ali felt Charlotte was slipping away from her and they were going back to that awful period last year. What if it all became too much and Charlotte started to self-harm again? She lay in bed every night, begging and praying to a God she wasn't sure she believed in for the truth about what really happened to come out and to finally put an end to this mess.

While Charlotte went to the bathroom, Ali saw her phone on the kitchen table. She thought about what Lisa had said. She didn't like spying on Charlotte – she had always trusted her daughter but was she being naïve? Before she could change her mind, she picked it up and quickly keyed in Charlotte's passcode. Although Ali had always had access to her login, she had never before felt the need to check up on her daughter's phone. Charlotte wasn't a kid who was glued to it, that spent her whole life on it, unlike a lot of teenagers. She seemed to use it so sporadically that Ali had never felt the need to monitor it. Until now. Lisa's words had unsettled her; she felt she needed to check, just in case.

She scrolled through Charlotte's apps looking for Snapchat. She couldn't find the app on her daughter's phone but Ali was sure she used to have an account.

She checked through her photos stored on her camera roll. She knew teenagers sometimes screenshot things. Her heart stopped when she scrolled onto a photo taken from the waist down of a naked male. There was no head so she didn't know who he was, or even who had sent it. She guessed by the slim torso with its ill-defined muscles and light covering of body hair that it was a teenage boy. Horrified, she closed that photo and swiped through some more and found another image but it wasn't the same boy this time. This boy was darker in skin tone and his body hair was more coarse. She closed that photo and continued scrolling until she found more photos, all of different boys. She felt vomit fill her mouth. Where had these photos come from? Was somebody sending them to her daughter? Or a worse thought entered her head: was Charlotte exchanging intimate images with all of these boys? But no matter how much she mulled it over, she still couldn't imagine Charlotte doing something like that. Charlotte wasn't confident in her body, preferring to hide beneath baggy clothes instead. It just didn't make any sense.

She heard Charlotte returning from the bathroom and she quickly left the phone down where she had found it. A part of her was torn between demanding her daughter explain where the photos had come from but also knowing that this wasn't the kind of thing to be done when she was feeling emotional. She needed to tread carefully, to pick the right time to discuss this with Charlotte because she was the type of child who would clam up if she sensed any pressure upon her. Ali was too stunned to tackle this now. She needed to wrap her head around it first before she could discuss it rationally.

34

That night, Ali lay awake in bed wondering what she should do. She doubted Charlotte had ever even kissed a boy so what the hell was she doing with these images? She couldn't reconcile these two versions of her daughter: the timid girl and the one who had received extremely graphic images. This was one of the times when she found her job as a single mother tough. If Charlotte's dad had been in their lives, she would have someone to talk to about all of this, another viewpoint or someone just to share the load with but it all rested firmly on her shoulders. She had to make decisions for both of them and if she made a mistake, it was all on her.

Charlotte was still asleep when she got up the next

morning. She decided not to wake her and instead headed into the restaurant. It was eight o'clock and she wasn't due to start until ten but she wanted to be busy and take her mind off the doubts and questions that were circling around her brain.

Lisa was already in when she got there, seated in her office. Ali guessed her boss wasn't sleeping well either these days. She looked tired, her lines seemed more pronounced than usual and shadows darkened her eyes, making her look older.

She knocked gently and entered.

'Ali,' Lisa said placing down her pen. 'How are you doing? You look like you haven't slept either.'

Ali sighed and sat down across the desk from her. 'I'm guessing there's no news on Josh then?' she asked.

Lisa shook her head. 'Nothing. How's Charlotte doing? Has she told you anything more?'

Ali shook her head and inhaled sharply. 'I took your advice and checked her phone last night,' she began. She had been in two minds about whether to tell Lisa or not but she desperately needed to talk to someone about it all. She was going out of her mind with worry. And she certainly couldn't talk to her parents about something like this; they would be horrified. She could still hardly believe it herself. It just didn't make any sense to her.

'And?' Lisa leaned across the desk towards her. 'Did you find anything?'

'I found some photos.'

Lisa wrinkled her brow. 'What kind of photos?'

Ali checked behind her to make sure nobody could hear before lowering her voice to a whisper. '*Nude* photos.'

'Oh, Ali, I'm sorry. It's horrible to think of our babies carrying on like that,' Lisa consoled.

Ali shook her head. 'They weren't photos of Charlotte...'

Lisa looked at her in confusion. 'Well, who were they of then?'

'They were male.'

Lisa gasped and clapped her hand across her mouth. 'Oh my God, Ali. Are you serious?'

'I still can't believe it. I was sure I was seeing things. There wasn't just one. There were several different boys... I mean, I think they were boys... it was hard to tell but they looked young, so I'm guessing they were probably around the same age as Charlotte,' Ali went on.

'Do you know who sent them to her?'

Ali shook her head. 'The weird thing is that none of them show their faces.'

'Did you ask Charlotte about them?' Lisa asked.

Ali shook her head. 'I was too stunned. I just don't know what to say or how to bring it up with her. Part of me is furious at her for engaging in that sort of behaviour but another part of me says, this is *Charlotte*. It just doesn't seem the like the kind of thing she'd do.'

'Ali, I know it's hard to imagine your sweet, little, innocent girl doing something like this but believe you me, kids nowadays grow up too fast and they have phones and get up to all kinds of things we wouldn't even begin to imagine.' Lisa visibly shuddered. 'You need to talk to her about it...' She paused. 'Now, more than ever, you need to keep the lines of communication open between you.'

'I know. I will... I just needed to get my own head around it first and figure out the best way to approach it with Charlotte. I don't want to go in there all guns blazing and risk her shutting me out altogether.'

'I know, it's tricky.' Lisa was sympathetic.

'When I think of all those preachy parenting books I read when she was small about sleep routines and healthy feeding habits and none of them ever covered anything like this. Where's the parenting manual for this?' Ali said sardonically.

'Unfortunately, there's no book for these situations,' Lisa agreed. 'There's a gap in the market. I should write one.'

Ali smiled glumly. 'It would be a bestseller.'

Lisa picked up her pen and began twirling it between her thumb and forefinger. 'Ali, I think you should know something.' She lowered her gaze. 'A rumour that I heard... I had initially dismissed it but now I'm thinking it may be connected to the photos.'

Ali felt dread pool into her tummy. What was Lisa going to tell her? She didn't think she could stand much more. 'What is it?'

'People are saying things...' Lisa began tentatively.

Her heart picked up speed. 'What kind of things?'

'I hate to be the one to tell you this but I think you probably should know...'

'What is it, Lisa?' Ali demanded, wishing her boss would just spit out whatever it was that she wanted to say.

'Well, they're saying that... well... that Charlotte... might have brought this on herself...'

Ali was stunned and blood came whooshing into her ears. 'Wh... what do you mean?'

'Look, I'm just telling you what Ollie heard...' Lisa added.

Ali blinked in disbelief. 'What did he hear?'

'They're saying...' She paused. 'They're saying that she was blackmailing a boy.'

'Charlotte was blackmailing a boy,' Ali repeated

dumbly because she wasn't able to process what Lisa was telling her.

Lisa nodded.

'How would she do that?' Ali asked, trying to make sense of this information but no matter how much she tried to understand what Lisa was telling her, she couldn't get her head around it. '*Why* would she do that?'

Lisa shrugged. 'I don't know but maybe this is all connected. Could she have been using nude photos to blackmail them?' Lisa suggested delicately.

Ali shook her head at the absurdity of the situation. 'You think Charlotte was using these nude photos to blackmail boys?' She would have laughed only the situation was so serious. 'Do you know how ridiculous that sounds? It's preposterous. This is Charlotte we're talking about!'

'Don't shoot the messenger.' Lisa raised her palms to face Ali. 'I'm just telling you what's being said. I thought you'd want to know.'

'Well, that's crazy.'

Lisa nodded. 'It does sound pretty unbelievable; I have to agree with you.'

'Why didn't you tell me earlier?'

'Well, I only heard it yesterday and I didn't tell you then because I didn't believe it, to be honest.'

'Oh my God. I feel sick. It just doesn't make sense...'

'Ali, I know it's hard, none of us ever want to imagine our children being involved in something like this but it's there – the evidence is there on her phone and you need to think carefully about how you handle this.'

Ali nodded, knowing that her boss was right.

'I'm sorry, I didn't know whether I should tell you or not but I think you need to know so that you're prepared...' Lisa went on.

'Prepared?' Ali repeated. 'Prepared for what?'

'Look, I'm not saying this is going to happen... but if the Gardaí get wind of this and they did decide to investigate along this line of enquiry, at least you'll be ready for it and won't get a shock.'

Ali gulped. 'Do you think they will?' she asked fearfully.

'I don't know,' Lisa said quickly. 'But I guess they have to explore every lead. You need to talk to Charlotte, Ali; you need to find out exactly what happened so you can be a step ahead if they do call.'

35

Ali came home from work that evening burnt out with exhaustion and her mind consumed by what Lisa had told her. She didn't have the energy to make dinner but it didn't matter because she wasn't hungry anyway. Once again, Charlotte was upstairs in her room but instead of going up to check on her straight away like she usually would, Ali went into the kitchen and flopped into a chair. She saw Charlotte had left her phone on the table so she took it up and checked it again. A part of her still believed that she had imagined the whole thing, that this was all some horrible nightmare. But when she went into her daughter's camera roll, the images were still there and she knew this was real.

She heard her daughter coming down the stairs a while later. Charlotte entered the kitchen but stopped dead when she saw Ali clutching her phone. Their eyes met and Ali searched her daughter's wan face. She was searching for an answer or a possible explanation that might help her to understand what was going on here. Who should she believe? She really didn't want to accept what Lisa had said earlier about Charlotte blackmailing people could be true, but faced with the images on her daughter's phone, it was hard to think otherwise.

'Why are you on my phone, Mum?' Charlotte asked quickly as she closed the space between them.

'Who is this?' Ali asked holding up one of the images for her daughter to see.

'Give it back!' Charlotte demanded and dived to grab it from her mother's hand.

Ali dodged her. 'Are you going to tell me what's going on? Who are these guys?'

'I swear I don't know, Mum.' Charlotte was panicked.

'You must know!' Even though Ali knew she should remain calm, she couldn't keep the anger from her voice.

'I swear I don't.' Charlotte looked excruciatingly embarrassed.

'Well, how did they end up on your phone then?'

'They keep sending them to me.'

'Who does?'

'I think they're from some of the boys at school. They keep spamming me with them from fake accounts on Snapchat. They don't show their faces.'

Ali felt relief unwind the tension from her muscles. She knew Charlotte was telling the truth. She sighed. 'Thank God.'

'Mum?' Charlotte was bewildered by her reaction.

'I thought you were using the photos to blackmail the boys.'

'What?' Charlotte was horrified. 'Why would I do that?'

'I'm sorry,' she said. She was sorry for doubting her daughter. For ever thinking that she might be capable of doing something like that. Just what kind of mother was she? Ali lowered her voice. 'When did this start?' It was beginning to make sense; she was starting to realise that there was something bigger at play here. She didn't want to sound paranoid but was this all part of a vicious campaign of bullying to deliberately target her daughter?

'A few weeks ago.'

'So this has been happening since before the party?'

Charlotte nodded.

'Why didn't you tell me? That's harassment!' Ali was outraged. 'It's illegal to send sexually explicit images to a minor.' She had always hoped Charlotte would be comfortable coming to her if she ever had a problem. They had always had an open and honest relationship and Ali liked to think that nothing was off limits. Until now.

'I didn't know what to do, Mum.' Charlotte bit down on her lip and then started to cry. 'I was going to tell you... but I didn't know how... That's why I took screenshots of them.'

'We need to go to the police with them.'

'No, Mum, please,' she begged. 'It's too embarrassing.'

'You've nothing to be embarrassed about. These guys, on the other hand, could find themselves in a lot of trouble.'

'It's just going to make everything worse, Mum! Please don't do anything. I'll delete them. I've already deleted Snapchat anyway so they can't reach me any more.'

'No, way, Charlotte. We need to get to the bottom of this. Come on, get in the car.'

'Where are we going?'

'To the Garda station, of course.'

Charlotte shook her head and planted her feet firmly on the floor. 'No, Mum, we can't go there.' Charlotte looked petrified. 'I'm not going there.'

'Why not?' Ali challenged. 'We have proof right here.' She lifted the phone again and jabbed her index finger at the screen.

'Mum, I'm scared. They already think I pushed Josh into the pool; if I go down there, I'm worried they're going to find something else and arrest me. Please, Mum, I'm begging you, don't make me go down there.'

Ali looked at her daughter who now suddenly appeared far younger and more vulnerable than her sixteen years. She saw her own terror mirrored in her eyes and it tore Ali's heart in two. When Charlotte had been younger, she had gone through a period of having nightmares. She would wake up in her bed during the night screaming hysterically that there was a monster in her wardrobe or a ghost under her bed. Ali would have to turn on the light and show her that there was nothing there before she would believe her. It had taken Ali months to convince her that monsters and ghosts weren't real. The situation they were in now reminded her of that time except now she couldn't assure her that she had nothing to fear because Ali was just as scared as her daughter was. Ali was caught between storming down to the Garda station and demanding they find out who the culprits were, and fearing they could be unwittingly walking themselves into more trouble. She was frightened that someone would spin it that Charlotte had somehow solicited these images and was using them for her own means. Although Ali had always trusted the Gardaí, she was keenly aware that it was her word versus the other parents of St Thomas's. She was a single mother who lived pay-cheque to pay cheque; these people had deep pockets and it seemed they might stop at nothing to see her daughter go down. She needed to think carefully about the implications for both of them.

Ali looked at the terror pooling in her daughter's hazel eyes, the same colour eyes as her father's had been and suddenly, she was just as scared too, as the reality of this situation smacked her full force in the gut. If things got more serious, just how far were these people willing to go to protect their children? And what if her love wasn't enough to keep her daughter safe?

36

Someone was shaking her. They were gripping her on either side of her shoulders and wouldn't let go. Ali woke with a start and saw Charlotte hovering over her. Her face was creased in fear.

'Charlotte? What's wrong?' she said, bolting upright in the bed. She could hear banging hailing from downstairs. She checked her phone and saw it was just before 8 a.m. 'What's happening?' she said, coming to, wondering if she was fully awake or stuck in a dream.

'Mum, it's the Gardaí. They're downstairs. I'm so scared,' she wailed. 'I think they've come to arrest me!'

Ali's heart started to ratchet up inside her ribcage. What the hell was going on? 'It's okay,' she said to calm her daughter. 'Don't worry. I'm sure it's all going to be just fine.' She tossed off the duvet and stood up onto the varnished floorboards. She took her dressing gown down from the hook on the back of her door.

The banging intensified.

'Mum, hurry, I'm worried they're going to break down the door.'

'All right, I'm coming!' Ali shouted down to them in frustration even though she knew they wouldn't be able to hear her. As she slipped her arms inside her robe, she hurried down the landing and took the stairs two at a time. Charlotte stayed on the landing watching from the top step.

She removed the security chain and opened the door. She saw that Detective Inspector Ryan and Garda Waldron were back again.

'Ms Daly, can we come in?' DI Ryan asked.

She immediately thought about Josh. She prayed he hadn't taken a turn for the worse and the case had been upgraded to a murder inquiry.

'Is there an update on Josh Quinlan? Has he woken up yet?' she asked quickly, trying to get a step ahead of them.

'I don't believe he has and we are still investigating all the circumstances surrounding the events of that night.'

'So what is this about then?' Ali asked in confusion. 'You're after frightening the life out of both of us.' She felt relieved that Josh's condition hadn't deteriorated any further but it still didn't explain why they were here again banging down her door.

'If you wouldn't mind allowing us in, we can explain everything then.'

Ali stood aside and gestured towards the sitting-room door. She could see Charlotte standing at the top of the stairs, too terrified to come down. She went inside and this time didn't offer them a seat and so the three of them remained standing.

'We believe your daughter may be in possession of explicit images of minors which would mean she is in breach of the Child Trafficking and Pornography Act,' Garda Waldron began.

Ali clenched her jaw and squeezed her eyes shut briefly, before opening them again. 'If you're talking about the nude photos that are on her phone – they were sent to her – they're not hers,' she rebutted instantly.

'Ms Daly, we have a duty to inform you that if you were aware of the existence of these pictures and didn't immediately notify An Garda Síochána, you could be charged with the Withholding of Information on Offences Against Children and Vulnerable Persons Act 2012.'

'What?' Ali asked in disbelief. Not only were they blaming this on her daughter but she had somehow now managed to implicate herself in this matter too? 'But I only found out about them yesterday! We were trying to decide what to do...' She felt as though she was sinking, that their hands were pushing her down and she was disappearing through the floor. No matter where she turned, or what she tried to do, they seemed to be coming at her from every angle. They had this all wrong; she needed them to believe her. She and Charlotte were not the bad people here – in fact, they were the victims. She hated using that word; it felt so, so... *helpless* but she really didn't know where to turn now. When was this nightmare ever going to end?

'I need to seize your daughter's phone for a forensic examination,' Detective Inspector Ryan said.

'Who told you about the images?' Ali challenged. 'You need to question whoever it was because that's the person who sent them.' Whoever had tipped them off about their existence had their own motivations for doing so.

'I'm afraid we're not at liberty to disclose that information.'

Ali sighed. 'Okay but I swear she's being targeted here. This is all a set-up. You have to believe me. Some boys are using fake accounts and sending her these unsolicited images.'

'We will investigate all avenues, Ms Daly and if what you're saying is true then you've nothing to be worried about. Now if you could provide us with her phone, we'll be on our way.' He smiled at her but for some reason, it did nothing to reassure her. Every time she felt confident that they would soon clear her daughter's name, something else happened to keep her more firmly in the frame. Would this hellish situation ever end?

37

After the Gardaí had left, Ali had gone back upstairs and found Charlotte in her bed. Ali climbed in beside her and lay alongside her daughter's length, squashed into the narrow single bed. Charlotte was distraught; she had cried muffled sobs into her pillow until there were no tears left. When her exhausted body finally relented and gave in to sleep, Ali couldn't bear to leave her side and she stayed where she was while her daughter slept. Ali thought of all those long nights she would curl up beside her daughter in bed to read *The Tiger Who Came To Tea*, Charlotte giggling at how the tiger cleared out the cupboards and drank all the water from the tap, never getting tired of the tale. When the story was finished, Charlotte would settle back on her pillow, Ali would tuck the duvet right up under her chin and trace her fingertips gently across her skin, as her eyelids grew heavier and started to close. If Ali so much as moved, Charlotte's eyes would flicker open once more and Ali would have to start all over again. Now, as she listened to her daughter's shallow breathing, Ali yearned for the simplicity of those days.

Charlotte had woken after lunch and the two of them got up and tried to get on with their day as best they could. Ali had spent hours consoling her daughter and reassuring her. The truth was that she was terrified too; it felt like they were becoming deeper and deeper embroiled in this mess and no matter how much they protested Charlotte's innocence, it seemed nobody would believe them. She couldn't understand why they were being targeted. Had they done something to offend someone or were they just easy prey? It was starting to feel as though it was her and Charlotte against the whole world. But she knew she couldn't fall apart; now more than ever, she needed to put on a brave face for her daughter's sake. She had to stay strong – Charlotte was depending on her, so instead, she had lied and reassured her daughter that everything was going to be just fine even though Ali wasn't sure if she believed that any more.

'Just you wait and see, love; this will all blow over soon and we'll look back on this and laugh.'

Ali couldn't imagine ever looking back on this period of their lives and laughing but she needed to give her daughter something to cling to.

The next morning, it felt as though Ali had only just closed her eyes when the alarm on her phone sounded. Charlotte had slept in her bed with her, neither of them wishing to be on their own, and so, she had quickly silenced it, taking care not to disturb her daughter. She really didn't want to leave Charlotte at home alone in her current state but she had to go to work. Lauren was on annual leave so she couldn't very well take the day off too. Since the Gardaí had seized Charlotte's phone and they didn't have a landline, Ali wouldn't even be able to check in with her to see how she was doing. She decided to leave her own phone at home for Charlotte so she could call her during the day and left a note for her daughter that if she needed to contact her, she would be able to reach her on the restaurant phone.

By the time Ali arrived in work, she couldn't remember the drive, tiredness and stress had combined to leave her head in a fuggy state. She went around to the back door that the staff used to enter the restaurant and headed upstairs to grab her apron from where it was hanging. She hooked it over her head and went into the kitchen just as Lisa came into the room carrying a lipstick-ringed mug.

'Ali, how are you doing?' she asked as she opened the dishwasher. 'Did you get a chance to talk to Charlotte about those photos on her phone?' She bent down and put the mug inside before using her hip to close it again.

'I did, actually. I confronted her about them and she said she was being sent them from anonymous Snapchat accounts.'

'Really?' Lisa looked at her, failing to hide her scepticism. 'Why would anyone do that?'

'I just don't know.' Ali sighed. 'To make matters worse, the Gardaí came over again yesterday morning.'

'Why?' Lisa asked in bewilderment. 'What did they want now?' She folded her arms across her chest and rested against the cupboards, giving Ali her full attention.

'They heard she was in possession of the images but I can't figure out how they would know about them. It just makes no sense at all.'

'Ali, you don't think...?' Lisa trailed off.

'What?' Ali demanded.

Lisa removed her glasses and rubbed her eyes. 'Well, maybe what the other kids are saying about Charlotte is true...'

Ali looked at her in disbelief. 'No I don't think that!' she snapped. 'This is Charlotte we're talking about. She doesn't do that sort of stuff. I believe my daughter. She's telling the truth. This is all a set-up, I'm telling you, Lisa,' she blasted. Why would nobody believe her?

'Okay,' Lisa said, raising her palms in self-defence.

'Now the Gardaí have seized her phone with all those photos on it. It looks so bad.' Ali held her head in her hands and groaned. 'They said she could be charged with breaching the Child Trafficking and Pornography Act because she was in possession of explicit images of minors and I could be in trouble too for withholding information because I didn't report it straight away! But I had only just found out about them and I wanted to think about what the best thing was to do.'

'But surely it's the person who sent them to Charlotte in the first place who should be in trouble?' Lisa seemed as confused as Ali felt.

Ali shook her head. 'It's illegal to be in possession of sexual messages or media of someone who is under the age of eighteen; it's considered child pornography even if you didn't want to receive them. We could be in real trouble.'

'She didn't share them with anyone else, did she?'

Ali shook her head. 'No, I don't think so.'

'Well, thank God for small mercies. It sounds as though Charlotte is the victim here.'

'I just want to know who is doing this to her.' Ali started to get upset as frustration gave way to tears. 'Why are they trying to pin this on my daughter?' What was wrong with these people? Why were they so desperate to blame Charlotte? She kept trying to find a motive but couldn't.

'I wish I could answer that,' Lisa said, shaking her head.

'Well, when the Gardaí investigate, they'll soon realise that there's absolutely no way that my daughter was blackmailing any boy with nude photos. I'm frightened, Lisa. When is this going to end? It feels like someone has made voodoo dolls of the both of us and they just keep sticking in pin after pin.'

'I know you are frightened. We all are... None of us ever imagined being in this situation. I keep saying to Patrick that I wish we had never had that bloody party! But we can't turn back the clock unfortunately.'

'What if the Gardaí don't get to the bottom of it?' Ali asked fearfully.

'Come on, Ali, don't lose heart. Of course they will. It's their job to leave no stone unturned.'

'I keep praying that Josh will wake up and re-member what happened.'

Lisa's face darkened. 'And what if he remembers something we don't want him to remember?'

'How do you mean?' Ali asked in confusion.

'Well, you know...' Lisa shrugged. 'If he wakes up and remembers everything, he might tell them about the alcohol and we could still find ourselves in hot water...'

'Well, actually, Lisa, I wanted to talk to you about that...'

'Oh yeah?'

'I want to tell the Gardaí that some of the kids at the party were drinking,' Ali pleaded.

The woman shook her head resolutely. 'No way, Ali, you can't. We've been over all of this.'

'But I need them to know that Josh was possibly drunk and slipped into the pool of his own accord. Or perhaps the kids who are saying they saw Charlotte push him in were off their faces and didn't see any-thing!' Ali said desperately. 'At the moment, it's the only thing I have that can protect my daughter.'

'No,' Lisa said firmly. 'Myself and Patrick have been discussing it and there's no way we can allow them to find out. It's too much of a risk. It's not going to change the outcome – Josh is in the ICU whether I gave the kids alcohol or not.'

Ali looked at her in disbelief. How was she able to wash her hands of the guilt and clear her conscience so easily? She thought she knew Lisa, they had worked together for close on fifteen years, but it seemed when their backs were against the wall, everyone looked after themselves. 'So you're willing to lie to the police?' Ali challenged.

'Nobody said anything about lying, Ali!' Lisa snapped.

'But you're withholding information. Information that could be crucial to solving what happened that night.'

'I won't lie to anyone but I'm also not going to deliberately bring trouble to my door.'

'But I'm sure they're doing toxicology reports in the hospital. They could show that Josh was drinking alcohol or maybe worse... So what does it matter if I tell them?'

'Of course they will be doing tests but even if they discover alcohol in Josh's system, the blame doesn't automatically fall on us. We can say that he must have snuck his own drink in with him. But if they know we supplied all the teenagers with alcohol... well, that's another issue entirely...'

'But, Lisa, it's not fair! Charlotte is being targeted here; this might help to open up another theory about what really happened that night and take the finger of blame away from her.'

'Ali, our livelihood is on the line here and not to put too fine a point on it – your job will be too,' Lisa said in a tone designed to remind Ali of hierarchy between them. She circled her index finger between them. 'This secret remains between us.'

38

The next morning, Ali marched into Charlotte's bedroom and pulled open the curtains roughly. Sleeping on the matter had done nothing to weaken her resolve; even after deliberating over it all night, she found she was even angrier this morning about the injustice that was being meted out to her daughter. She hadn't heard any more from the Gardaí about the images so she guessed it would take a while to investigate them. Ali didn't know who was doing this to them or why they had chosen her family to target but she wasn't going to stand for it any longer. Ali knew she was up against some very powerful people with vast wealth and it seemed they would go to great lengths to do whatever it took to protect their children. Well, she was not going to allow her daughter to be used as a scapegoat any longer. They had nothing to hide. Charlotte had already missed a full week of school and even though she was a bright girl, if she wasn't careful, she could start falling behind. Ali had never been the type of parent who let her daughter stay home from school for any old reason. Charlotte used to tease that if her leg was hanging off, Ali would still send her to school but Ali only ever allowed her to miss school if she was very unwell; education was important to her. Her daughter was clever and Ali knew getting a good Leaving Cert was an opportunity for Charlotte to have a different life to her.

'Time for school, love,' Ali called out to her as she opened the window to let a fresh morning breeze stream into the room.

'Mum, stop,' Charlotte wailed, pulling the duvet up over her head. 'I'm not going back there.'

Ali walked over to her daughter's bedside. 'I've had enough of this; you can't hide in your bedroom forever. I am not letting these people get away with ruining our lives for another moment. I know it's not easy but you've done nothing wrong so you're going back in there, you're going to face everyone with your head held high and if anyone says anything to you, you let me know.'

'Mum, please,' Charlotte begged. 'I really don't want to see anyone.'

'We're not hiding any more, Charlotte. I'm done with it. I think they're deliberately targeting you – I don't know the reason why, but I'm not standing for it any longer. These people think they can bully us with their money and wealth; well, we're not going to sit by and watch them destroy our lives. Now more than ever, we have to show them that we won't tolerate it. Bullies thrive on fear. If we don't stand up to them, they win.'

'Please, Mum, nobody wants me there.'

'You belong in that school as much as anyone!' Ali replied firmly. Was that the issue here she wondered. Did the St Thomas's parents resent having a scholarship student amongst them? Did they somehow see her daughter as inferior because Ali wasn't paying the extortionate fees that the rest of them were?

She pulled back the duvet and begrudgingly, Charlotte planted her two feet on the floor. She took in her daughter's unwashed hair, her grey pallor from not having been outside in several days. 'Go have a shower, you'll feel much better afterwards and I'll have your breakfast ready for you downstairs.'

* * *

Almost an hour later, Ali turned her Clio through the gates of St Thomas's. Ali was working the evening shift so she was able to drive Charlotte to school rather than let her take the bus. As she drove up along the tree-lined avenue towards the school building, she saw a group of boys in rugby jerseys throwing a ball to one another on a pitch. She slowed to cross a speed bump, giving her time to study them. They were all boys that looked to be the same age as Charlotte but they seemed so much bigger, their shoulders broad and muscular and their stance imposing and wide as if they were already so sure of themselves and their rightful place in this world. She continued on, eventually pulling up in the car park with the red-bricked building looming before them. She turned the key in the ignition to silence the engine. Turning away from the window, she looked at her daughter. 'Are you okay?'

Charlotte shook her head. 'I don't want to go in there.' She looked over towards the building, biting down on her bottom lip. 'I don't belong here.'

'I know that this is hard on you but I want you to keep your chin up and remember you have a right to be here as much as anyone, okay? Now, go and have a good day. I'll be back to pick you up.' As she looked across at her meek daughter sitting in the passenger seat beside her looking abjectly terrified, Ali thought about those confident boys walking across the grass she had just passed. She wondered if that was the kind of confidence that came with being rich? These children felt it was their entitlement; they automatically belonged in this world where Charlotte clearly didn't, until a scholarship had levelled things for her.

Charlotte didn't reply as she opened the car door and climbed out.

'Bye, love,' Ali called after her but Charlotte had already slammed the door shut.

Ali watched her for a few moments, her head hanging down as her gaze was lowered to the ground. She looked so out of the place amongst the other children with school bags slung over one shoulder, walking in groups of two and three, laughing and chatting easily with their friends as they entered the building. She prayed that the bullies who had been preying on her daughter would leave her alone today. She knew Charlotte was almost at breaking point and wouldn't withstand much more.

Ali wondered yet again if moving her from Riverdale had been a bad idea. Although her daughter had been a loner, she had seemed so much happier than she was now. Why had she tried to fix what wasn't broken? She had hoped that a school like

St Thomas's would open doors for her in the future but it wasn't just that; she had also hoped the smaller class sizes might have helped to encourage her daughter to come out of herself a little more. Was it so bad that she had hoped she might make a few friends too?

She watched as Charlotte made her way up the steps and then disappeared inside the school building. She was just about pull out of the car park when she saw a woman come up alongside her car, signalling to get her attention. Ali rolled down the window to her.

'You've got some cheek,' the woman began. She looked vaguely familiar to her, then it clicked: she was one of the women she had met at the charity coffee morning. Her name was Kyra or something like that if Ali remembered correctly.

'Sorry?' Ali asked, looking around to make sure she hadn't accidently blocked anyone in the car park or parked incorrectly.

'There were nude images of my son found on your daughter's phone. We had to go down to the Garda station to identify him. Can you imagine how humiliating that was for a sixteen-year-old? Your daughter was blackmailing him. She's already put a child in intensive care. This school had no issues until she joined. When are you going to get the message that she's not wanted here?'

Ali felt her blood run cold. 'Those photos were unsolicited.'

'You keep telling yourself lies, Ali, but nobody believes that. We know all about your type and we don't like it in our school.'

Ali opened the door of the car. She wanted to talk to this woman face to face, mother to mother and from this angle, sitting in the driver's seat with Kyra hovering over her, it felt as though she was being talked down to.

'Sorry,' Ali said trying to diffuse the situation. 'Kyra, isn't it?' she said as she stepped out of the car.

'I know all about you, Ali Daly,' she said smugly.

'What's that supposed to mean?'

'I know what you did back in university.'

Ali felt her breathing come quicker, become more shallow. Her ears started ringing and she thought her legs might buckle beneath her. 'Wh... what are you talking about?'

'Professor Lorcan Keane, wasn't it? Yes, I know *all* about it,' she teased like a cat pawing at an injured mouse.

'I... I...' Ali felt blindsided; she stumbled and stuttered, unable to form a response.

'Oh, don't play the innocent with me.' The woman tsked. 'I know what you're trying to do here but you're messing with the wrong kind,' she warned, wagging her finger. 'You've got your daughter in on your little act now too. What a pair of con artists both of you are! As the saying goes: black cat, black kitten. Well, you won't extort money from me.'

Before Ali's head could catch up with what was happening, she felt her body launch forward towards this woman. 'How dare you!' she screamed, grabbing the woman by her neck.

Suddenly, she felt arms pulling her backwards. 'What the hell are you doing?' she cried, turning around to find a man restraining her.

'This is a school, not a boxing ring!' he chastised. He was dressed casually in jeans and a hoody and Ali guessed he was a fellow parent.

'Careful or I'll have you up for assault too,' Kyra teased as the man held Ali firmly by her shoulders.

'Did you hear her?' Ali protested, trying to wriggle free from the man's grip. 'She's threatening me!'

'I think you'll find it's *you* who's threatening *me*.' The woman jabbed a finger in Ali's direction. 'Stay away from my family, Ali, or you'll be sorry,' she warned before turning on her heel, walking across the car park and climbing up into a black Mercedes SUV with tinted windows.

'Are you okay?' the man asked, loosening his grip on her as they watched the woman drive out of the car park.

Ali panted, too shocked and stunned to form a reply.

'Look, I don't know what's going on between you and Kyra Higgins but I don't think a school is the best place for sorting out your grievances. You should probably go now,' he advised.

Ali nodded contritely to him before he turned and walked away. Her whole body was trembling when she sat back into her car. She was shaking too badly to drive so she locked the doors and waited until her hands stopped quivering and her breathing started to return to normal. How had that woman known about him? Ali had deliberately shut that part of her life from her head. Until now. How had that woman known about Professor Lorcan Keane?

Suddenly, Ali felt panicked. Panicked and scared. She had run from her past for so long but it was catching up with her. This situation seemed to be turning down a dark road and she wasn't sure she wanted to go there. Would these people stop at nothing to blacken her name?

39

Ali drove home and spent the rest of the day with her head in a spin. She couldn't figure out how this woman – Kyra Higgins – had known about her past. She had never told anyone. Not even her closest friends or family. Or so she had thought. She felt exposed. Vulnerable and open. How did this woman know so much about her? And the timing of the whole thing was another thing that rankled with her; the woman's tone had been taunting and Ali had felt threatened. Why had this woman deliberately chosen now to use this information against her? There was clearly a connection but she couldn't work out what it was.

She tried to eat something but her stomach felt

knotted as though someone was holding her abdomen on either side and twisting and turning it. She checked the clock and thought about Charlotte in school. Ali really hoped she was having a better day than she was. It felt as though she had sent her own heart in with her daughter. It had been such a battle to get her to go back to St Thomas's. Ali had felt conflicted; a part of her felt awful for forcing her to go into the school to face everyone and yet another voice reminded her that Charlotte had done nothing wrong. Ali knew that this was her biggest test to date as a parent and she needed to remain strong and show her daughter that hiding away from your problems wouldn't solve anything. She also hoped that by having some routine and getting back into her studies, it would be a good distraction for Charlotte from her worries.

When it was time to collect her daughter from school, she decided not to drive into the school grounds and risk meeting that woman again. Instead, she parked in the shopping centre across the road and texted Charlotte to let her know where she was. As she waited in her parked car, a soft mizzle started to fall and rivulets ran down the windscreen. She made sure her doors were locked and she looked around the car park in case Kyra was watching her but it was difficult to see out through the rain-spattered glass.

Eventually, she caught a glimpse of the navy, plaid kilt of Charlotte's uniform and her heart leaped into her mouth. She studied her daughter as she approached the car, taking in her sunken shoulders and downturned gaze, feeling it tear inside her.

Charlotte spotted the car and made her way over. Ali unlocked the doors to let her in.

'Hi, how was your day?' she asked as Charlotte sat in the passenger seat and took off her glasses to wipe away the raindrops. Damp tendrils of hair clung to her face and her jacket was studded with wet marks.

'I'm not ever going back there again, Mum,' Charlotte said in a small voice, putting her glasses back on again.

'Oh, love, it couldn't have been that bad,' Ali cajoled. She was trying to sound light and breezy in the hope that it would rub off on her daughter. 'What happened?'

'Who is Lorcan Keane?' she asked before Ali had even turned the key in the ignition.

Ali felt her breathing snag in her chest. 'Sorry?' she asked, hoping she had misheard her.

'Who is he, Mum?' she demanded.

Ali pinched her eyes shut before quickly opening

them again and starting the engine. She had blocked that name out of her head for so long and now hearing it twice in one day brought her right back there again.

'I think we should go home and—'

Charlotte cut across her, 'Just tell me, Mum!'

'What did they say to you?'

'Enough, Mum, I want to know the truth!'

The day Ali had feared for so long was here. She knew there was no way she could run from it any longer. Charlotte was a clever girl; she would see right through her if she tried to fudge it or skirt around answering her question. She had always known that this time would come but she had imagined it so differently. Her daughter would be in a good place, they would have an open and honest conversation and Charlotte would be able to handle what Ali would tell her. Not now. Not when they were sitting in the car park outside Tesco. Not when their world was falling apart.

40

Ali turned off the engine and silence filled the car once more. She took a deep breath and exhaled heavily. 'Lorcan Keane,' she began, choosing her words carefully, 'was a professor at the university where I studied. He lectured me in Sociology.'

'But you didn't go to college,' Charlotte interjected.

Ali had never told Charlotte about her university days. She had been afraid it would lead to questions so it had been easier to pretend she had never gone on to third-level education.

'I did. I studied English and Sociology.'

Charlotte wrinkled her nose in confusion. 'I don't understand. You always said the reason why you wanted me to do well in school was so that my life wouldn't turn out like yours?'

'That's right. I started a degree but I never finished it.'

'You dropped out?'

Ali nodded. 'It was when I found out that I was pregnant with you and I guess my priorities changed.' Ali rearranged her features into a smile. She wanted Charlotte to see this as a positive thing.

'So I was the reason you never got to finish your degree? Basically, I ruined your life.'

'I never said that. As I said, my priorities changed. I had a gorgeous little baby and academia no longer seemed interesting to me; I wanted to be with you and work hard to give you the best life that I could.'

After she had dropped out of university, Ali had moved back home to Achill to live with her parents until Charlotte was born. They had helped her out with her baby and supported her financially until Ali was ready to be more independent. When Charlotte was a year old, her friend Fiona had convinced her to move into a two-bedroomed house share and so she'd taken her baby girl with her and moved back to Dublin. She'd started doing evening shifts in the Riordans' restaurant, while Fiona helped her out by minding Charlotte while she worked. After a few years like this, Fiona had got a boyfriend and they wanted to move in together and so Ali used a teenage girl from next door to babysit Charlotte when she worked evenings and weekends. By that stage, Ali had been promoted to a supervisor and she was earning enough to be able to cover the entire rent by herself so she hadn't bothered searching for a new flatmate when Fiona left. She had been proud that they finally each had their own bedroom after spending the first decade of her daughter's life sharing a double bed. Lisa had recently promoted her to restaurant manager and life was a bit easier now that Charlotte was old enough to be left home alone when she worked evening shifts.

'So who is he then? Why did they tell me to ask you who he was?'

Ali knew the time had come to be honest with her daughter. She had always known that one day they would have to have this conversation but she didn't feel ready for it. She knew she'd never be ready.

She took a deep breath. 'Lorcan Keane is your father.'

Charlotte blinked as she digested this revelation. 'My father,' she repeated.

Ali nodded to confirm.

Charlotte wrinkled up her nose. 'Eugh, Mum, you

did it with your lecturer? Were you two seeing one another?'

'It wasn't serious.' Ali closed her down.

'So why did you break up?'

'As I said, we weren't really a couple... it just sort of... fizzled out...'

Ali could see Charlotte's mind working hard trying to process all of this new information. 'But how did those girls in school know about my dad before I did? Why am I the last to know? Were you telling everyone else except me?'

Ali shook her head. 'Of course not! I don't know how they know about this because I don't ever talk about him to anyone.' Not even her family and close friends knew about Charlotte's father and it was unsettling to Ali to think there was someone who had a connection to her old life but she didn't know who it was and now they were using it against her.

'Does my dad know about me?' Ali noticed a hopefulness about her daughter that broke her. Even though she had never asked Ali about her father before, it was clear from her face that she was excited to discover more about him.

'No, I never told him about you,' Ali said, knowing it had to be this way. It was better for everyone if Ali only told Charlotte the bare facts that she needed to know.

Charlotte's face lit up. 'He doesn't know about me?' she repeated in disbelief. 'Do you think I could meet him – I mean, maybe we should tell him...?' she said, catching herself and trying to downplay her excitement but Ali knew her daughter too well; she knew every mannerism and feeling that her daughter experienced. Charlotte couldn't hide her feelings from her mother if she tried.

'Let's just take our time here; you've only just found out who your father is. Let's not rush into anything.'

'But why, Mum? I might have brothers and sisters now,' she said hopefully. 'And don't you think it's not really fair on him having a daughter all this time and not even knowing that I exist?'

'You need to give yourself time to sit with it and see how you feel about it all.'

'I know how I feel about it, Mum,' she said impatiently, 'and I'd like to know who he is.'

'Let's just go home,' Ali sighed, starting the engine.

They both fell quiet as the car stopped and started in the city gridlock. The rain had made the traffic worse as pedestrians scurried beneath umbrellas and drivers peered out through rain-spattered glass. Her windscreen had started to fog up and she reached out to wipe clear a patch with the back of her hand. A cyclist weaved in front of her and Ali had to jam on the brakes. It felt like the universe was having a laugh at her expense. She beeped angrily, then immediately regretted her outburst. She saw Charlotte raise her brows at her temper and Ali was contrite. She was just so damned scared by what was happening to them. How had these people known who Charlotte's father was? She felt as though she was playing a game of blind man's buff; they were spinning her around and she was caught in the middle of their game, except she didn't know who she was playing against. And now to make everything worse, Charlotte wanted to meet her father. How on earth was she going to convince her that it was a bad idea without revealing the nasty truth?

41

Ali and Charlotte didn't speak to one another for the rest of the journey home. The scrape of the wipers across the drizzle-spattered windscreen filled the silence between them.

When they got home, Ali let them into the house and Charlotte headed straight up the stairs, while Ali entered the kitchen and started to make herself a cup of tea. She had to leave for work soon, she was due in at five, but she needed to unwind for a few minutes first. While she waited for the kettle to boil, she circled her shoulders backwards a few times to loosen out the tension that had knotted its way around her shoulder blades and neck.

'I want to meet him,' Charlotte blurted, entering

the kitchen a few minutes later just as Ali was pouring boiling water over her teabag.

Ali squeezed her eyes shut before opening them again. She placed the kettle down and turned around, resting her back against the worktop, giving Charlotte her full attention.

'My Dad – I want to meet him,' Charlotte continued.

'I know you're probably...' she paused for the right word before settling for, '...*curious*... about him... but you've only just learnt who he is. Let's take this one step at a time, eh? It's going to take a while to get your head around it all before you do anything else.' She was used to seeing Charlotte moping around these days, always with her head stuck in her books; it had been a long time since Ali had seen Charlotte so enthused about anything and it broke her heart that the reason for it was because of her father. It was natural, Ali knew, for Charlotte to be interested in learning more about who he was but how was she supposed to convey to her daughter who he *really* was, without coming clean with the full story? *You don't know him like I do*, she longed to scream at her but knew she couldn't. She had to tread carefully because if Charlotte picked up on her reluctance to allow her to meet her father, she knew she risked pushing her away altogether.

'Mum, I've waited sixteen years to meet him. I'm ready.'

'But you can't just land on his doorstep after all this time and expect to play happy families with him, Charlotte – that's not how life works. You don't know his situation. He might not be receptive to the news that he has a child.'

'Well, I'd like to at least find out,' Charlotte retorted.

'But why?' Ali countered. 'What difference is it going to make? He has never been in your life. What's going to change?'

'Only because you never told him about me! I can't believe you denied him the chance to be my father and you robbed me of the chance to have a dad around when I was growing up.'

'Woah there, hang on a minute. It wasn't like that.'

'What other way can it be, Mum?' Charlotte's voice climbed higher. 'I always wondered why he never came to visit me. I knew lots of kids in school whose parents were no longer together but their fathers were still in their life. I'd watch their dad pick them up from school on set days or they would stay over at his place at weekends but I couldn't understand why my dad never came for me. I thought it was because he didn't love me but now I know that it was because he didn't even know that I existed! He never got a say in whether he wanted to be involved in my life or not!'

'I know you're upset but I did it with good reason. You have to believe me that everything I do – every decision I've ever made – it's always been for you.'

'Y'know, I used to look at the other kids who had their dads around and wonder what that would be like. To have two parents at home instead of one. I know you did your best, Mum, but imagine if I had had a dad around too?' she said wistfully.

'You've had a huge shock, love, but please, take your time. The whole situation with Josh and the school kids is stressful; you can't rush into something like this. This is huge. Let's just take some time to get your head around it all. Let's see how you feel in a few months.'

'You want me to wait a few months?' Charlotte repeated incredulously.

'Charlotte, you've waited sixteen years to meet him; what difference will a few more months make? You can use the time to decide if it's what you really want.'

'All my life, I've had you and don't get me wrong,

Mum, I appreciate that but now I have the chance to get to know my dad and I can't believe that you're trying to stop me!'

'I know it hasn't been easy but I like to think I've done a good job. You don't know him like I do.'

'Well, if he's so bad, why were you with him?' Charlotte challenged.

'You have to trust me. He's not the man you think he is.'

'What's that supposed to mean?'

Ali knew she was treading on dangerous ground here; Charlotte would keep digging and she could find herself forced along a road she didn't want to go down. 'Nothing...' she conceded eventually.

'You know what? You're not perfect either, Mum!' Charlotte snapped.

'I know I'm not perfect but you have to believe me when I say that everything I've done, it's always been for you. You're my whole world.'

'Oh yeah, like forcing me to go to St Thomas's. That was definitely the best decision you made for me!' she retorted sardonically.

'Come on, Charlotte, you know I was trying to get a better education for you. I hoped a school like that would open doors for you; how was I supposed to know something like this would happen?' she pleaded.

'Well, if it wasn't for you, I wouldn't be in this mess.' Charlotte turned on her heel and stormed out of the room.

The words crushed her. Ali felt as though Charlotte had taken a scissors to her heart and cut it into shreds. For all these years, she had been both a mother and father to her daughter and thought she was doing a good job at both roles but she had been fooling herself. Charlotte saw it differently. Charlotte wanted more. More than Ali. More than she could ever give her as a single mother. Why had she thought their unit was enough and that Charlotte would be content with that? She had been naïve, watching too many episodes of *Gilmore Girls*.

'Charlotte, wait...' she called after her daughter.

She heard her footsteps continue up the stairs and finally, the slam of her bedroom door. Ali groaned. She had always imagined that when this day came, they would discuss it calmly, rationally. She knew Charlotte would have questions and she would do her best to answer them honestly. In her fantasies, Charlotte had even thrown her arms around her and told her that she didn't need her father in her life, that the mother-daughter bond that they had was enough. But now Ali saw those dreams for what they really were: nonsense.

42

22 OCTOBER 2023

Charlotte's Journal

I can't believe that today was the day when I finally discovered who my dad is. It hurts that those girls in school knew about him before I did. He's my dad, yet I was the last to know. All those years where Mum could have told me who he was but she chose not to. She's lying to me when she says that she never told anyone about him. She swears it's the truth but how can it be? She obviously told someone. I never asked her outright about him before because I was worried she'd be upset or angry but I've always wanted to know who he is. Whenever I see other girls hanging out with their dads, I can't help wondering what that must be like or what it's like to have two parents at home instead of one? I know my mum has done a good job on her own; she's made so many sacrifices and works hard to give me everything but it doesn't stop me wanting to know more about him. I've never even seen a photo of him. I'm curious about what he looks like because Mum has auburn hair with freckles, but my hair is jet black so I guess that had to come from my dad. Does he wear glasses like I do? I don't think he has ever been present in my life – even when I was a baby. They must have broken up before I was born. Mum really doesn't seem to like him so I guess he broke her heart. Even if she has no feelings for him, I don't think it's fair that she kept me a secret from him. I grew up believing that the reason he never came to see me was because he didn't love me, so to discover that she deliberately kept me hidden from him hurts. How could we have had a relationship if he didn't even know that I existed?

I hate fighting with Mum because I know she loves me but I just don't understand why she doesn't want me to meet him? She's had me all to herself for sixteen years and now it's like she can't bear the thought of sharing me. I just want to get to know more about him but she's making me feel bad about it. Maybe she's worried that I'll forget about her but I'd never do that. I don't think it's wrong to want to see whose genes I share, to see if I look like him or discover if we have similar interests. She grew up with both parents and I think she's being selfish by trying to stop me from getting to know my father. I don't think she gets what it's like to only know 50 per cent of yourself. I feel like everything in my life up to now has been a lie and I don't know who to trust or believe any more.

43

Ali went into work that evening, wishing she didn't have to be there. Lisa had already gone home by the time she got in so Ali couldn't even ask her for an update on Josh. As the chefs chit-chatted to her, she found she wasn't in the mood for making conversation, wishing she could just be left alone with her thoughts. Her argument with Charlotte was playing on a loop inside her head. The conversation had gone so badly. She had been blindsided by Charlotte's insistence on finding her father. Because Charlotte had never asked questions about her father before, Ali had always naively assumed that she wasn't bothered by his absence. Now Charlotte had let her know in no uncertain terms that that was not the case and that she very much wanted to get to know him. Ali had never told anyone about who Charlotte's father was, passing him off as a random one-night stand, so she couldn't even turn to anyone for advice. She was trying to navigate this alone and she had no idea of what the best way was to handle it.

She went out front of house and got stuck into seating customers for dinner. She was called over by one of the waiters to attend to a customer who had complained that their food had been cold upon arriving at the table and soon she was caught up in the usual bustle of work. She was glad that her mind was distracted from everything that was going on at home and when she checked the clock next, saw that it was almost time for last orders. She was relieved when the restaurant cleared out early and she was finally able to head home.

She sat in the car and gripped the steering wheel. She had decided that she would try to talk to Charlotte again when she got home. She hoped that with the space of a few hours by herself, her daughter would have calmed down and might not be so hell-bent on tracking down her father. Ali hoped she might be willing to talk it all through properly and listen to her mother's advice.

The city was quiet as she drove through the muted

streets. She eventually turned down her road and saw their house was cloaked in darkness. She guessed Charlotte was asleep and her immediate reaction was one of relief that she was off the hook from having the conversation tonight, followed instantly by a flash of guilt. She normally looked forward to catching up with her daughter after the evening shift, Charlotte telling her about her homework or what she had watched on TV.

She entered the darkened house and went into the kitchen to make herself her usual herbal tea. When the kettle had boiled, she poured the water over the teabag and flopped into a chair, clasping the mug between her palms. When she had finished it, she went upstairs and crept into Charlotte's room to check on her like she had done going to bed every night since she had been born. She guessed her daughter was exhausted; learning the truth about her father and all the associated emotions had to have taken its toll on her. Ali tiptoed across the carpet, not wishing to wake her. She reached her bed and bent down to place a kiss on her head but there was only blank space beneath her hands as she searched around in the darkness. She flicked on the lamp on her bedside table and saw that Charlotte wasn't in her bed.

'Charlotte?' she called out, hoping her daughter would answer from the bathroom.

She listened out but no reply came. 'Charlotte?' she tried again, making her way into the bathroom they shared but it too was in darkness. She headed into her own bedroom, searching the space with her eyes but she wasn't there either. She returned to her daughter's bedroom once more, feeling sure she must have missed her somehow.

'Charlotte? Where are you?' she called but there was no reply. A heavy foreboding overtook her and she sank down onto the bed. She took her phone out of her pocket and dialled Charlotte's number but then remembered that the Gardaí still hadn't returned it. 'Damn it to hell, anyway!' she cursed, tossing her phone down on the duvet. She thought of Charlotte's journal then. She searched around the bedroom for it, hoping that it might provide her with some clues to her daughter's whereabouts, knowing that in these circumstances, keeping Charlotte safe was more important than respecting her privacy. She checked all around the room, inside her wardrobes, she turned out the contents of her drawers but grew frustrated when she couldn't find it anywhere. It was then that she saw something lying on her daughter's desk. A jagged page hastily ripped out of one of her school notepads. She lifted it up, three words swimming on the paper before her:

I'm sorry, Mum.

Ali felt blood leave her head and an angry buzzing sounded in her ears.

'No!' Ali screamed. 'No, no, no...'

44

Ali hurried back out into the dark night again, where a silver crescent moon shaded everything in black and white. She got into her car but realised she didn't know where she should go. Fear curled around her and clung to her like smoke as she thought about the scrawled letter Charlotte had left for her to find. What had her daughter been apologising for? Horrible thoughts invaded her brain. She prayed Charlotte hadn't done something stupid to harm herself. She thought back to that awful period of self-harm, those lumpy, jagged scars like ladders up and down her thighs, their ugly scarlet colour had faded to a silvery blue shade but they were there as a reminder of all the inner pain that Charlotte had tried to rid herself of if you looked closely enough. Charlotte had spent months in therapy afterwards but she was doing so much better these days. *Wasn't she?* Or at least she had been until she had started at St Thomas's. What if she had done something to harm herself again, or worse... *No*, she refused to let her mind go there and pushed the awful thought from her head. She had to stay positive.

Her immediate thought was to go to the Garda station and a few weeks ago, that would have been her first step in a situation like this but then she remembered everything that had happened over the last while. Her trust in Ireland's police service had shifted after their recent dealings with them. Although she knew they had a job to do, it didn't feel like they were on her side, so she was reluctant to involve them in their lives any more than she had to. And besides, would they even take the missing report seriously after Charlotte had only been gone for a matter of hours? She would give it a little longer and if she still hadn't located her daughter, then she knew she would have no choice but to get them involved. Charlotte had no friends that Ali knew of so there was no one she could contact on that front.

She started the engine, her fingers clenching the steering wheel as she drove down the street. She drove slowly, her head swivelling from left to right, scouring the footpaths for a glimpse of her daughter under the orange haze of the street lights. Charlotte might have had a change of heart and could be making her way back to the house, realising that running away wouldn't fix anything and she belonged at home with Ali but as she scanned the pavements, there was no sign of her daughter. She continued towards the main road and rang her parents in Achill on handsfree to see if they had heard anything from Charlotte. Even though her daughter was without her mobile phone, perhaps Charlotte had found a payphone to call them from or maybe she had even decided to get on a bus and head west. Although they lived on the opposite side of the country, Charlotte was close to her grandparents and would often call them for a chat or they would call her too.

She knew as soon as she heard her mother's sleepy voice down the line that they had been in bed.

'Is everything all right, love?' her mother's tone was concerned. 'It's not like you to ring so late.'

'Sorry, Mam, I didn't mean to wake you. I didn't realise the time. I was only ringing for a chat,' she lied.

'No worries, how's Charlotte doing?'

'She's good,' Ali lied again, feeling her stomach clench. 'Look, Mam, you go back to bed and I'll call you tomorrow.' She knew from the way the conversation was going that they hadn't heard from Charlotte and she didn't want to worry them unnecessarily when she was sure the child would turn up soon.

'No worries, love, we'll talk to you then.'

As she hung up, another idea took root in her mind. What if Charlotte had gone to find her father? Ali felt the blood drain from her head at the thought. It would make sense after their argument that she might run to him, desperate for a connection. Something deep within – perhaps it was a type of primal mother's instinct, something that went right down into the marrow of her bones – but something told her that she was on the right track. She thought about Lorcan Keane, the sneer on his face the last time she had seen him. The cruelty in his eyes. What if Charlotte had found him? The idea of her vulnerable, sixteen-year-old daughter being anywhere near this man terrified her. Charlotte didn't know Lorcan like she did. Charlotte didn't know what Ali knew. She didn't know what he was capable of.

It had been seventeen years since she had last seen him. If Ali's hunch was right and she had decided to go to him, how was Charlotte going to find him? The only thing she knew about him was that he used to lecture at Dublin University but Ali didn't know whether he was even still working there.

She had to find her daughter fast. She put the car into gear, indicated and pulled back onto the road. Even though it was after midnight, she decided to drive towards the campus and pray that she would find her daughter there because right now, it was the only lead she had.

45

Ali stepped out of her car and scoured the dimly lit campus. The place was quiet; Ali knew that the students were long gone home. As she looked around her, she saw that it had changed a lot since she had last been there. Modern, glass-fronted buildings now sat beside the older ones that she remembered from her days on this campus. She saw a coffee shop was located adjacent to the library; that hadn't been there in her day. She could almost hear the echoes of her time spent here, hanging around taking cigarette breaks between lectures, carefree laughter with friends. She made her way past what was once the Science building towards the Mitchell building where the Sociology department had been located. Her heart picked up speed as she inched ever closer, thinking back to the last time her feet had trodden this same path. She pushed the thoughts from her head; she needed to focus on finding her daughter.

Soon she had reached the entrance to the building and she walked beneath the aluminium cladding that marked the door. She pushed the handle with her palm, testing if it would open but as expected, it was locked. She moved up towards the glass and peered into the darkened building. This felt hopeless. Had Charlotte found him? Ali wondered or had she gone somewhere else to look for him now? Ali was all out of clues about where she should try next.

'Can I help you?' she heard a voice ask.

Her heart began galloping. She swung around and was confronted with a man coming towards her shining a torch in her direction. She was dazzled in the light and couldn't see his face.

'I... I...' she stuttered, putting her hand up to shield her eyes from the glare of the beam.

'What are you doing here?' he asked gruffly.

As her pupils adjusted to the light, she realised from his uniform that he was a security guard. Her breathing began to slow.

'I used to go here,' she began. 'Back a long time ago...'

The guard assessed her warily. 'That's nice but it's a bit late for an evening stroll,' he quipped.

'I'm looking for Lorcan Keane – he's... he's a professor in the Sociology department.'

'I know who he is.'

'I need to find him.'

'The staff are long gone home. Why don't you come back tomorrow?'

'It's urgent. I need to find him now – do you have an address for him or maybe a phone number?'

He shook his head and she knew as he considered her that he thought she was unhinged. 'Even if I did, I couldn't give you that information.'

She nodded. 'I understand... You see, I'm trying to find my daughter and I... um... thought she might be with him. Did you see a teenage girl around? She's very petite, a little over five foot, tiny build,' she added. 'She has dark hair... Oh, actually, wait, I have a photo of her.' She fished her phone out of her coat pocket and held it up for him to see. The photo was the screensaver on her phone and her daughter's lovely smile beaming back at her from the screen seared her heart. It was taken last Christmas in her parents' house in Achill. It was one of the few recent photos she had of her daughter where she actually looked happy.

He shook his head. 'There are thousands of teenagers here. I can't be expected to know them all,' he replied dismissively. 'Now come on, I need you to leave.'

She nodded. 'Of course.' She knew she was coming across as a woman with a few screws loose. She began walking back towards the area where she had left her car. When she reached it, she unlocked it and sat inside. She bowed her forehead against the steering wheel in frustration. What was she supposed to do now? She had no way of finding out where Charlotte was.

Suddenly, it occurred to her that perhaps Charlotte had somehow found out Lorcan Keane's home address and had gone there. If only Ali knew where he lived. There were no guarantees that this was where her daughter was but something deep within her being was telling her that this was where she had gone. She took out her phone and decided to google Lorcan Keane, her fingers trembling over the keys. Instantly, she was greeted with the faculty photograph of him. His raven-black hair was now streaked grey and his face was more weathered too but as she looked into his watery brown eyes, they were exactly the same as she remembered. She'd never forget those eyes. She scrolled through the hits that the search returned. Lots of links related to his position in the university, academic conferences he had spoken at and essays he had published. She continued down through them, moving onto the second page and eventually found a Mr Lorcan Keane had applied for planning permission for an extension to a house at 29 Seaview Avenue in Bray six years ago. It wasn't an unusual name and she knew there could be several Lorcan Keanes living in Ireland. It was a long shot, but right now, it was all she had.

She turned on the engine and headed in the direction of the coast. The idea of coming face to face with the man she had run from all those years ago terrified her, but she knew she had no choice if she wanted to get her daughter back safely.

She drove through the city suburbs and finally arrived in the village of Bray. She soon located the house, a red-bricked, two-storey home that she guessed had been built some time in the 1940s. Her heart sank when she saw no lights on and there was no car in the driveway either. She got out of the car and found the chilly autumn air smelled of woodsmoke from the nearby chimneys. As she made her way up to the door, her breathing turned ragged but she told herself that she had to do this; she had no choice. For all she knew, this house might belong to a different Lorcan Keane or he could have moved house in the six years since the planning application was made. Even if it was the right house, he might not be at home.

She took a deep breath to steel herself, pulled her shoulders back, then she reached up, pressed the bell and waited.

46

Time seemed to have become elastic, stretching on forever and it felt as though her heart was pounding harder with every second that she waited for the door to be answered. She listened out for any sign of life coming from inside the house but all sounded quiet between its walls. She pressed the bell again, feeling braver this time probably because she knew that if it hadn't been answered by now, it was unlikely that anybody was home. Yet again, there was no answer. She turned and made her way back towards her car feeling deflated; she was all out of ideas. Her only option now was to go to the Gardaí.

She put the car into reverse and was just about to

start backing out of the driveway when she saw the beams of two headlights turning into the space beside her. Had whoever lived here come home? She put the car back into neutral and turned off the engine. Her heart started up again as she climbed out of the car. Was she about to come face to face once again with Lorcan Keane after all this time?

The other driver got out of their car and left the beams on, dazzling her. It was only when he moved closer that she saw it was really him. The resemblance to Charlotte was painfully obvious; their eyes were the same amber colour and the pointed arch of his brows was exactly the same as Charlotte's. Of course Ali had noticed that as a toddler, Charlotte's likeness to her father was obvious but she had pushed it out of her head. She had tried to forget about it over the years but seeing him standing before her tonight, it was undeniable. It felt like a slap to realise that the features of the person she loved most, her perfect, beautiful daughter, were also shared by the man she hated. She felt her legs buckle beneath her and she had to reach out towards the car to steady herself. She was face to face with the man who had very nearly destroyed her.

'Alice,' he drawled, taking a step towards her. He had always insisted on calling her by her full name.

'It's been a while. To what do I owe the pleasure?' She knew by his face that he was enjoying this. He was enjoying toying with her. Messing with her emotions.

'I'm searching for my d-daughter,' she stuttered. 'I believe she may have come here.' She wasn't going to get into the fact that Charlotte was his daughter too.

'I think you mean *our* daughter.' He shook his head faux despondently. 'All these years and you never told me I'm a father, Alice.' He tutted. 'Why would you do that?'

He knew. He knew the truth which meant Charlotte must have found him. 'Where is she?' she demanded.

'Our daughter is right here.' He gestured towards the car but Ali couldn't see who was inside it with the glare of the headlights. She ran around to the passenger side and felt relief flood through her when she saw Charlotte sitting in the seat. 'Thank God,' she cried. 'I was worried sick!' She went to open the door but it was locked and Charlotte made no move to open it from the inside.

'Come on, Charlotte, I know you're upset but we need to talk,' she cajoled. 'We can fix this. Just open the door, love. Let's go home.'

'She doesn't want to go with you, Alice,' Lorcan said, following behind her.

'Charlotte, please,' she begged. 'We need to get out of here.'

Her daughter remained infuriatingly still in the passenger seat.

'She's had enough of your lies,' Lorcan continued. 'She told me everything.' He smirked at her and Ali longed to slap it off his face. 'It sounds like you're not doing a great job right now.'

'Open the car, Charlotte!' she demanded, ignoring him. 'You need to listen to me.' She banged on the glass with her palm. She was trying to sound brave even though fear was pulverising her insides.

'Just go home, Alice. It's clear that she doesn't want to see you right now,' Lorcan mocked.

'Charlotte, come on,' she said, losing patience. 'I'm sorry for not telling you about your father before now but I had good reason. I was trying to protect you.'

She noticed the front door of the house next door being opened and an elderly couple wrapped in dressing gowns came out to see what all the commotion was about.

'You're causing a scene,' Lorcan hissed at her angrily.

'Charlotte, he's a dangerous man,' she went on, unperturbed. She had to get through to her daughter. 'You need to trust me.'

Just then, she saw a flicker in her daughter's eyes and Ali knew that the words had hit home with her. 'I promise I'll tell you everything; just come home.'

She heard the clicking sound of the door being unlocked from the inside and as soon as the mechanism had been released, Ali opened it, leant inside the car and pulled her daughter tightly against her but Charlotte remained stiff in her arms. 'Oh, love,' she sobbed, tears streaming down her face. 'I'm so sorry.'

'I want the truth, Mum.' Charlotte said, climbing out of the car, her innocent eyes looking so broken and Ali hated herself for her part in all this pain.

Ali nodded. 'I promise I'm going to tell you everything. No more secrets.' She put an arm around her shoulder and steered her over to her Clio.

Lorcan stood blocking their way into the car. 'Where are you going, Charlotte? Don't listen to her! You know she's just going to tell you more lies.'

'Just get out of the way. Leave us alone,' Ali snapped.

His face contorted in untamed fury. Ali watched in horror as he clenched his fist and drew back his arm. She jumped in front of her daughter, scared that he was going to lash out at them. His hand hovered there in the air between them, until he finally relented and let it drop by his side again. It seemed with his neigh-bours looking on, he was unwilling to risk it.

Ali helped Charlotte into the car before hurrying over to the driver's side. She locked the doors and then put her arm on Charlotte's shoulder. 'I'm sorry – for everything,' she sobbed. 'Let's get you home, love.'

47

Once home, Ali shut the front door behind them and collapsed against it in relief. Her daughter was home. She was back safely where she belonged. Ali was counting her lucky stars that she had arrived at Lorcan's house in Bray when she did because if she hadn't... she shuddered to think what might have happened.

Charlotte headed down to the kitchen and Ali followed after her.

'Are you hungry?' she asked as her daughter sat at the table.

Charlotte shook her head.

She hadn't wanted to bombard her daughter with questions on the drive home. They hadn't spoken about the events that had taken place that evening; they were each too wrapped up in their own thoughts.

She put her hand over her daughter's on the table and squeezed it. 'Are you okay?' she ventured. 'He didn't—' She broke off. 'He didn't... hurt you or anything?'

Charlotte shook her head again.

'Thank goodness.' Ali sighed. Horrible visions and thoughts had swirled around her brain all the way home. 'I was so worried, Charlotte; I've never been so scared in all my life. Why didn't you tell me you were going to find him?'

'Because I knew you'd try to talk me out of it. How did you know where I was?'

'I took a guess and luckily, I was right. So how did you find him?' Ali asked.

'It wasn't hard. I googled him and discovered that he worked at the university so I went there and it was easy to find his office.'

'He didn't know you were coming?'

Charlotte shook her head.

'He must have got a big surprise.'

'At first, he didn't believe me when I told him who I was. Then I told him your name and I knew he remembered you.'

'How did he react to the news that you were his

daughter?' Her breath stalled as she waited for her daughter's response.

'He was surprised but he seemed happy. I can't believe how much I look like him. It was like looking in a mirror.'

Ali nodded. 'So what happened then? Where did you go?'

'We went for pizza and we talked some more. I told him about school and stuff. Then he told me I could stay with him for the night if I needed some time out. We were going back to his house and that's when we saw you.' Ali noticed how animated Charlotte became as she talked about her father and she knew she was excited to finally have met him. She could tell that Charlotte was already planning a whole future for them: time spent getting to know one another over dinners out, perhaps daddy-daughter dates to the cinema. Ali hated herself for what she was about to do but she had no choice; what Ali was about to tell her was going to crush everything she longed for.

Ali took a deep breath. 'Charlotte, there's something you need to know... Something I didn't want to tell you before now because you will find it upsetting but I think the time has come for honesty. You'll understand why when I tell you.'

Charlotte blinked hard. 'What is it?' she asked anxiously.

'So remember when I told you that Lorcan Keane was my Sociology lecturer? I was working on my dissertation in my final year but I got appendicitis and missed a few weeks of lectures and fell behind. He noticed my grades had dropped in some of my assessments and when I explained that I had been sick, he told me to call up to his office and he'd go through it all with me.' Ali paused to tuck her hair behind her ear. 'We did this for a few weeks, going over the lectures I had missed, and he helped me to get on top of it all again.'

'Okay...' Charlotte said, studying her intently, trying to work out where this was leading.

'Everything was going really well,' Ali continued, 'until one day, just as I was leaving, he moved to kiss me. I was stunned but I managed to dodge him and ran towards the door. I had just gripped the handle and thought I was free when suddenly, he pulled me back into the room.' She paused and swallowed hard to steel herself for what she was about to say next. 'Then he pinned me down onto the floor and he... eh... he raped me.' She could hear the tremble in her own voice. 'God I don't think I've ever said that out loud.' She shook her head as the emotion overtook her and the old wound that she was sure had healed was picked open once more.

Charlotte cupped her hand over her mouth and tears bulged in her eyes. 'So, I'm the product of a rape?' Her daughter's face was creased in pain as realisation hit her. 'My father is a rapist.' She started pulling her hair up by its roots and Ali reached out her hand to stop her.

Although Ali wanted to keep a brave face on for her daughter's sake, she couldn't help but lean into her and cry into her daughter's hair.

'Did you ever tell anyone before now?' Charlotte asked.

Ali shook her head. 'When he was finished, he warned me that if I told anyone about it that he would make sure that I failed my final exams. I was terrified. I was scared nobody would believe me because I just let him do it. I keep asking myself why I didn't fight harder. Why didn't I try harder to stop him? I don't think I even screamed!' she added in disbelief. 'It was like I couldn't believe it was actually happening.'

'Oh, Mum.' Charlotte put her arms around her and squeezed her.

'In the end, it didn't matter anyway,' she said bitterly, 'I couldn't face him in lectures; I couldn't even set foot on campus. Then a few weeks later, I found out I was pregnant so I dropped out and never sat my finals so failed my degree anyway.'

'But didn't people ask you who the father was?'

'They did but whenever anyone asked me, I just lied and said it was a random one-night stand and that I couldn't remember his name. Your grandparents were horrified.' She smiled weakly. 'But it was better to have them disappointed in my behaviour than knowing the truth. I know there were rumours going around the college at the time about him being your father. Apparently, people thought that because I was spending time in his office getting private tutoring, that there was something going on between us. So then when I fell pregnant, they assumed it was because we had been in a relationship with one another.'

'So how did those girls in my school know about it?' Charlotte said with tears glazing her eyes.

'That's what I've been trying to figure out too,' Ali replied. 'I'm guessing the only way it could have resurfaced now is that one of the parents in St Thomas's must have also been a student in Dublin University at the same time or else they know someone who was.'

'I'm sorry this happened to you,' Charlotte said angrily, coming across more mature than her sixteen years. Their roles had been reversed and for the first time in their relationship, it was Charlotte who was comforting her. She hated burdening her daughter with this, telling her that she was the product of a sexual assault. Her daughter was a sensitive soul and felt things deeper than most people; Ali had carried this with her for years and for the most part was able to block it out as she went about her day-to-day life. It was only if something or someone triggered the memory that she thought about it. She was in a good place now and had had many years to deal with it but she was worried about the impact that the shock of this revelation would have on Charlotte.

'It's okay,' Ali consoled her. 'It's okay, it was a long time ago. I'm fine, I promise, I'm over it now and from all of that pain, I received the most beautiful gift of you.' She pulled her daughter in close. 'Obviously, I wish it didn't happen the way that it did, but something wonderful came from something bad and you're the best thing to ever happen to me. I never thought I'd say it, but I wouldn't change anything.'

'How can you say that, Mum?' Charlotte cried angrily. 'That man did something horrible to you and I have to live with that.' She scrunched up her face in disgust. 'I have his genes inside me. Maybe I'm bad too?' she added fearfully, pulling her sleeves down over her frail wrists and hugging herself.

'You stop talking like that,' Ali warned. 'You are not a bad person. Genes mean nothing in this case. You're a good person Charlotte; you don't have it in you to hurt someone.'

'Don't I?' She dangled the question in front of Ali.

'What's that supposed to mean?' Ali asked quickly as a bad feeling washed over her.

'Nothing.'

'Charlotte, if you need to tell me something, it's important that you do it now.'

Her daughter's eyes darted down to the ground but she remained mute.

'You promise you've told me everything you know or saw from that night at the Riordans'?' Ali pushed, but Charlotte got up and ran past her, hurrying upstairs.

What was Charlotte not telling her? she wondered, growing frustrated by her daughter's silence. Ali had opened up and told her daughter her darkest, most painful secret and yet still Charlotte couldn't confide in her. They were fighting with their hands tied behind their backs and if Charlotte didn't tell her the truth soon, Ali was scared that time was going to run out for her.

48

---

23 OCTOBER 2023

Charlotte's Journal

I feel sick. Disgusting. I can't believe I'm related to that vile monster – that his DNA is in me too. And because I was so selfish, running off to find him without telling Mum where I was going, I dragged her back to face him. I ruined her life all those years ago and then I made her face him again. Why wouldn't I listen to her? She tried to warn me; she tried to protect me by keeping it hidden from me and now I understand why. To discover you were conceived because a man raped your mother is a mind-fuck. I keep thinking of all the opportunities she could have had if she hadn't got pregnant with me. She might have finished her degree. She might have gone travelling or got a well-paying job with regular hours and weekends off like she always wanted and life would have been easier for her; she wouldn't be scrambling from payday to pay-day, trying to stretch out the grocery shop for a more few days until she had some money. It's all my fault; I brought this on us. Mum tried to keep me away from him but I had to keep digging and now look what I've done and I can't undo it. I am always there to remind her of what he did to her and yet she has only ever shown me love. I'll always have to live with the knowledge that the man who is my father is evil. I can't live with myself – I am disgusting. I have the badness from him inside me. It's crawling inside me like a parasite. I want to tear my hair off my scalp, peel my skin from my bones and get him out of me.

I don't deserve my mum. I don't deserve to be here.

49

In the middle of the night, Ali woke panting and sweating with icy fear. She was standing there, watching Lorcan pinning her daughter down on the floor but she wasn't able to stop him; neither her legs nor arms would move. She was useless and inert. She opened her mouth to scream but nothing came out. She opened her eyes and pulled great, heaving gulps of air into her lungs. She sat up in the bed and flicked on her lamp, relieved to find she was safe in her own bed. *It was only a nightmare*, she told herself. Charlotte was at home now; she was safely tucked up in her room but she still couldn't shake off the sickly feeling that clotted in the pit of her stomach. It had felt so real. *So terrifying.* She couldn't rid herself of the image of Lorcan's sneering face looming over her. She could hear the *clink* of his belt being undone and tossed onto the floor. The pressure of his fingers gripping her neck as he tugged at her clothing and fumbled with her underwear. She kept thinking about what would have happened if she hadn't got there in time tonight? Would he have done the same thing to Charlotte as he had done to her all those years ago? It petrified Ali just how close Charlotte had come to jeopardy and the worst thing was, her daughter hadn't even realised it.

She needed to see her daughter. She needed to feel her silky skin beneath her fingertips and to see the shallow rise and fall of her chest as she breathed, before she would really believe that she was safe.

Ali climbed out of bed and planted her feet onto the carpet. She was exhausted, the combination of her fitful sleep and telling her daughter the truth about how she came to be, years of pent-up worry about how she might react, had spilled out of her and although it had been a relief in many ways, now that Charlotte knew the truth, they would have to navigate this knowledge together. Ali knew that Charlotte would need time to adjust to the difficult news of learning how she was conceived. She felt as though she had been hollowed out; like someone had used an ice-cream scoop and taken everything out of her.

Then there was the situation with Josh; they hadn't heard anything from the Gardaí since Charlotte's phone had been confiscated and she prayed that things wouldn't get any worse for her.

She crept down the landing and gently opened her daughter's bedroom door, cursing inwardly as it creaked. In the darkness, she made her way over to Charlotte's bed but an awful stench filled her nostrils. She switched on the main bedroom light and it was then that she saw her daughter lying awkwardly, half-hanging over the bed like a rag doll, with her hair spilling over her head, falling towards the floor.

'Charlotte?' she called out as her brain tried to work out what was happening.

But no response came from her daughter.

She hurried over and pushed back her hair and saw her eyes were half-open like a doll's, their whites rolling back in her head. She was covered in vomit and white froth trailed from the corner of her mouth. Ali cupped her hand over her own mouth. *'Dear God, no!'* she screamed aloud. No way. Not her beautiful daughter. Out of the corner of her eye, resting on top of Charlotte's bedside table was an empty wine bottle and a blister pack of paracetamol. Dread pooled into her stomach and she felt bile rising up her throat. She found herself retching as she picked up the tablet packet and saw they were all empty. She thought about the open bottle of wine that had been in the fridge. Ali and Lisa had only had a small glass from it the first time the Gardaí had called so she knew the bottle had been over half-full. That was way too much alcohol for a child as young and petite as Charlotte but it was the combination of it with the tablets that scared her more. How many had she taken? Had she choked on her own vomit? She put her ear close to her mouth to see if she was breathing but she couldn't hear anything. She put her hand on her chest and thought she could feel the shallowest rise and fall of her ribcage but it was so faint, she wasn't sure if she was imagining it. She manoeuvred Charlotte into the recovery position and was startled by the bluish tinge of her skin and how cool to the touch it was. She knew she needed to do something but she couldn't think what. Her thoughts were slow and fudgy. Then it hit her that she needed to get help. She needed to call an ambulance.

She made her way up from the bed and ran back to her bedroom. Her legs were wobbly, like they were made from marshmallows, and she was worried they would give way beneath her. She found her phone charging beside her bed. She unplugged it and it took her several attempts because her hands were trembling so much but eventually, she managed to key in the number for the emergency services.

'Hello, Emergency 112, what service do you require?'

'It's my daughter, I... I think she's overdosed on paracetamol tablets combined with alcohol – she's unconscious.'

'I will connect you to the ambulance service. Is this your correct phone number in case we get cut off?' He called back her number to her.

'Yes.'

'What's your address?'

'5 Parnell Close. You've got to hurry,' she pleaded, knowing that she needed to provide them with these details but wishing they could speed things up.

After she had hung up, she ran back into her daughter's room. She knelt down onto the floor beside her bed and put her arms around her. She noticed fresh scars on Charlotte's thighs where the t-shirt that she had worn to bed had risen up and Ali realised with despair pooling into every part of her body that Charlotte had been self-harming again. *You should have been watching out for this*, a mocking voice chided. If she had picked up on the fact that Charlotte was cutting herself again before now, she could have prevented things from escalating this far and now it could be too late. She might have lost her daughter forever.

'Come on, Charlotte, wake up,' she begged. 'You have to wake up! Charlotte, please!' She shook her shoulder. 'Don't do this to me,' she warned. 'I can't lose you – I just can't—'

She choked on her tears but Charlotte remained unresponsive.

50

The slow *drip, drip, drop* of the fluid as it left the bag, travelled down the intravenous line and entered her daughter's body, punctured the silence in the hospital room. How long had she been waiting for an update? It felt like years but she knew it was only a few hours since she had first made the call to the emergency services. When they had arrived at her house, she had left Charlotte, hurried downstairs and opened the door to let them in. She could see the blue ambulance light strobing around the street outside. Ali told them she was upstairs and they had taken the steps two at a time, with Ali hurrying after them. They had checked her vital signs and confirmed that she was still breathing but her pulse was faint. Ali told them about the wine and the blister pack of paracetamol that she had found beside her daughter. She felt like the worst mother in the world when she wasn't able to tell them whether it had been a new pack of paracetamol that Charlotte had bought over the counter herself or if it had been an already-opened packet taken from the medicine cupboard in the kitchen.

'I don't know,' she had wailed.

They explained that Charlotte was at risk of organ failure if she didn't get the right treatment quickly and that she needed to get to the hospital urgently. They had gently lifted her onto a stretcher then carried her downstairs to the ambulance. Ali had been allowed to travel with Charlotte, holding her cold, limp hand as neon-orange street lights streaked past the windows.

When they arrived at the hospital, the doors had been flung open and Charlotte's trolley had been ushered inside the building, leaving Ali running in its wake. Ali was now sitting at her bedside, under the dimmed lights of the intensive care unit. A kindly nurse had sat down beside her and explained carefully that they were administering a substance called N-acetylcysteine – NAC for short – intravenously. Due to Charlotte's petite size, the unknown time the paracetamol had been ingested and the quantity that had been taken, they had warned Ali that there was a risk of liver toxicity and the role of NAC was to help protect her liver function.

'What happens if her liver is damaged?' Ali had asked fearfully.

'In severe cases, patients can require a transplant or we have had patients who pass away if the liver goes into failure but let's not think like that just yet,' the nurse tried to reassure her.

Ali gulped. 'Will she be okay?' she begged. She wanted them to tell her that everything was going to be all right but nobody was doing that and it made her even more scared.

'NAC has good outcomes when it's administered early.' The nurse side-stepped her question. 'We will monitor her blood levels for the next while and only then will we know the extent, if any, of the damage that has been done and whether she is out of danger.'

'I'm an awful mum,' Ali wept. 'She's been through so much lately and I told her something yesterday and she was so upset by it. I shouldn't have told her; I should have known she was too fragile to handle it.' Ali had failed her. She should have done more to protect her daughter. She should have seen this coming, she kept berating herself; just what kind of a mother would allow things to get so bad that her child felt that this was the only way out?

'Look, I don't know what happened that led your daughter to doing what she did but you can be assured that we'll do all we can to help get her on the road to recovery.' The nurse patted her shoulder kindly.

Ali nodded and thanked the nurse as she went on her way. She held her daughter's frail hand inside her own as Charlotte continued to sleep off the effects of the overdose. Although she longed for her to wake up, to be able to tell her that she was sorry for everything, that she loved her more than she would ever know, Ali prayed that her body was putting its energy into healing itself. It tore at her heart that Charlotte felt so worthless that she had resorted to doing something like this. She longed for her daughter to see herself through her eyes – she was beautiful, clever, kind and loving. If only she had a little bit more confidence in herself, Ali knew she could bloom, but now she might not ever get the chance. Would Ali get to cheer her on as she graduated from university? Would she get to help her into her wedding gown when she got married? Would she get the chance to watch her become a mother – to watch that nurturing and caring side of her daughter flourish as she fell in love with her own little baby? Ali wanted all of this so desperately for Charlotte's future and she couldn't bear to think that she might never get to see any of it.

When the nurse had gone on her way, Ali had taken out her phone and googled *paracetamol toxicity* and was met with sorrowful stories in the media from loved ones who had died as a result of paracetamol overdose. As Ali read their stories, she realised there was a real possibility her daughter wouldn't get better. What if Charlotte died? What would she do then? Ali would never survive a world without her daughter in it. It was unthinkable.

'Put that phone away, and don't be googling!' a different nurse came up behind her and chided, startling Ali. 'You're better off staying away from the internet; it's only full of sad stories.'

Ali nodded, abashed, and placed her phone down.

'You look like you could use a coffee. There's a vending machine down the hall; why don't you stretch your legs for five minutes?'

Ali shook her head. 'I can't leave her.' She recalled all those long nights she had spent walking the bedroom floor with her tiny baby daughter, trying to get her to sleep. Back then, she had thought that they were going to be her hardest days as a parent. She had naively assumed that once her daughter grew and became more self-sufficient, life would be easier, but she never could have imagined then that her real worries would only start as Charlotte gained more independence from her. She would give anything to cradle her baby in the crook of her arm again, to feel her baby's downy hair against the skin of her neck. Although the sleep deprivation and feeding challenges that a new baby brought had been hard, at least she had been able to keep her daughter safe back then but now it felt like Charlotte was so far out of reach.

'I'll stay with her until you get back. I promise I won't move. Now, go on, go,' the nurse ordered.

Ali felt her bladder pressing on her organs. She badly needed to use the bathroom.

'Okay,' she relented. 'I'll only be a few minutes. Please come find me if anything changes or she wakes up.'

The nurse smiled kindly. 'Of course I will.'

51

Ali came out of the bathroom and made her way down the hall. As she looked at the people walking past her, she suddenly remembered she was still wearing the pyjamas that she had travelled to the hospital in earlier. When the paramedics had arrived, she had only had time to grab her raincoat from where it was hanging on the newel post at the bottom of the stairs and had thrown it on over her pyjamas, before following her daughter's trolley into the back of the ambulance. She felt self-conscious now as she made her way down the corridor towards the coffee machine that the nurse had told her about. Morning sunlight streamed in from a courtyard where birds whirred from tree to tree. A carpet of russet-coloured leaves covered the ground outside. Her joints were stiff from sitting, so she circled her neck and shoulders as she walked.

She continued along and eventually arrived at the machine. She rooted around in her pocket for her phone, thankful to see the machine accepted Apple Pay as she hadn't thought to bring her purse with her. She selected a black coffee and was lowering her phone towards the contactless payment reader when she saw someone she recognised coming down the hall towards her. It took a moment for her brain to realise that it was Josh's father, Roger Quinlan. He looked older in the days since she had last seen him outside his clifftop mansion. His skin was ashen and deep lines and creases shadowed his face. It hit her that Josh must be in this hospital too. A part of her wanted to hide from him, she couldn't take another angry confrontation with him on top of everything else right now, but she also wanted to know whether there had been any update on his son's condition.

As the machine poured tarry coffee into the cup, Ali hurried over to him.

'I'm sorry,' she began anxiously, blocking his path. 'You might not remember me; I'm Ali Daly, Charlotte's mum.'

She watched his face darken in recognition.

'I... I just wanted to see how Josh is doing?' she continued, not giving him a chance to tell her to get lost.

'He's still the same. Still in a coma.'

'I'm really sorry to hear that. I'm praying every day that he wakes up.'

She saw him taking in her pyjamas and dishevelled state and realised he might think she was a crazy woman that had shown up at the hospital with the sole purpose of finding him. 'My daughter Charlotte was brought in here last night,' she explained, gesturing to her pyjamas. 'I didn't have time to change.'

'I'm sorry to hear that. Is she okay?' he asked.

Ali shook her head. 'We're not sure yet. She... um... she overdosed on paracetamol. She's had a really tough time of it lately.' Ali choked and couldn't stop the tears from spilling down her face as she relived the horrible events of the night before once more.

'I'm very sorry to hear that.' He reached out an arm and placed it on her shoulder. 'Hang in there; none of us want to be here,' he said, shaking his head sadly.

Ali nodded, grateful for his touch, his kindness. 'I'd better get back but I want you to know that Josh is in my prayers.'

'Thank you, Ali and I'll keep Charlotte in mine.'

Then she lifted her coffee and continued down the corridor towards Charlotte's room.

She made her way back to Charlotte's bedside, feeling teary after her encounter with Josh's father. He had shown kindness to her when he could have chosen otherwise. It had been unexpected and made her feel a wreck. She rounded the door to the intensive care unit and true to her word, the nurse was still there sitting at her daughter's bedside. She smiled kindly at her as Ali entered.

'There love, are you feeling a bit better?'

Ali nodded, not trusting herself to speak.

'I'd better get going before they come looking for me.' She winked. 'Call me if you need anything.'

Ali watched her pale, vulnerable daughter, sleeping like a doll and looking even smaller than usual in this large bed surrounded by machines and wires.

She heard her phone ring and when she fished it out of her pocket, she saw it was her mother.

'Hi, love,' Maura sang down the phone. 'Sorry I was half-asleep when you phoned last night. I woke up this morning and wondered if I had dreamt it.' She laughed.

'Oh, sorry,' Ali said, remembering the conversation they had had the night before as Ali had begun her search for her daughter. She had promised she would phone in the morning but she had forgotten. So much had happened since then; in those few hours, the bottom had fallen out of Ali's world.

'So how's all with you?' her mother went on. 'The weather is miserable here today; I tried to take the dog for a walk on the beach earlier and he wouldn't go outside. Planted his arse on the floor and wouldn't move. I can't say I blame him.'

'Mam, I have something I need to tell you...' Ali began tentatively.

'What is it, love?'

'It's Charlotte – she's in hospital.'

'Hospital?' She heard her mother gasp at the other end of the phone and then calling Ali's father, Eddie to repeat to him what she had just been told. 'Is she okay? What's happened to her?' Questions spilled from her mouth.

'She overdosed on paracetamol.'

'Charlotte overdosed?' Her mother repeated incredulously. 'On paracetamol? Are you sure, love?'

Ali couldn't keep the tears at bay any longer. 'Mam, a lot has happened and I haven't told you about it because I didn't want to worry you.'

'Oh, love, what is it? What's wrong?'

'Please come, Mam,' she begged. 'I need you.'

52

52

When Ali saw her parents standing in the doorway of the intensive care unit that evening, emotion consumed her.

'Oh, love,' her mother said as she pulled her in tightly. Ali could smell the comforting scent of the lavender notes in the perfume that she had used since Ali was a little girl. She hugged them tight and they hugged her back even tighter. Why had she thought she had to do this on her own? Her parents had always been there for her: a safety net when she was falling.

Even though it was only a couple of months since she had seen them, Ali couldn't help but notice that they had both aged in that time. Her dad had become more stooped and her mother was a little slower on her feet. She hated doing this to them. Hated bringing them here. Hated putting worry on their shoulders but she couldn't carry it all on her own any more. She felt as though she was sinking under the weight of years of her secrets and she was too weak to go on any longer. She was so tired: tired of always having to be strong, tired of doing everything on her own, tired of holding it together all of the time.

They released one another and after receiving permission from the nurse to enter the unit, they followed Ali inside to Charlotte's bed. They moved gingerly to their granddaughter's bedside, overwhelmed by the sight of their precious grandchild surrounded by bleeping medical equipment. It was clear from their pinched faces that they were distraught. Ali had last seen them in August when she had had a week off work and she and Charlotte had made the journey to the west coast of Ireland to stay with them. They had had a great week on the white sands of Achill; the weather had been kind and they had spent most days on the beach. Charlotte had taken surf lessons and Ali had marvelled at how her daughter had come alive in the ocean, as she mastered standing on her board. She had even convinced Ali to give it a try; although she hadn't got the hang of standing up on the board, she had loved the feeling of coasting on the surging waves towards the shore. The days spent breathing in the briny sea air gave them a hearty appetite and they would return home to her parents' cottage for her mother's homecooked food: sweet Guinness bread, rich casseroles and juicy apple tarts made with delicate pastry. Looking back now, Charlotte had seemed happy there – or her own version of happy. Why hadn't that been enough for Ali? Why had she gone and ruined it by forcing her to change schools?

'How's she doing?'

Ali looked at her frail daughter lying in the bed, with wires and tubes trailing from her thin arms. 'She's stable for now. It all depends on her toxicity levels whether she's done any lasting damage to her liver or not, so she's not out of the woods yet.'

'What happened, love?' her father asked gently. 'Why on earth would she do something like that?'

Ali filled them in on the party at Lisa and Patrick's house. She told them about Josh Quinlan being found unconscious in the pool and they were shocked when she told them how everyone was pointing the finger of blame at Charlotte. She told them about the bullying and online intimidation that she had been subjected to since. She could see they were stunned by the revelations, grappling to understand it all and didn't know where to begin asking questions.

'Those phones are the ruination of society,' her father said desolately. 'The parents of those other children should be ashamed of themselves. Pushing a young girl to the edge like that where she felt her only option was to do something like this!' he continued angrily.

Ali knew the time had come for honesty. She couldn't hide from her secrets any longer. Running away just made everything worse. She took a deep breath. 'There's something else that I need to tell you both,' she began tentatively.

'What is it?' her mother asked, cocking her head to the side.

'It's about Charlotte's father—'

'Her father?' her dad repeated.

Ali nodded. 'He wasn't just a random guy that I met in a nightclub.' She cringed as she said this.

'All right. So who is he then?'

'He was my lecturer in university. Professor Lorcan Keane.'

She watched her parents' faces screw up in confusion as they tried to digest what she was telling them.

'He's Charlotte's father?' her mother asked in disbelief after a moment, fingering the gold crucifix that she wore around her neck.

'Were you in a relationship with him?' her father asked.

Ali shook her head, knowing she was going to crush them with what she said next.

'Do you remember how I had to get my appendix out in my final year and I missed a few weeks of lectures?'

Her mother nodded dumbly.

'Well, he was helping me catch up on the work that I missed. And... erm... one day, we were alone in his office and... he... he raped me.'

'The dirty bollix!' her father roared.

'Whist, Eddie,' Maura shushed. She jabbed a finger towards Charlotte to remind him of where they were. 'Your granddaughter is seriously ill in that bed.' Her mother moved towards Ali and held her by her shoulders.

'So that's why you dropped out of college?' her father asked as it all finally made sense to him. He had been so upset by her announcement back then that she wasn't going to finish her degree when she was just weeks away from sitting her final exams. Neither of her parents had gone on to third-level education and they were so proud that their daughter was getting a degree. When her father had asked her the reason why she was dropping out, Ali had blamed it on being pregnant. She told them she wasn't feeling well, which had been true; she had had debilitating morning sickness but she knew she could have pushed herself to do the exams if she had really wanted to. They had offered to speak with the college to see if she could repeat the exams at a later date, when she was feeling better, or after the baby was born, but Ali refused and so they had had to accept that they would never get to see their only child graduate.

'I'm sorry, Dad, I just wasn't able to. I was scared I might come face to face with him again.'

'He ruined your life!' Eddie blazed. 'And we let him get away with it.'

Ali shook her head. 'I have Charlotte because of what happened back then. Believe it or not but I wouldn't change it; without what he did, I wouldn't have my daughter.'

'Oh, love,' Maura sobbed. 'It shouldn't have happened, though.'

'He needs to be brought to justice,' Eddie concurred.

Ali nodded in agreement. 'I know, you're right, I probably should have said something or reported it at the time in case he did it to someone else but honestly, I just wasn't able to face it... I forgot about him and focused on Charlotte and for the most part, I've been able to block it out for all these years. Until now.'

'Oh, love.' Maura pulled her into a hug.

Her father's face darkened as he read between Ali's words. 'Has this something to do with Charlotte taking those tablets?'

Ali nodded. 'I had to tell her who her father was but I didn't mention how she was conceived. I didn't want that burden hanging over her when she was already so fragile. We had an argument and I went to work but when I came home and checked in her room, I realised that she was missing. I eventually managed to track her down but she had gone to find him.'

Her mother was horrified. 'She went to find Lorcan Keane?'

Ali nodded. 'I was so scared, Mam.'

'That's why you called last night, wasn't it?' Maura asked, as she pieced it all together.

Ali nodded.

'You should have told us; we would have come straight down to help you find her.'

'I know, Mam, but I didn't want to worry you when I was sure I would find her. When I realised she might have gone to find him, I was terrified he would do the same thing to her as he did to me. He's a monster. I persuaded her to come home but I had to tell her the truth then. She got so upset when I came clean about how she was conceived because the realisation that she was the product of rape was too much on top of everything else that she is going through. I went to bed and woke during the night. I had a nightmare and felt really unsettled after it. I can't explain it but had an uneasy feeling and I don't know what made me check on her – but that's when I found her—' Ali dissolved into tears as she recalled the turn of events that had led her to this point.

'Why didn't you tell us?' Maura chimed in. 'Carrying the weight of that around with you for all this time. You should have told me and we could have helped you.' She clasped Ali's hands inside her own and squeezed hard so that when she released her grip, white fingerprints were left along her skin.

Ali shook her head. 'I don't want you to blame yourselves, please. This is hard enough; I need you both to be strong here. The honest answer is that I just wasn't able to. I was scared. He threatened to fail me if I told anyone and as it turned out I never sat the exams in the end, so it wouldn't have mattered anyway,' she said bitterly.

Her father clapped his palm on her shoulder. 'You've been through it, love,' he said sadly. 'I'm sorry we weren't there for you.'

53

Soft-soled shoes crept across the vinyl floor and when Ali turned around to see who it was, she saw the nurse from earlier on was back again.

'How's she doing?' she asked, taking Charlotte's chart out of the holder at the end of the bed and reviewing it.

'Still asleep. Shouldn't she have woken up by now?'

'Try not to worry; it's her body's way of repairing the damage that was done. She'll wake up when she's ready.'

Ali nodded, knowing that she was right. She would much rather Charlotte's body concentrated its energy on repairing and mending itself back together.

'I've some good news for you. I've just had Charlotte's bloods come back from the lab and her toxicity
is decreasing. Her body is responding to the NAC. We
won't know for sure yet if there will be any lasting
damage but for now, we're pleased that she's heading
in the right direction.'

Ali sagged with relief. 'Thank God,' she said,
leaning in and kissing her daughter's porcelain forehead. Even if Charlotte got better, Ali knew that
would only be the start of her road to recovery. She
would have an awful lot of work to do to get her back
to a good mental state again. They would have to address her reasons for overdosing in the first place;
there was still the situation with Josh looming over
them and then the news that she had been conceived
from rape would have to be dealt with too. There was
so much heaped on her young shoulders.

The nurse went over to the monitors and began
doing her checks, then she fished a pen from her
pocket and updated Charlotte's chart. 'Try to stay positive,' she said as left them alone and went on her way.

The three of them embraced after the nurse had
gone. 'Thank God she's responding to the treatment,'
Ali said. After all those long hours Ali had spent
praying at her bedside, finally it was a step forward.

'She's a fighter,' Eddie replied.

Ali held her daughter's hand inside hers and gave it a gentle squeeze. Even though she was sleeping, she wanted Charlotte to know that she was right here with her, to know that she'd always be with her no matter what. Ali would always be there to catch her when she fell because that's what mothers did.

Just then, they heard someone behind them.

Ali straightened up and saw Josh's father standing there. Immediately, her heart picked up speed. 'Roger,' she stammered. Her mind began racing. What did he want?

'I hope you don't mind me coming in here,' he began nervously. 'I've got to know most of the nurses here over the last few days and I told them that I knew you and they said I could come in for a few minutes but if this isn't a good time, I can come back?' He thumbed over his shoulder in the direction of the corridor.

She could tell from his demeanour that he wasn't here to cause trouble for her. 'No, it's okay.' She stood up and gestured for him to come inside their cubicle. 'Come in.'

She noticed her parents looking at one another, trying to figure out who this man was and why he was here.

'How's she doing?' He gestured towards Charlotte.

'She's stable for now. It'll be a while before we know the full impact but we'll take each hour as it comes.'

He nodded and raked his fingers through his hair. 'I know that feeling well.'

'Mam, Dad, this is Roger Quinlan; he's Josh's father: that's the boy that was found unconscious in the Riordans' pool.'

'I'm very sorry to hear about your son,' Maura said.

'Well, that's why I'm here. I just wanted to let you know that Josh is awake.' He broke into a smile and suddenly looked brighter than Ali had ever seen him and she got a glimpse of the man that he was before this awful nightmare had descended upon them.

Ali lit up, relief washing through her. 'He is? You must be so relieved. How is he?'

'That's the thing.' He grinned. 'It's like he was only asleep. He's talking to us; he remembers who we are. Obviously, he's tired and groggy and confused but I think that's to be expected all things considered. The nurses are amazed at how well he's doing. For a while there, it wasn't looking good. They need to do more tests on him and we're not sure if there will be any lasting damage... but one step at a time. He's awake and we are thanking our lucky stars. It's been hell but to get our son back feels like I've won the lotto.' He placed his palms together and raised them towards the ceiling. 'I'll never ask God for another favour ever again.'

'I'm so glad to hear that, what wonderful news.' She meant every word; she was so thankful that Josh was finally awake and at least one of their children was on the road to recovery. 'I really appreciate you letting me know.' It would have been understandable if he didn't give her a second thought all things considered.

'There's something else, something that you need to know...' Roger said, shifting anxiously.

'What is it?' she asked, hunting his eyes for a clue as to what was going on.

'I think you need to come with me and hear it for yourself.'

54

Ali left her parents at Charlotte's bedside with strict instructions to call her if there was any change in her daughter's condition, then she followed Josh's father down the corridor. Her heart was racing as she trailed after him. He was walking fast, rounding corners, and she had difficulty keeping up with him. When he swerved out of the way of a porter pushing a young girl in a wheelchair with a drip attached, Ali did the same. Where was he taking her and why? All kinds of thoughts flitted through her mind. Was he going to tell her something more about what happened at the party? Was this some kind of trap: was he trying to snare her into a room packed with Gardaí waiting to interrogate her? Perhaps he was going to implicate her daughter further or try yet again to place the blame on Charlotte? Ali didn't think she would survive any more. She now understood why people made false confessions when under extreme duress.

She followed him up two flights of stairs and eventually, he turned into a room. As she trailed behind him, Ali took a deep breath and set her jaw, steeling herself for whatever it was that she was about to face.

She entered the room and saw Josh sitting up in bed with a woman sitting next to him that Ali recognised from the night when she had dropped Charlotte at the party. She guessed she must be Josh's mother. The woman was a shadow of the glamourous woman she had seen that night sitting up high in her BMW; the bouncy, blow-dried hair was now lank and frizzy and her face was devoid of make-up. Josh's skin looked shades paler compared with the tanned boy she remembered. The woman stood up as Ali entered the room and walked towards her. Ali tried to read her expression; was she angry? Was she about to launch into a tirade of abuse?

'It's great to see he's awake,' Ali said nervously.

The woman surprised her then by reaching out and grasping Ali's two hands in her own and squeezing them. 'I'm Corinna. I heard about your daughter; how is she doing?'

'She's sleeping now but she's stable and she's responding to the treatment, thank God. The nurses are happy that she hasn't deteriorated, which can sometimes happen in these situations. They said that's a really positive sign.'

Corinna shook her head sadly. 'I understand what you're going through. The last few days have been the very worst of my entire life. I'm keeping everything crossed that Charlotte makes a full recovery and you get your happy ending too. I know a lot has happened but despite everything,' she choked, 'we're both just two mothers who love our babies very much and want our kids to be back home where they belong.'

'Thank you,' Ali mumbled, feeling emotion catch on her words. She was stunned by the woman's sympathy. She nodded in Josh's direction. 'How's he doing?'

'To be where I am today with Josh awake feels like a miracle; I am so grateful. We had some very dark days.' She glanced over at her husband and they exchanged a barely imperceptible nod. 'The thing is, Ali... I think we owe you an apology,' she said, with tears brimming in her eyes.

'You do?' Ali blinked incredulously, sure she had misheard the woman.

'Ali,' she began solemnly, 'Josh remembers what happened that night...'

55

Ali's head swivelled back to where Josh was lying in
the bed. He tried to sit up straighter and his mother
rushed up and helped prop pillows behind his back to
make him more comfortable. He shot a nervous
glance towards Corinna and she gave him a reassuring nod. Ali held her breath as he started to talk.

'On the night of the party,' he began quietly, 'I remember we... we were drinking some beers and Ollie... well, he was really drunk.' He paused for a
moment to catch his breath. 'He was getting messy –
getting aggro because one of the lads was teasing him
about a conversion he'd missed in a rugby match a
few weeks ago,' he croaked. 'I saw Charlotte standing
over in the corner on her own. She was the only

person not drinking. Some of the girls and guys were in a big group, sniggering and laughing at her, and I felt bad for her. You could tell that she really didn't want to be there.' He paused as his breathing became laboured. 'Anyway, they started doing dares and then one of the lads – I don't know which one – dared Ollie to kiss her so Ollie goes over and literally pins her to the wall and starts to kiss her, except it's not just a kiss; his hands are everywhere. Charlotte doesn't see it coming and you can see that she's terrified and they all think it's hilarious. I just couldn't stand there watching her look so scared so I went over and tried to pull him off her. Charlotte managed to escape and she ran off; I didn't see where she went because then Ollie got really mad at me. He started pushing and shoving me so I'm pushing him back. Then... then... there's a pile on and all the lads are around me and they're all chanting Ollie's name. Then I see a fist shoot out and it connects with my jaw and the next thing I know, I'm falling backwards and then... that's the last thing I remember.'

Slowly, the wheels of Ali's brain started to turn. She blinked as the shocking truth hit home. Charlotte had been telling the truth. She hadn't pushed Josh into the pool; although Ali desperately wished she had told her the part about Ollie assaulting her. Her heart ached for her daughter. No wonder this had been too much for her; what a burden to carry by herself. Why hadn't she felt able to confide in her mother about Ollie's unwanted advance with all those teenagers looking on and sniggering? She must have been petrified; was it any wonder that she ran away?

But as well as receiving the welcome news that her daughter hadn't assaulted Josh, it was a bigger shock to hear that it was Lisa's son, Ollie, who had instigated the whole thing. It dawned on her then that it must have been Ollie – not Josh – who had been the grainy figure seen close to her daughter in the images that the Gardaí had shown her. When he had pinned her to the wall, they must have gone out of shot of the CCTV, which would explain how the rest of the incident – Ollie assaulting Charlotte, Josh's intervention and the pile on between the boys, which had led to Josh being found in the pool – wasn't picked up by the cameras. Ollie had known it wasn't Charlotte's fault and hadn't told anyone. *Had Lisa known too? she asked herself.* Had they tried to cover it up to protect themselves?

'Do you know who threw the punch?' Ali asked.

'No. There were so many of them on me.' Josh shook his head. 'But my money is on Ollie because he was completely off his face and so riled up.'

'I think they all colluded to keep their story on the same page and I guess they decided to use Charlotte as the scapegoat,' Roger said. 'Even though having seen her myself and how petite she is, I can see that it really was very unlikely that she would have been physically capable of pushing a lad the size of Josh. I guess the other teenagers knew she was an easy target and blaming her was the best way to cover up what really happened that night.'

'I'm still surprised no one captured it on their phone,' Ali said in bewilderment.

'I would think that even if any of the teenagers did video it, Ollie would have made them all delete everything from that night,' Corinna said.

'We need to tell the Gardaí,' Ali said urgently. The truth was out now and she didn't want her daughter being in the frame for a minute longer than was necessary.

'We're a step ahead of you. We've already done that; they were the first people we contacted. They want to interview Josh when he's a little stronger; they're hoping to stop by tomorrow.'

Relief surged through Ali. Charlotte was being exonerated; finally, she could close the door on this ordeal and just focus on healing her daughter.

'After we spoke with the Gardaí, I told Roger that

we had to speak to you too and I couldn't believe it when he explained that you were already here in the hospital.' Corinna bowed her head. 'I'm so sorry, Ali, for everything.'

'It's not your fault; in fact, I should be the one thanking you for raising such a conscientious young man. He went against his friends and stood up for what was right; it's hard at that age not to follow the crowd.'

Corinna looked lovingly at her son with tears welling in her eyes. 'He's a good boy. He always has been, but I'm extra proud of him right now.'

'Thank you both for everything.' Ali turned back to Josh. 'And especially to you, Josh. You're a great young man. I don't know how I'll ever repay you.'

'It's okay,' he mumbled, embarrassed by the compliment. 'I hope Charlotte will be okay.'

'Me too,' Ali replied. 'I'd better get back to her.'

As Ali made her way back to Charlotte's bedside, she felt lighter; the weight of worry had lifted and although her daughter wasn't out of the woods yet, she felt hopeful for the first time in days. She willed her to pull through so that she could tell her the good news and that they didn't need to worry any more.

56

Ali made her way back down the corridor, her head a chaotic muddle of thoughts and feelings. She was so relieved that Charlotte had been vindicated but to discover that Ollie – and potentially Lisa – had lied about what had happened that night had been a kick in the gut that she hadn't seen coming.

Ali was glad that Josh's parents had already gone to the Gardaí and she didn't have to be the one to do that because she didn't think she could face another interview with them. She rounded the corner to Charlotte's room and bumped into her father coming out the door towards her.

'Oh, thank God you're here,' he said breathlessly. 'I was just coming to find you.'

'Is everything okay?' she asked, panicked, rushing past him to her daughter's bedside. She prayed she hadn't deteriorated. She studied her daughter, surrounded by wires and monitors. It was then that she saw it. Charlotte's eyes flickered open.

'Mum,' she croaked.

'Oh my darling girl! My darling, darling girl!' she cried, moving closer to her. Tears streamed down her face, landing in her daughter's hair as she cupped her chin in her hands. She kissed her forehead, then planted kisses all over her hair. So grateful to be able to do it, knowing how near she had come to losing her. It felt like getting a second chance; the truth was out there now and she was going to make sure her daughter got better and healed. She never wanted to be in this situation again. 'How are you feeling?'

'I'm tired and I have a headache but I'm okay.'

'You gave me such a fright,' Ali said, stroking her warm cheek.

'I'm sorry, Mum,' she whispered. Her eyelids fluttered closed again.

'Hey, you've nothing to be sorry for. Do you hear me?' Ali sobbed. 'I just want to get you well again and get you back home where you belong. You've been under so much stress but I have some good news.'

Charlotte opened her eyes once more and Ali's parents turned to look at her.

'Josh woke up and he remembers what happened,' she announced, excitement and relief dancing on her voice.

Charlotte tried to sit up in the bed.

'Take it easy, love,' she instructed as she guided her upright.

'What did he say?'

'He told me what Ollie did to you that night, honey.' Ali turned to her parents to explain what she had just been told by Josh. 'Ollie tried it on with Charlotte and Josh tried to intervene to stop it. Charlotte ran away and the boys piled on top of Josh. Someone punched him and that's how he ended up in the pool.'

'But why didn't anyone say this before now? Surely everyone knew the truth. Why did the other teenagers there not come clean and say what happened instead of letting Charlotte take the rap?' her father asked in disbelief.

'I'm not sure, but I think they were scared of getting into trouble themselves. Who knows? Or maybe Ollie had warned them not to tell the truth. He is the captain of the rugby team. He holds a lot of influence.'

'So you think that maybe they were all too frightened to speak out against him?' Maura asked.

'I think so.'

'But surely the Gardaí checked all their phones as part of their investigation? Teenagers these days capture everything on their phone,' Maura went on.

'They're clever; I'd say they had already deleted anything that would incriminate Ollie.' Ali stroked her daughter's forehead. 'I just wish you had told me the truth about Ollie assaulting you.' She squeezed her hand, then felt its frailty inside her own and relaxed her grip. 'I could have helped you.'

'I didn't want you to get in trouble with the Riordans and lose your job,' Charlotte admitted in a small voice. 'I know how hard it is for you on your own trying to pay all the bills and the rent.'

Ali's heart twisted, like Charlotte was holding it on either side and wringing it. Guilt flooded through her; her daughter was aware of the struggles Ali faced trying to keep a roof over their heads and because of that, had tried to keep what Ollie did a secret. 'Oh, love,' she said tearfully. 'You're more important than any job.'

'I was worried that you wouldn't believe me because Lisa is your boss and you two are friends,' Charlotte explained. 'I swear though that I didn't know any of the other stuff about the fight and Josh being dragged out of the pool until the next day. Then it all just spiralled and I was too scared to tell you in case you didn't believe me.'

'Ollie is the son of the Riordans,' she explained to her parents who she could see were struggling to keep up. 'Come here,' Ali said, pulling her in tight against her chest. 'I would always believe you and I would always choose you, again and again and again.'

'So, what happens now?' her father demanded. 'You need to tell the Gardaí, Ali.'

'Josh's parents have already spoken with them and they're hoping to formally interview him tomorrow. I presume then they'll have to interview Ollie.' She turned to Charlotte. 'And possibly you too, love, to learn more about the assault. Presumably, after that, they can decide whether they have enough evidence to press charges. Hopefully, this new information will bring an end to it for us.' She sighed.

'But Mum, you could lose your job over this,' Charlotte said anxiously. 'How will you pay the rent and all the bills?'

'That's the least of my worries. I couldn't work with Lisa again anyway.' Ali rubbed Charlotte's cheek. 'I'm sorry, love that you've had to go through this.'

'It's okay. I'm just glad that Josh is awake and that everyone knows the truth now.' Her lids grew heavy and closed down again as she drifted back to sleep.

57

The following day, Charlotte gingerly stepped out of the car and Ali guided her to standing up. She linked her right arm, while Eddie linked her left side and Maura ran ahead to open the door for them. They went inside and Ali found the house was warm and inviting. Her parents had come over earlier to put the heating on and make sure it was welcoming for Charlotte's return home.

The medical team were happy with how she had responded to the treatment and said she could go home. She had been referred back to CAMHS and would need to speak with a psychologist to get the help she needed. Before they had left the hospital, she had asked to see Josh and so Ali had brought her down to his room. Ali had been so proud of her daughter as she thanked him for everything he had done for her and leaned over the bed to hug him. He was recovering well too and his parents were hopeful he would be allowed home soon as well. She had wished him and his parents all the best and prayed they would be closing the door on this awful nightmare.

'Welcome home, love,' Ali said, pushing the door behind them as they went inside the house. She reached out to give her daughter a kiss on the cheek. Over the last twenty-four hours since Charlotte had woken up, she couldn't stop herself from touching her, knowing how perilously close she had come to losing her.

'Thanks, Mum.'

'Why don't you go upstairs, have a bath, put on some snuggly PJs and I'll make something good for us all to eat,' Ali suggested.

'Okay.' Charlotte smiled and Ali felt her heart soar. It had been a long time since she had seen her daughter's beautiful smile.

While Charlotte climbed the stairs, Ali and her parents headed into the kitchen.

'I'll put the kettle on, love,' her mother said, patting her on the shoulder.

'Thanks, Mum. It's so good to be home.'

Ali had just flopped down into a chair when the doorbell rang. She went to get up but her Dad waved her down again.

'You stay where you are; I'll get it.'

'A girl could get used to this.' Ali laughed, making an exaggerated show of relaxing back into the chair as her Dad headed down the hallway. She was enjoying having her parents around. Since they had arrived, as well as giving her support with Charlotte, they had taken care of her and reminded her that she wasn't on her own. She was used to being self-sufficient, to doing everything by herself, and it felt good to know they were there to help her when she needed them.

She listened out and heard a woman talking with her dad. 'Ali?' her dad called after a moment. 'Someone's here to see you.'

'That didn't last too long.' She groaned, stood up and followed him out to the front door.

Her heart picked up speed when she saw Lisa standing inside the door frame holding a foil tray aloft. What was she doing here? Had the Gardaí been over to her yet? Ali wondered. Did she know that Josh had woken up and had told the truth about what had happened at the party? Her immediate thought was that perhaps she was here to apologise on behalf of

Ollie but after everything that she had learnt, Ali didn't want to hear it. She didn't think she'd ever be able to forgive Ollie for what he had done. Ali had been so taken up with Charlotte's recovery and getting her home from the hospital that she hadn't thought about Lisa and what she might say to her when they finally came face to face.

'Lisa...' she began.

'I'll give your mother a hand,' her father said, excusing himself.

'I brought you over one of Keith's lasagnes,' she said, holding out the tray. 'How's Charlotte doing?'

'She just got out of hospital.'

'Oh, Ali, thank God.' She put the lasagne into one hand and launched forward and hugged Ali with her free arm. 'What a relief. She gave us all a fright,' she went on.

'Lisa, I need you to be honest with me. Did you know?' Ali challenged, not caring about the hierarchy between them any more.

Lisa paled before her eyes. 'What are you talking about, Ali?'

'I know the truth about that night. Josh is awake and remembers everything. Your son groped Charlotte and when Josh tried to intervene to help her, Ollie started a fight with him. Some of the other boys joined in and somebody threw a punch which caused Josh to fall into the pool. Ollie knew that it wasn't Charlotte because she had already run off and yet he allowed Charlotte to take the rap. You must have known, Lisa.'

'I told you, Ali, I was helping that boy who was sick; you know this!' Lisa was defensive.

'But Ollie knew; he knew what happened!'

'It wasn't like that. Nobody knows who threw that punch; it could have been anyone!' She threw her hands up into the air dismissively.

Ali felt her blood chill in her veins. So Lisa did know. She did know the sequence of events that had taken place that night that resulted in Josh being left in a coma and her daughter being blamed for it. 'So you knew, Lisa?' Ali said in disbelief. 'You knew Charlotte didn't put Josh in the pool and yet you didn't tell the Gardaí? You knew how stressed and scared I've been – how upset and worried Charlotte has been and you still said nothing?' she cried in disbelief. 'Your son's actions pushed my daughter to the brink and she felt her only option was to take an overdose! She could have died!' Ali's voice wavered on tears as emotion and anger overtook her. She knew Charlotte's overdose couldn't solely be blamed on what had happened at Lisa's house; learning about her father was also part of what drove Charlotte to take those tablets, but the pressure she had been under in school and after the party hadn't helped matters. It was like filling a bucket with water; her bucket was already full and then learning about her father had been the catalyst for it to spill over. 'Josh nearly died too; that's two teenagers that might not be alive today because of your son's actions and lies.'

Lisa's eyes darted to the floor and Ali realised that her boss had known the truth all along. A part of her had held onto a glimmer of hope that maybe Lisa hadn't been aware of the exact events that had taken place around the pool as she so claimed, but one look at her contrite face told her that that wasn't true.

'You served alcohol to underage teenagers, which caused your son to go around acting like a drunken lech,' Ali went on. 'And when Josh stood up to him, there was a pile on and unfortunately, he came out the worst of it. Not one person at that party was brave enough to come forward and speak out against Ollie. Shame on you, Lisa and shame on everyone else there that colluded to hide the truth about what really happened that night. You could have had blood on your hands and you were prepared to keep your little secret to yourself to protect your family and your business. How can you live with yourself?'

Lisa hung her head, knowing there was no point denying it any longer. 'I'm sorry, Ali, I never meant for it to get this far; you have to believe me. Put yourself in our shoes. Patrick and I were scared we would be in trouble for serving alcohol and because we supplied it from the restaurant, we could lose our licence. You have to believe me, I didn't want this to happen any more than you did. I was sure Josh would wake up straight away.'

Ali thought she might be sick at Lisa's admission. 'So you and Patrick were in on this together?' she asked in disbelief.

'I'm sorry. We never expected it to drag on for as long as it did.'

Ali shook her head despondently. Lisa was her boss but more than that, Ali had considered her to be a friend. How could she have put them through all of that? How many times had she called to her door over the last few days or chatted to Ali in the restaurant and acted like she was genuinely concerned for Charlotte's welfare? Realising that her boss had known the truth all along and tried to cover it up was a betrayal too much for Ali. Had Lisa such little respect for her that she could treat her like this? After all the years they had worked together, Ali the loyal, servile employee and Lisa was happy to throw her under the bus just so she could protect her own family. She felt like a pawn in the Riordans' game. Ali had almost lost her daughter because of them. 'But you had so many chances over the last week and a half to come clean; you knew the pressure Charlotte was under and you still did nothing! You let me cry on your shoulder, you knew how stressed I was and you could have helped us by being honest but you chose not to!'

'But, Ali,' she protested, 'we could have lost everything and I really thought Josh was going to get better.'

'But you didn't know that for certain. We could have lost two children!' Ali snapped back. 'You put his family through hell. You put my family through hell.' Ali stabbed her index finger towards Lisa. 'Have you any idea how awful the last few days have been?'

'I'm so sorry but at least everyone is okay now. We need to look at the positives; we can all move forward now.'

'This isn't the end of it, Lisa,' Ali cried in disbelief. 'Not by a long shot!' Was her boss really suggesting they all forget about it and go back to their normal lives again? 'Josh's parents have informed the Gardaí so I'd imagine you can expect a visit from them very soon.'

'Oh, Ali, please,' Lisa pleaded. 'It doesn't have to

be this way. Can't we all sit down together for a chat and talk it all out?'

Ali was consumed with white-hot fury. Did Lisa seriously think they could sort this out over a *chat*? Had she no conscience or sense of guilt for her role in landing Charlotte in trouble in the first place? Now that Ali knew the truth, she saw her for what she really was: a self-serving fraud.

'It's too late now. You had your chance to talk. Get out, Lisa,' she ordered, holding the door open for her to leave. Her hands were trembling. She knew there was no going back from here; her friendship with Lisa was over, her job would be gone too but none of that mattered.

The woman nodded, stunned, and turned around to leave still clutching the lasagne.

Ali closed the door behind her; her legs felt like they were about to give way so she used the wall to guide her as she sank down to the floor. The truth was out there now and that was all that mattered.

58

ONE YEAR LATER

Ali sat in the lecture hall, scrawling her notes down onto the paper, doing her best to keep up with what her lecturer was saying. She was the only person taking notes by hand; the rest of the students, who were closer in age to her daughter than they were to her, were all typing them up on their laptops. Most of them were just half her age but she had been working hard on blocking out the mocking voice at the back of her head that told her she was too old, that she didn't belong here. She was attending Trinity College and although it had taken over eighteen years, she was finally going to finish her degree. Quitting work in the restaurant after everything that had happened had given her the push she needed. She had thought about looking for a new job in a different restaurant. Although she wouldn't be asking Lisa for a reference, she had a lot of experience and was hopeful she would get something else but it was Charlotte who had challenged her to go back and finish her degree.

Initially, Ali had laughed off the suggestion. 'I'm too old; how could I go back to college at my age?'

But Charlotte had pushed her and said the same words that Ali said to her when she told her how important it was to get a good education. So she had given it a lot of thought and after discussing it with her parents and getting their encouragement, she decided to look into it a little further. They had offered to help her out financially while she studied and when she researched it more, she also discovered that there were grants she could avail herself of too so she had bitten the bullet and applied. No one had been more shocked than her when she had been accepted.

When the lecture was finished, she closed her notebook and shoved it into her bag. She dipped her shoulder into her coat sleeve and did the same on the other side then hurried out of the lecture hall.

As she hurried across Parliament Square, a bitter wind cut her in two. She emerged under the arch onto College Green then she hurried down Townsend Street towards Tara Street station where she would take the DART home. As she stood on the platform, she checked the clock to see when the next train was due; she needed to hurry if she wanted to make Charlotte's performance tonight.

It was hard to believe that this time last year, she had been sitting by her daughter's bedside in the intensive care unit praying that she would recover. Charlotte had finally been ready to return to school after Christmas. She hadn't returned to St Thomas's and instead had gone back to Riverdale Community School. She seemed happy there and when Ali dropped her off every morning, she went in without complaint. She was working hard but wasn't putting herself under as much pressure as she used to. Ali had also learnt some harsh lessons; she had been so consumed with wanting her daughter to fit in, making her change school and pushing her to get the best opportunities in life, that she had overlooked her child's wellbeing. She now realised she didn't care if Charlotte never went to university, just so long as she was happy and for the first time in a long time, Ali could say with certainty that her daughter was happy.

She was back attending weekly therapy sessions and her therapist had suggested that joining the school drama group might be a good way to express herself and explore her creative side as well as building her confidence. Initially, Charlotte had said there was no way she was doing it but Ali had struck a deal with her and agreed that she would go back to college if Charlotte would join the drama group and as it turned out, it had been the best thing to ever happen to her daughter. She had made friends with like-minded teenagers, shy and sensitive kids that came alive when they were on the stage, dazzling the audience with their brilliance. Tonight, she was taking part in a production of *Pride and Prejudice* and she was playing the sizeable role of Elizabeth's elder sister, Jane Bennet. Ali had been helping her to learn her lines at home and had marvelled at Charlotte's capacity to retain them all. Ali was overjoyed to finally see her shy, timid daughter start to emerge from her shell.

Ali got off the DART and hurried in a half-run, half-walk towards the school. Autumn leaves tumbled down, leaving burnt orange and mustard coloured piles along the path. She loved the saturated colours of October, with its brilliant blue skies and auburn-hued leaves. When she reached the school, she saw the car park was full with parents who were all here to watch the play. She went inside to the hall and spotted her parents in the audience and they waved her over. She saw Josh Quinlan was there sitting with them.

'We kept you a seat, love,' her dad said, patting an empty chair beside him.

She hugged them and greeted Josh, before sitting down quickly as the curtain was raised and the actors took to the stage. Josh had made a full recovery and he and Charlotte had forged a strong friendship over the last year.

Ali didn't speak to Lisa any more. There had been so many teenagers involved in the pile on at the party in her house that to this day, the Gardaí had never been able to ascertain who had thrown the punch that landed Josh in the pool and so nobody was ever charged with the assault. The boys had closed ranks, protecting one another, fearing the repercussions if the truth was revealed.

Ali also suspected that Lisa had been the one to either tell some of the other parents that Charlotte was the scholarship recipient, or else she had told Ollie, who had subsequently told his friends. It was the only plausible explanation for how Charlotte had been identified by the other children, which had led to the bullying that she had endured at the school.

Lisa had also admitted to tipping the Gardaí off about the nude images that Ali had found on her daughter's phone. Ali had been devastated to learn that the person she had trusted with this information and revealed her innermost worries to, had betrayed her so cruelly and used it to ensnare her further. It seemed her boss was willing to do whatever it took to protect her family.

They had discovered that the images had been sent by boys in her form as part of the campaign of bullying against Charlotte. She had been cleared of all wrongdoing and the boys who had believed it was 'just a bit of harmless fun' had all been cautioned by the Gardaí on condition that they attend a workshop especially for teenagers to educate themselves on the laws surrounding sexually explicit images, whether received consensually or not.

Her boss had been charged with 'Conspiracy to Pervert the Course of Justice' and she and Patrick had also admitted to the charge of supplying alcohol to persons under the age of eighteen under the Intoxicating Liquor Act. Although Ali didn't wish for them to go to prison, she hoped some form of justice would be meted out.

Ali had also finally gone to the Gardaí and told them about what Professor Keane had done to her all those years ago. She had been reluctant to report it at first but with the backing of her parents and her daughter, she knew she had a duty to tell them what had happened to her, if only so that he couldn't do it to someone else. It transpired during their investigation that she wasn't the only one. She still felt guilty for not reporting the assault years earlier; maybe she could have prevented him attacking anyone else but as her mother had counselled, the only person who should be feeling any sense of shame was Lorcan Keane. He was now suspended from work in the university and a file had been sent to the Director of Public Prosecutions to see whether there was enough evidence to bring a case against him. It turned out that Kyra Higgins had been studying at Dublin University at the same time as Ali and had heard the rumours circulating about Ali's relationship with Professor Keane. Kyra had taken this story and twisted it so that everyone believed that Ali had form in blackmailing men for money. It was bad enough that Kyra was using what had been a traumatic experience for Ali to accuse her of this behaviour but it was beyond disgusting to her that she was accusing Charlotte too. When the truth had come out, Kyra hadn't even tried to apologise.

Soon, her daughter appeared on stage and Ali felt as though she herself was up there. Her heart was thumping so wildly, a combination of terror for her daughter standing on the stage in front of the packed hall and sheer pride. It was hard to believe that this confident young woman on the stage before her was the same girl who had been fighting for her life just a year ago. She risked a glance at Josh, who was watching Charlotte, agog.

This time last year had been the lowest point in her entire life but she knew that all of the good things she had now couldn't have happened without going through that period. She and Charlotte were both healing. Ali herself was enjoying the challenge of university even if she did feel like the class granny and it gave her so much happiness to watch her daughter blooming and growing into a great young woman. Charlotte had big plans of her own for university next year and Ali was excited for the adventures that were ahead for her daughter. Charlotte knew the truth now about who her father was; there were no more lies. Ali no longer had to cover her tracks or be careful with what she said in case she walked herself into trouble. She hadn't realised how small she had deliberately made her world, always checking and watching what she told people in case they pieced her story together. It was a relief to have all of her secrets out in the open; she had nothing to fear now and that in itself brought freedom.

59

Charlotte's Journal

Today was one of the best days of my entire life. I still get goosebumps every time I think about it. I stood up on a stage and performed in the drama group – me!!! Even I can't believe that I actually did it!!! I really did not want to join the drama group but Mum cut a deal with me whereby if she went back to university to finally finish off her degree, then I had to join. I knew it wasn't easy for Mum returning to education after all this time so I think I got the easier end of the deal. Nobody was more surprised than me to find that I really like it here. They're all nice; it feels easy. They don't care about what brand your handbag is or what clothes you're wearing or what the latest trend is. We're a mixed bunch; there are loud, dramatic types, then there are the shy kids like me, that tend to be more introverted but when those lights come on, it's like our inner muse is released. I won't admit it to Mum but her convincing me to join the drama group was one of the best things to ever happen to me.

We've been working so hard on this play and it was my first time taking on a speaking part. I thought I'd hide backstage, be one of the crew members. I still don't know how they managed to persuade me to do it but I'm so happy now that I did. For months, we have been rehearsing and although I didn't dare tell anyone, I was never sure whether I'd actually be able to go through with it, so it felt like a huge personal achievement to have stood up on that stage and performed tonight. Although I was terrified I might forget all my lines when I got up there, I was excited to show everyone our production. Mum asked me if I got nervous when I saw the audience but the truth is when I was on the stage, they disappeared behind the lighting. The glare of yellow put me in a trance; I went into my own world and actually forgot I was up there. I forgot about everyone and lost myself in the performance. The freedom of being on that stage is inde-scribable. It was only when the lights went down and the audience stood up to clap that I came to and re-membered where I was. When the cast and crew linked hands to take a bow, I spotted my mum and my grandparents sitting beside her about four rows back from the front. And then my gaze landed on Josh. He came. My already racing heart had thumped faster at the sight of him. He said he wanted to watch me but my nerves ratcheted up about ten levels at the thought of performing in front of him. I tried to change his mind but when I saw him in the audience, I was so glad he didn't listen to me and came anyway.

As the curtains went down, the cast headed back-stage, laughing and giggling. Our director high-fived me as I came off and said, 'Great job tonight, Charlotte.'

'Thanks, Will.' I beamed. I felt like I was walking on clouds. I actually did it. I was ecstatic. I hugged the other cast members and gathered up my belongings from the dressing room. I headed out to meet my family and I saw Josh was waiting in the hall for me. He threw his arms around me and hoisted me up into the air.

'You were amazing up there.'

We have become close over the last year. Josh had been the only one who stuck up for me that night at the party but he had paid the ultimate price. You'd never know except for a small scar on his forehead where he was injured in the fall. We both have been through a really tough time and we were the only ones who understood what each other had gone through. It had been hard discovering what my dad did to my mum but I'm learning how to cope with it. I realise that even though I share the same DNA as my father, that's all we share. I'm not him and I don't hate myself any more – in fact, I'm proud of the person I am today. I'm still going to my weekly appointments with my counsellor but the person who has really helped me to work through it all has been Josh.

'You were amazing tonight,' he whispered into my hair and my whole body started to tingle. He reached up and cupped my face in his hands and my skin came alive beneath his fingertips. The feelings be-tween us have been growing; we've got really close and somewhere, it has changed from friendship into something more. A connection fizzes between us, so strong that I'm sure if I reached out to touch it, it would jolt me.

Josh moved closer and his lips softly pressed against mine. My mouth yielded to his as we kissed.

My first kiss. Electricity pulsed through my veins. When we pulled away, I couldn't stop grinning at him.

'Still just friends then?' Liam, one of the other members of the group, called out as he came into the corridor and saw us together. The cast had been teasing us about how close we were; we have always denied it was anything more than friendship but now we know we can't pretend any longer. We laughed, then Josh took my hand and we went out to the foyer where Mum and my grandparents were waiting for me. Mum looked at Josh and me holding hands and grinned. 'Well, about bloody time!' she exclaimed, putting an arm around me. 'I was wondering when you two would get together.'

'Thank you, Mum,' I said, reaching up to give her a kiss on the cheek.

She looked confused. 'What's that for?'

'For pushing me to do this. For everything you've done for me my whole life. I know I haven't always made it easy for you but I'm so grateful and I love you so much.'

'Oh, sweetheart,' she said, pulling me into a hug. 'I love you too. My darling girl. Look how far you've come. I've always been proud of you but tonight, I could burst.'

Then Mum and I linked arms and we all walked outside together into the gilded autumn sunlight.

* * *

MORE FROM CAROLINE FINNERTY

Another book from Caroline Finnerty, *The Child I Long For*, is available to order now here: https://mybook.to/ChildILongForBackAd

ACKNOWLEDGEMENTS

I can't believe this is my tenth published book. After my first book, *In a Moment*, was released back in 2012, I never knew if I'd ever manage to write another (difficult second book syndrome is a thing), let alone, write a further nine, so it feels like a huge personal milestone to get here. One thing I've learnt along the way is that it certainly never gets easier – with every book I've written, there is always a point where it feels like I've forgotten how to write and I think this will be the book that breaks me but somehow it always comes together in the end. There are so many people who have guided me along the journey over the last few years but these people in particular deserve a special mention:

Firstly, to my amazing agent Hannah Todd who has recently joined the Janklow & Nesbit agency, Hannah you are always so supportive and approachable and on hand with the best advice. Thank you for your help with this book. Thanks also to Elinor

Davies and also the team at the Madeleine Milburn Agency for all their assistance too.

A huge thank you is also due to my editor Francesca Best for her guidance and encouraging words. To Emily Reader for yet another superb copy-edit which has benefitted this book so greatly and to Arbaiah Aird for her excellent proofread.

I also want to thank the wider team at Boldwood, especially the marketing and production teams. You are so good at what you do, and I am grateful to be part of it all.

To all my friends, with a special mention to fellow author, the very talented Janelle Harris/Laura Anthony who is always there for a brainstorming-walk and a glass of wine.

To all the booksellers and bloggers, for their support especially Rachel Gilbey for her amazing blog tours. Thanks also to the libraries across the UK and Ireland, especially my local library in Celbridge, for their support over the years. Also, a huge mention is due to Susan Buggy for being the best bookseller an author could ask for and to Vincent Sutton in the Liffey Champion newspaper who has done so much for me and always champions local writers.

To my family and friends for cheering me on. My

parents who always keep the newspaper clippings and tell random strangers about my books.

Also, a special thank you is owed to my husband Simon; none of this would be possible without you and our four beautiful children, Lila, Tom, Bea and Charlie. I am eternally grateful for you all.

Lastly, thank you to my readers, especially those people who leave reviews and contact me with lovely messages and kind words, you'll never know how much those messages mean and spur me on whenever I'm doubting myself. I am so grateful every day that I get to do this for a living, and ten books later, that people are still reading my books. With all the brilliant books out there to choose from, I never take it for granted. Thank you!

ABOUT THE AUTHOR

Caroline Finnerty is an Irish author of heart-wrenching family dramas and has compiled a non-fiction charity anthology. She has been shortlisted for several short-story awards and lives in County Kildare with her husband and four young children.

Sign up to Caroline Finnerty's mailing list for news, competitions and updates on future books.

Visit Caroline's website: www.carolinefinnerty.ie

Follow Caroline on social media here:

f facebook.com/carolinefinnertywriter

X x.com/cfinnertywriter

O instagram.com/carolinefinnerty

BB bookbub.com/profile/caroline-finnerty

g goodreads.com/carolinefinnerty

ALSO BY CAROLINE FINNERTY

The Last Days of Us

A Mother's Secret

A Sister's Promise

The Family Next Door

The Child I Long For

My Daughter's Silence

Boldwⵔⵔd

Boldwood Books is an award-winning fiction publishing company seeking out the best stories from around the world.

Find out more at www.boldwoodbooks.com

Join our reader community for brilliant books, competitions and offers!

Follow us
@BoldwoodBooks
@TheBoldBookClub

Sign up to our weekly deals newsletter

https://bit.ly/BoldwoodBNewsletter

www.ingramcontent.com/pod-product-compliance
Lightning Source LLC
Chambersburg PA
CBHW01085713072 6
47900CB00017B/2742